Oy Feminist Planets: A Fake Memoir

Marleen S. Barr

NeoPoiesisPress.com

NeoPoiesis Press, LLC

2775 Harbor Ave SW, Suite D, Seattle, WA 98126-2138
Inquiries: Info@NeoPoiesisPress.com
NeoPoiesisPress.com

Oy Feminist Planets: A Fake Memoir by Marleen S. Barr
ISBN 978-0-9892018-6-5 (paperback : alk. paper)

    1. Science Fiction: Novel. I. Barr, Marleen.

Library of Congress Control Number: 2015902749

First Edition

Cover Artwork: David Junkin
Cover Design: Milo Duffin and Stephen Roxborough
Interior Typography: Erin Badough

Printed in the United States of America.

Contents

Stop The Starship, I Want To Get Off

Call me Samuel.

Why?

Because: You don't know about me without you have read a book by the name of *Oy Pioneer!*; but that ain't no matter. That book was made by Dr. Marleen S. Barr, and she told the truth, mainly. There was things which she stretched, but mainly she told the truth. That is nothing, I never seen anybody but lied one time or another. *Oy Pioneer!* is mostly a true book, with some stretchers, as I said before.

Inveigling myself within the start of Mark Twain's *The Adventures of Huckleberry Finn*? Is this any way to run a fake memoir about being a Jewish feminist science fiction scholar? You bet it is!

What do you expect a Manhattan dwelling feminist hero to do? How can I evoke the classic American literary canon in a manner which mirrors my particular female experience? Sure, I can walk to the Hudson River. But floating down that river on a raft is not an option. Nor can I ask you to call me such decidedly *goyish* appellations as Langhorne or Clemens. At least "Samuel" is a Jewish name --even though only *shiksas* are called "Sam." Remember Sam on *Bewitched*? A female witch, the supernatural, is appropriate to *Oy Feminist Planets*.

Barr stretched in *Oy Pioneer!* Now the way that book winds up is this: Her protagonist fraternizes with a talking horse, has antigravity sex with a vampire, marries her cat, and flies around in a starship. I am that protagonist. Due to events beyond my control -- I refer to the Gentile male literary tradition (no tradition tradition) dominating the American literary canon -- I must allude to male authors to evoke that tradition. Call me Shirley? Call me Sylvia? Is this any way Melville -- or Philip Roth and Saul Bellow -- would start the great American novel?

Times have changed.

Call me Sondra.

That's Lear. Sondra Lear.

I know from Twain and Melville and Roth and Bellow and the whole American literary tradition kit and caboodle because I am Professor Sondra Lear, feminist science fiction scholar by day and husband hunter by night. I failed to find a husband when I spent my young adult years in graduate school studying Literature at the State University of New York at Buffalo. The Buffalo English department, housed in Samuel Langhorne Clemens Hall, oozed with liberal male scholars. Barr had to stretch. She had to imagine that I and my entire supernatural coterie emerged from within a puff of the late Leslie Fiedler's cigar smoke. Hence: *Oy Pioneer!* is mostly a true book, with some stretchers, as I said before. I should know. Like Barr, I am a feminist science fiction specialist. I also wrote *Oy Pioneer!* -- in a parallel universe. I am Marleen's parallel universe double. What happens to her happens to me—with a difference (or, as Jacques Derrida would say, a *différance*). If a parallel universe is too far-fetched for you, just think Jorge Luis Borges. In "Pierre Menard, Author of the Quixote," Borges describes two authors (Menard and Cervantes) who create the same text (*Don Quixote*). This text is at once the same and different. Marleen S. Barr's *Oy Pioneer!* and Sondra Lear's *Oy Pioneer!*, in the manner of the *Don Quixote* Borges describes, are simultaneously identical and unalike. (Enough already with Borges and Derrida. I promise. At least I don't have to create a Works Cited list in here.)

The page proofs, and the public lectures -- and the god knows what else -- have required me to read *Oy Pioneer!* multitudinous times. I can't get through the thing without cracking up. Because I laugh so hard at my own prose, I have to cross my legs during the public readings. "Cross" does not allude to anything Gentile. I cross to try not to pee on the stage. The same thing happens to Barr.

Hence: What is authorially and experientially characteristic of *Oy Pioneer!* also goes for *Oy Feminist Planets*. Barr and I both wrote these texts. Make "texts" "books." "Texts" is too akin to literary theory jargon. I promised -- no more literary stuff like Derrida and Borges. That's the truth.

More truth: Yes, finding a husband in Manhattan is mission impossible incarnate.

But, believe me, it could be worse. The stretcher is worse.

The stretcher: If you think Manhattan does not constitute a happy husband-hunting ground, imagine how difficult it is to get married if you are cooped up in a starship populated by nonhumans. And to make matters more complex, the crew consists of Marleen S. Barr clones—who are also clones of me. I admit that it was a little self-centered to name all the clones Sondra. The clones and I are all aboard a starship hurtling faster than the speed of light towards a Fulbright grant year on a far far away feminist separatist planet (that is to say a god knows where devoid of men) near Alpha Centauri. As if this situation were not bad enough, although I am presently married, I *still* can't find a husband. More about this stretcher: In addition to not being Jewish, my husband is neither real nor human.

Sure, my life is beyond beyond; but acquiring a supernatural husband did *finally* shut up Herbert. Herbert is my mother. Don't worry. My mother is female. I know; with me you can never tell. You're already aware that I am exceedingly unpredictable -- and you're only at the book's beginning. Keep reading. You'll find out that the supernatural husband I describe is my first husband. There is a second husband. He's an alien; but at least he's human. One must be thankful for small things. (Don't mind me -- you're being subjected to my intrusive narrative voice. I'm a literary critic. I'm used to telling readers what to do.) Meanwhile: Back to the present. I nicknamed my mother Herbert simply because she is so unmotherly. She never said "call me Herbert." She is married to George, my father. I call him Egor.

Figuring that a supernatural, nonhuman husband is still, by definition, a husband, Herbert decided to look away. She had spent years doing nothing other than ordering me to get married. How does she now respond to the facts of my life? She considers them to be *mitzvah-esque* blessings in disguise.

These are the facts, ma'am. (Detective fiction is another male bastion.)

And even more about the stretcher: Despite my feminist science fiction expertise, I never expected my reality to be juxtaposed with the unreal. I never thought that the Sondra clones would turn my neutered cat, Norris Compton Lear, into a Cary Grant look-a-like husband. (Norris, a native Virginian cat/husband, is not Jewish.) Who would say "of course of course" in response to the Sondra clones' decision to turn Ms. Ed, my trusty feminist talking horse, into a young daughter? The Sondras made it possible for me to win a Fulbright grant to a separatist feminist planet -- *and* they covered my starship fare. Who knew? I will refrain from describing my adventures with the horny vampire Ilya Lugosi. You'll meet Ilya later after he materializes. He never fails to appear whenever I click the soles of my magic red clogs together. Okay, I will call a halt to throwing supernatural circumstances at you -- for the moment, anyway.

The events I describe would never have ensued if my history were otherwise and I had not started my teaching career at Blackhole State University. The school is located outside New York City in what is to me southwest Virginian rural hell. Trying to find a husband (and a Jewish one yet) in Blackhole, Virginia is even more of a mission impossible than trying to find one in Manhattan. I would say that achieving success is analogous to the chance of traveling in a starship. I never expected to inhabit a stretcher. I never expected to be both protagonist and alternative universe author of *Oy Pioneer!* and *Oy Feminist Planets*. I know that many protagonists inhabit starships. But what was I doing in a debut novel about an irreverent romp through the groves of academe with a fiercely-feminist-and-husband-hunting-literary theorist? The odds against experiencing the fantastic plot circumstances connected to this quest are exceedingly low too. I am the only person (and I use that term loosely) who has done so. But back to specifics about the past.

In addition to my participation in *Oy Pioneer!*, I also had to publicize the thing. The attention generating efforts were a hoot. My friend Gary Shapiro, an arts columnist for the *New York Sun*, advised me that writers should disseminate promotional items which relate to their book topics. Andy Borowitz, the author of *Who Moved My Soap?*, sent Gary a bar of soap-on-a rope. A book about soap promotes itself via soap? Well, then, it stands to reason that a memoir about a husband-hunting feminist theorist should promote itself via potential husbands. So I invited all the single male graduate students and professors in my department at SUNY Greenwich Village (a.k.a. SUNY - G.V.) to one of my book signing events. (I was not compromising myself: the students were too young for me. And, even if they were the last men on Earth, under no circumstance would I ever marry any of the male colleagues I had ever known; I do not mean "known" in the biblical sense -- Old Testament, that is. I don't know from the New Testament.) Book promotion step one: I advertised the single men as potential-husbands-on-a-rope. Book promotion step two: I tied them all to the banister surrounding the bookstore's café. Is this a stretcher? I will never tell you. But now hear this: Ya ain't seen nothin' yet. As a literary scholar, I can say with certainty that Twain's use of colloquialisms differ from mine. Twain did not dote on the word "*oy*."

Gary further advised me that books designated for signing and purchasing should be positioned near available food. Why didn't I think of that? People, especially Jewish people, never fail to gravitate toward food. Following Gary's instructions to the letter, I placed copies of *Oy Pioneer!* close to food and in proximity to the fettered potential husbands. Whipped into a frenzy by the sight of eligible men roped in tow, women stampeded. Samuel Langhorne Clemens derived his pen name "Mark Twain" from the ropes that were used to secure steamboats. I would bet my Ph.D. that Clemens did not have husband-hunting techniques analogous to soap-on-a-rope in mind. It takes a feminist critic who has spent her career studying a feminist science fiction author village to fathom such an analogy. Although Clemens' doings bear no connection to my experiences, the same cannot be said for Hillary Rodham Clinton and Bill Clinton. Using the longhorn-like stampede my book promotion methods prompted as an experiential guide, bookstores generated improved crowd control methods to handle the hordes who wanted autographed copies of Hillary's and Bill's best seller autobiographies.

But enough already with the reality.

So, what's it like for a former husband-hunting fiercely feminist science fiction theorist to be inside a starship accompanied by Norris, her former cat and present husband, and Ms. Ed -- her former feminist talking horse and present daughter? To let you know, I turn to my science fiction critical expertise and evoke an exceedingly familiar narrative structure:

Captain's Log
Star Date 609-37-2946

It is another routine day on board the Sondra clones' starship. Because the Sondras want me to feel at home, they re-created the décor located in my childhood apartment in Forest Hills, Queens; they covered the Bridge's Captain's chair with a plastic slipcover. (William Shatner and Leonard Nimoy are Jewish; they could relate to a slipcovered Captain's chair.) When the Sondras decided to program the food synthesizer to produce matzo ball soup and bagels, I thwarted their good intentions. I requested salad sans dressing and tuna packed in water. To provide a uniform décor to match the plastic covered Captain's chair, the synthesizer spewed out Saran Wrapped food. The Sondras' attention to decorative detail obviously went beyond Martha Stewart's expertise. I found it difficult to stay on my diet in the presence of a never empty food synthesizer.

I break the travel monotony (remember I said that the feminist planet is located far far away) by observing how Norris and Ms. Ed, despite their recent transformation into human form, still adhere to their former respective feline and equine characteristics. Norris never fails to show up whenever he hears me opening a food synthesizer produced tuna fish can. He acts out during our normal marital spats by reaching under the plastic slipcover and clawing the Captain's chair. Because Norris is a very considerate -- and a very sexy -- husband, I look away. I try to forget that, despite all the interplanetary *tsuris* they experienced, Captains Kirk, Picard, and Janeway never had to cope with a shredded Captain's chair. Ms. Ed is as problematical as Norris. She responds to the Triple Crown races broadcast directly from Earth by lusting after horses named Funny Cide and Smarty Jones. Yes, Ed adhered to my cultural heritage by cheering for Funny Cide (a horse from New York) and celebrating the fact that Brooklyn Jew Bobby Frankel trained Empire Maker (the horse who won the Belmont). (The Sondras tell me that Bobby is the father of Bethenny Frankel, a star of a future reality television show which will be called *The Real Housewives of New York*. I wonder how the show would apply "real" to my New York experiences.) It is still difficult for me to deal with Ed, a daughter who, based upon her past experiences with Pegasus, emulates the sex life of Catherine the Great. I tried to make Ed feel better about her lack of access to Funny Cide by reminding her that he is a gelding. She is still holding out hope for a future big date with Smarty Jones. There's something peculiar about a girl who has posters of Seabiscuit and Secretariat adorning her starship bedroom. Kirk, Picard, and Janeway never had such problems.

A communication from Earth is interrupting my Captain's log. Lacking a Communications Officer, I have to attend to it myself. The unmistakable incessant voice of Herbert permeates the Bridge. Norris runs under the Captain's chair to seek refuge beneath the plastic.

"Hello Sondra. This is your mother, Herbert. Where are you?"

"I'm in a starship with Norris and Ms. Ed and we're headed toward my Fulbright to a feminist planet located somewhere near Alpha Centauri."

"Is Alpha Centauri a Jewish neighborhood? Oy, Sondra, why can't you be normal? I know that I agreed to look away when aliens turned your cat Norris into a human and you married him. That was not easy for me; besides not being born a human, Norris is not Jewish. I can cope with Ms. Ed better in her present form. It's easier to have her be a human grandchild rather than her former incarnation: a talking horse who resides on my terrace. But Sondra, this new starship and marriage to the former cat thing would not sit well with my beach club and Forest Hills Jewish Center friends. I can't tell them about your life. Is it too much to ask that I want that my daughter marry a nonsupernatural Jewish husband? Sondra, get married to a normal human Jewish man. Alpha Centauri is not the right place for you. You won't like Alpha Centauri any more than you liked Blackhole. Sondra, get married. Okay -- you are, after a fashion, married. But I am your mother and I know that it is best for you for me to continue to yell at you to get married. Sondra, come home. You can meet a garden variety Jewish husband in Forest Hills."

Desperate to end this conversation, I acted intuitively -- and in terms of my academic field's discourse. "Beam me up, Scotty," I said hoarsely and desperately. Nothing happened. I was already beamed up. And I was aboard the Sondras' ship, not the Starship Enterprise. Engineer Scotty, no part of the Sondras' feminist science fiction milieu, was not my crew mate. I had to end my conversation with Herbert in the tried and true manner.

"Bye Herbert. Gotta go. An alien is materializing in the transporter room."

The *Star Trek* transporter room is a stretcher. As I said, unfortunately, the ship is devoid of both Scotty and a transporter. This lack does not explain why it is not the right enterprise for me. I have to admit that, for once, Herbert is right. Traveling inside a starship with the newly human Norris, Ed, and my extraterrestrial clones is no way to live. I really have to get a life. "I wish I had a life," I said aloud to myself.

A rotund white haired woman materialized on the Bridge. It was none other than Barbara Bush, my fairy godmother. I remembered the last time I encountered Mrs. Bush in my parents' Forest Hills apartment. I convinced her that turning Norris into a Cinderella coach animal and requiring me to wear high healed glass shoes would not enhance my husband hunt.

"Mrs. Bush! How nice to see you. What brings you to the Sondras' starship?"

"I am here to grant your wish. You are a special case, Sondra. I have never made a wish-granting house call to a spaceship. I notice that the décor resembles your mother's taste. Plastic slipcovers abound. I don't use slipcovers at Walker's Point. But let me get down to business. I'll do my best to help you -- under one condition."

"Which is?"

"Don't mention your intense dislike for my son George."

"Fair enough. I do need to focus upon the personal rather than the political. I have to figure out how to get out of this starship place if it's the last thing I ever do. My mother correctly says, "Girl, there's a better life for me and you," even though my life is not about her. I have to ditch the starship without hurting the feelings of the whole supernatural horde residing in here. I want to go home to Forest Hills. I want to find a real human husband. I am ready to sacrifice my Fulbright to a feminist planet. There's no place like home. Even though I do have direct ship-to-shore communicative access to my mother, I don't think I'm in Forest Hills anymore."

"I am afraid that your problem is beyond my fairy godmother powers and abilities. Spaceships are not mentioned in the *Fairy Godmothers' Handbook*. The *Handbook* strictly adheres to including fantasy, not science fiction. You, of course, recall that I am very good at materializing shoes. Don't worry. I won't repeat the glass slipper fiasco. Sondra, do I have shoes for you," said Mrs. Bush as she waved her wand and disappeared in a puff of smoke.

When the smoke cleared, I saw my beloved magic red clogs positioned on the Captain's chair arm rest. The Sondras had forgotten to include them in my clothing allotment. Their presence signaled that Mrs. Bush had called in my friend, lover, and -- last but not least -- immortal vampire par excellence. I was face to face with none other than Ilya Lugosi. Ilya, in addition to being a vampire, is an incessantly horny and sex obsessed brilliant literary critic from T.R.A.N.S.Y.L.V.A.N.I.A. (that is, Theorists, Researchers, Authors, Nudnik Scholars, Yahoos, Librarians, Vampires, Announcing New Interpretations and Analyses). The red clogs function as our communications device. If I click them together when I am in trouble, he rescues me. This time Mrs. Bush sent him C.O.D. The Sondras gave her a check for the delivery charges. When Ilya materialized in a puff of smoke, he added to the smoke emanating from her departure. The ships' smoke alarms were blaring. Norris remained under the Captain's chair.

"Hello my dear Sondra. Only for you would I interrupt my writing and appear on a starship. I haven't had stellar sex in a long time. Let's get off this damned Bridge and go to your quarters. Let's have sex. Remember how much you enjoyed that floating anti-gravity sex I conjured up? We can both get it up here -- without any magical intervention on my part. All my parts are available to you."

"I can't have sex with you."

'Don't tell me that you are still hung up on that condom obsession. If the Sondras failed to provide condoms in addition to your red clogs, I can instantaneously zap one on. What's for lunch?"

"Saran Wrapped matzo balls, water packed tuna fish, and salad sans dressing. Ilya, I can't have sex with you. I'm married. I want to remain loyal to my husband, Norris." Norris peaked out from beneath the Captain's chair and smiled.

"Norris is a fictitious character. What person marries a human who was once a cat?"

"And who has sex with a vampire in a starship? I need to get a real life. I'm grateful that the Sondras gave me access to a starship inhabited by a loving daughter and husband. I am very attached to Norris and Ed. But an open tuna fish can-obsessed husband just doesn't cut it. I need someone with greater depth and wider life experience. While other husbands devoted themselves to their professions, Norris spent years sitting on top of my computer watching me write while swinging his tail across my screen. And Ed misses sowing her wild oats. In summary: Ilya, stop this starship. I want to get off. I want to go home. New York is where I'd rather stay. I get allergic in the starship's cargo bay. I want to be a wife (for real). Goodbye starship life. Forest Hills here I come."

"I want what is best for you, Sondra. Are you sure you're doing the right thing? Do you really wish to compromise your career by giving up your Fulbright to a feminist planet in order to return to Forest Hills?"

"Yes. Sometimes women's unconventional professional decisions are for the best. Hillary followed Bill to Arkansas. If Hillary elected to go to Arkansas, I can decide not to go to Alpha Centauri."

"You have a point. Click your red clogs together. After doing so, you and your fully functional magic red clogs will return to Forest Hills. Norris and Ed will remain in the starship with the Sondras. Feel free to continue to use the clogs to summon me. I am always available to help you. Goodbye, Dearest S. You know how to reach me."

Ilya's departure caused more smoke to fill the Bridge. The blaring smoke alarms were over extended. Norris emerged from beneath the Bridge Captain's chair and embraced me. His yellow eyes were downcast and his usually elegantly coifed gray hair was rumpled. He yowled mournfully.

"I heard everything. I'm trying hard to understand that you have to leave me and move on. I did my best to change from your cat into your husband. Intermarriage is so hard. Many Jews marry Gentiles. But I guess that felines and humans are not birds of a feather who can flock together. A cat who becomes a husband lacks authenticity. Despite my conversion, since I was born in a field in the Blue Ridge Mountains of Virginia, I just can't make it as a real Jew. Your decision to name me Norris instead of Morris didn't help matters. I felt so culturally short-changed when you watched *Mad About You* and I heard Jamie's and Paul's dog answer to Murray. I have spent my entire life as your cat and your husband. I don't want to lose you, Sondra. I don't want to be without you. Not ever."

"I'll call Ms. Ed and we can have a family discussion." I reached for my communication device. "Ed, this is your mother calling. Stop salivating over those Triple Crown reruns. Report to the Bridge immediately." Even though I was acting like Herbert, at least I was not echoing her.

"Mother you seem so sad and serious. What's with the bad news face? You look like you did when you said you were leaving Blackhole and I couldn't come with you. You insisted that Forest Hills, which is devoid of both forests and hills, is no place for a horse. And that was the part before you explained that I could get run over on Queens Boulevard, routinely called the Boulevard of Death."

"Remember that everything worked out well. You did end up coming to Forest Hills. We got around the lack of forests and verdant hills. You did fine living on my parents' terrace. Think of all the fun you had hanging out with the Washington Square Park police horses while I taught my classes at SUNY-GV. Things are different now. I must leave you and Norris. I need to go home alone. You both absolutely can't come." I looked away as Ed and Norris sobbed uncontrollably.

"Stop crying. You have nothing to cry about. In addition to being a wife and mother, I am a prolific science fiction critic. Believe me when I tell you that you inhabit a novel. Science fiction tropes can make it possible for you to live happily ever after. You two will remain on the starship with the Sondra clones. Don't worry. The Sondras love you. Marleen S. Barr and I will write another novel. I will reunite with you within its pages. Due to stereotypical science fiction chronology altering tropes, you will not notice my absence."

Norris and Ed perked up. I kissed them Goodbye. Two Sondras appeared on the Bridge. They changed Norris back into a cat and Ms. Ed back into a feminist talking horse. They returned me to my parents' Forest Hills apartment.

Casting aside fond memories of the starship food synthesizer, I opened the refrigerator. It was empty -- with the exception of a note from the Sondras: "Dear Sondra, We knew that you would look in the refrigerator immediately if not sooner. We respect your decision to leave our starship and your belief that you can go home again. Good luck back in Forest Hills, Queens, New York, USA, Earth. We will take good care of Norris and Ed. If you need us, in the manner of Ilya, we can participate in your real life. Just drop us a note and leave it in your refrigerator. Much love from your extraterrestrial clones, The Sondras."

I ate water packed canned tuna while sitting in my parents' living room on their plastic covered couch. Luckily, they were wintering in Florida.

Out of Africa

"I had a farm in Africa, at the foot of the Ngong Hills. The equator runs across these highlands, a hundred miles to the North, and the farm lay at an altitude of over six thousand feet. In the day time, you felt that you had got high up, near to the sun."

Call me Isak?

Definitely not. Calling me Isak works no better than calling me Samuel. Isak Dinesen was a *shiksa*. Jewish women do not live on plantations in Kenya -- or, for that matter, on plantations anywhere on Earth. I will never live at the foot of the Ngong hills; I, as you will soon see, merely met a supernatural potential husband named Ngudu. I feel much more at home near to the sun on a starship with the Sondra clones than on a plantation. No more starting my chapters with biblical names. The biblical names are beginning to resemble a plague. Samuel Clemens and Isak Dinesen, *goyish* writers incarnate, did not begat Sondra Lear -- or Marleen S. Barr. They are no literary antecedents of mine. I will just have to stop meeting new chapters in places like this. By me, call me refers to telephones.

The phone in the Forest Hills apartment rang. "Hello. Dr. Lear?" inquired a woman with an unmistakably South African accent.

"Yes."

"I'm Carrie Veldt from the University of Cape Town. The South African government has given me a travel grant to interview American science fiction writers and critics. I plan to speak with Ursula Le Guin, Joanna Russ, Samuel Delany, and Hardon Ellidaughter. May I meet you when I'm in New York?"

"Of course. I would love to get together. One warning: beware of Hardon Ellidaughter. He can be very difficult. He got out of control in relation to his contribution to a science fiction anthology

I'm editing. He phoned after midnight and screamed 'Lear, go fuck yourself.' Yes, he has a mouth and he must scream. But his outburst was uncalled for. Maybe Hardon was suffering from a Viagra overdose. I got my revenge, though. I arranged to have my mother answer when he next called. Suffering through a phone conversation with my mother is the exact excruciating fate he deserves. Luckily, I was out when the clash of the yelling mouth titans ensued. Both parties reported that the conversation was enjoyed by neither. Why I am telling you this I don't know. I guess I want to shield you from Hardon."

"Thanks. Dr. Lear. I appreciate your advice. How did things turn out with Hardon?"

"Peace followed my freeze-dried matzo ball shipment appeasement gesture. Please call me Sondra. Would you like to meet on Thursday at three in the Museum of Modern Art?"

"That would be great."

"I'll be in the second floor gallery in front of Monet's water lilies. It takes up the entire wall. You can't miss it."

"See you then."

Soon after arriving at the appointed time, I was greeted by a pleasant looking red haired thirty-five year old. We hit it off immediately and engaged in lively conversation. Carrie's enthusiastic warmth and openness motivated me to try to generate an exciting professional opportunity.

"I have never been to South Africa. Is there any chance I could come as a guest professor?"

"What a wonderful idea. I'll propose it to my department head, Gavin Gavinbach. I think he might go for it. You'll like Cape Town. It's absolutely gorgeous and our department includes André Brink and J. M. Coetzee. I admire your feminist science fiction scholarship and I would love to have you as a colleague. I'll introduce you to all my friends. We can camp out in a game preserve."

"Sounds good -- although I'm not sure if I'm the game preserve type." I omitted to mention that, due to years of failed husband-hunting, I might be able to adjust to a game preserve during drought conditions. Hunting is forbidden in game preserves; a sojourn in one could provide a nice respite. "I do know not to get out of the car to take pictures of the cute lions. Just out of curiosity, what happens to tourists who are not equally enlightened?"

"They become lion lunch."

"I can relate to this fate. Throughout my professional life, I've taken risks which usually resulted in me being served as dead meat. I'll make sure to stay in the car—with the windows closed."

"Good idea. It was great to meet you. I'll get back to you with Gavin's response. Bye for now Sondra."

"Just one more question: Is Gavin Gavinbach single?"

"Absolutely. And he's quite good looking and presently un-involved. Last but not least, he's brilliant and sweet."

"If he's in favor of my guest professorship, ask if he would like to join me for lunch immediately upon my arrival." No hungry hunting lion could better discern a potential lunch quarry than moi, husband hunter par excellence."

"Sure thing. Hope to see you soon in Cape Town. Bye Sondra."

South Africa was shaping up to be a happy-husband-hunting ground. Armed with Carrie's description of Gavin and the romantic depiction of relationships between the sexes in Africa Norman Rush describes in *Mating*, I very much hoped that Cape Town teaching was on the horizon. What could be bad? I would enjoy an adventure, assuage my rush to get married and, at the very least, mate with Gavin.

Carrie communicated Gavin's invitation. I boarded a thir-teen hour flight to Johannesburg. My itinerary called for changing planes there before going to Cape Town where Gavin would meet me. Surviving one of the world's longest flights would precede my initial close encounter with Gavin. When I took my assigned seat, I was reassured to see that the man sitting next to me looked innocu ous. I did not want to endure a pesty nut for thirteen hours.

"What are you going to do in South Africa?" he asked.

"Teach. And you?"

"I'm going to hunt." I masked my disgust and tried to estab-lish commonality.

"I hunt during my spare time."

"Oh? What kind of animals do you bag? What kind of gun do you use?"

"For years and without success I have pursued animals of the two legged male variety. My quarry is elusive: single men who want to marry me. I think they're on the endangered species list. I don't ever use a gun. I hear tell that 'you can't get a man with a gun'."

"This man with a gun responded as if I were a serial killer. Feeling sorry for the animals he would slaughter, I decided to give him a taste of his own medicine. I turned him into fair game quarry. I put him in my crosshairs and took direct aim in compliance with Herbert-inspired accuracy."

"Are you married? Are you Jewish?" I did not expect his answer to the latter question to be affirmative. Few Jewish men travel to South Africa to hunt.

"I'm single. But I'm not Jewish." Still envisioning the poor murdered animals, I was not ready to let him off the hook.

"Wonderful! I would consider marrying a *shayketz*. Just think: if we have a daughter, you can teach her some of your hunting skills. When a girl is alone out there in the social meat market, she just can't have too many hunting skills." Taking a cue from Norris, I was now ready to stop playing with my quarry and go in for the kill. The hunter would now face a fate worse than death: "My mother would be so happy to know that I'm spending thirteen hours with a single man who is a captive audience. I'm going to phone her so that the two of you can talk." I reached for the seat telephone, dialed, and heard Herbert's voice.

"I'm on the plane. I'm sitting next to a single man. I thought that you would like to chat with him."

I handed the phone to the hunter and stood up abruptly. "I must excuse myself. Lions and tigers and bears, you know. Oh my." (Ten hours later, the hunter was still on the phone with Herbert. A *shaygetz* lacks the requisite social skills necessary for extricating himself from a conversation with a Jewish mother in hot pursuit of a son-in-law.)

I scanned the crowded plane to look for a vacant seat. I noticed one located about fifteen rows behind me and made my way to it. A forty-something black man attired in native garb sat next to the vacant seat.

"May I sit here?" I asked.

"Yes. Of course."

"Hi. I'm Sondra."

"My name is Ndugu."

"Do you know about Schmidt? Does Schmidt send you letters? Have you heard of Jack Nicholson?"

"No. Why?"

"It's not important. Never mind." Since I occupied the plane's sole empty seat, I again resorted to the commonality tactic. A potential conversation piece caught my eye as I rose and opened the overhead compartment."

"Are these long thin covered items yours? Are they ski poles?""

"I am from the west African coast. My desert home does not lend itself to skiing. You refer to my ceremonial spears. As the chief and witch doctor of my tribe, I don't leave home without them." Eureka; commonality at last. Not knowing when spears could serve me well as effective husband-hunting weapons of choice, I pursued the conversation."

"How did you get your spears past security?""

"Easy. I turned them into a snakes.""

"Do you know Ilya Lugosi?""

"No. Why? Does Ilya Lugosi have any relation to Schmidt and Jack Nicholson?""

"Not at all. Tell me more about the magic poles.""

"After stowing the snakes in the overhead compartment, I changed them back into spears. The airline stipulates that two pets per flight are allowed in the cabin. I simply made an advance reservation for two snakes. Do you find my story hard to believe?""

"Absolutely not. I'm a science fiction critic. A spear which you turned into a snake and back? No sweat. When I spent a Fulbright year in Germany, I brought my cat Norris along on a Lufthansa flight. I married him after my extraterrestrial clones turned him into a human male. They changed him back into a cat, though. I needed to find a real human husband. The cat is now in my clones' starship with my feminist talking horse."

Ndugu and I did enjoy true commonality after all. We spent hours discussing how real magic realism impacts upon our lives. I was even on the verge of offering to introduce him to the Sondras and Ilya. But the flow of the conversation stopped when we approached Ile de La Sol, the flight's first stop in Africa. Ndugu became earnest and tense.

"Sondra I'm leaving the plane in Ile de La Sol. I don't want to leave you. Will you marry me?"

"What? Hold the phone." I could use Ndugu's proposal to kill two birds with one stone. Deciding that the hunter had suffered long enough talking to Herbert, I could simultaneously put him out of his misery and tell her that a man had asked me to marry him. "Excuse me Ndugu. I'll be right back." I walked down the aisle fifteen rows forward and grabbed the phone out of the hunter's hand.

"Hello. Herbert. You will never guess what. . . ."

"You're so ungrateful Sondra. I've talked my head off trying to get that hunter to marry you and you don't even thank me. I know he's not Jewish. I looked away when you married that *goyish* cat from Virginia. I can also look away from the *goyish* hunter who, at least, is a real human. Your husband hunt could finally be over. This hunter *goy* might just make a good son-in-law. I've had enough with animals ever since you inflicted that talking horse on me and your father."

"A man asked me to marry him."

"What? You bagged the hunter?"

"No. I'm talking about another man, not the hunter."

"What does he do? Is he Jewish?"

"No. He's a chief, a witch doctor, and a spear carrier."

"You met a Hollywood studio head who dabbles in acting as an extra. Wonderful. Sondra I'm so proud of you. Finally you made me happy. Before I close my eyes forever I will be able to bring your Hollywood husband to the beach club.

"Maybe I was too fast to deflect emphasis from the hunter. You're jumping the gun. Ndugu is a literal chief, witch doctor, and spear carrier. His spear is not always what it appears to be, though."

"In your life what is what it appears to be? Just get married. Is there a rabbi on the plane? If not, the Captain can marry you. Ndugu? Did I hear you say Ndugu? Is Ndugu Jewish?"

"Ndugu is black."

I heard a thunk. The sound unmistakably emanated from a one hundred thirty pound woman fainting on carpet covered with protective plastic runners. I returned the phone to its proper resting place, nodded at the hunter, and sat down next to Ndugu. He showed no sign of deviating from wife hunting.

"We can journey together down an African river on a raft. You can establish a farm. I am a rich man. In exchange for your hand, I can give your family many cows."

"My parents are still *plotzing* from when I housed my horse on their terrace. After that experience, the landlord made them sign a lease which specifically bars hooved animals. My family is unable to house cows. Furthermore, I am in no mood to donate cows to

Blackhole State University. Ndugu you are very nice. I can't marry you. I have to meet my department head in Cape Town."

"I can offer you your own hut in the center of my village. You can be friends with my four other wives"

"Jewish women from Forest Hills do not live in huts. And, as for my being friends with your wives, sisterhood is just not that powerful. Please know that I am very complimented by your generous offer. I am sorry. I must decline. My decision stands. There is no procedural irregularity."

The plane landed in Ile de La Sol. Ndugu removed his snakes from the overhead compartment. They hissed at me. He looked crestfallen as he exited the plane. I flew on to Johannesburg.

When I boarded my connecting flight to Cape Town, I was surrounded by Afrikaner men -- giant boisterous specimen of exaggerated masculinity who ooze excess testosterone. I attracted their attention while climbing up on my seat to attempt to heft my suitcase into the overhead compartment. Placing the suitcase on my head while standing on the seat, I tried with all my might to force it into the narrow space. The entire plane load of Afrikaner men laughed hysterically. The one standing directly behind me contained himself and managed politely to ask if I needed assistance. I was taken aback. No American man had ever offered to extricate me from a similar circumstance. Perhaps the American men did not want to appear to be male chauvinist pigs. These denizens of routinely male chauvinist Afrikaner culture had no such qualms. I assented to the assistance offer. The brawny bulky offerer who towered over me raised his pinky and effortlessly guided my suitcase into the space intended for it. Applause filled the plane. I crunched myself up in my seat to avoid further attention.

"This flight has open seating. May I sit here next to you?" the man who lifted his pinky asked.

"By any chance do you have a wife who resides in a hut?"

"No. Afrikaner women from Cape Town do not live in huts."

"Then please take this seat."

"My name is Andreas Andreasbach. Obviously, you are not South African. What brings you here?"

"Your name is Undress? Afrikaners are conservative. Surely your mother did not name you Undress."

"Certainly not. My accent is confusing you."

"That's a relief. I find it difficult to pronounce your name. I'm Sondra. I'm going to teach at the University of Cape Town."

"How interesting. I know all of these great Cape Town bars and night clubs. Perhaps we could go out together during your stay." Andreas was obviously trying to pick me up. As a stranger in a strange land, I decided that it was too complicated to get involved with a man before I even saw my new temporary home. I put Andreas off.

"That is a very nice offer, Undress. But during my stay I want to devote myself to my teaching and writing."

"I wish you a wonderful time. Goodbye, Sondra," Andreas said as the plane landed and he effortlessly extricated my suitcase before exiting.

I exhaled nervously as I prepared to meet Gavin Gavinbach. While scanning the crowd, I noticed a good looking athletic middle-aged man holding a sign which read "Welcome, Sondra." The sign holder of course could be none other than Gavin. I was not prepared for the fact that he wore a khaki shirt, khaki shorts, and a pith helmet. Gavin, in other words, resembled a refugee from an Abercrombie & Fitch ad.

"Hello Gavin. I'm Sondra. I'm very excited to be here. Thank you for inviting me."

"Welcome. Let's get your stuff and I'll drive you to your apartment."

Gavin removed his pith helmet upon our arrival at a pleasant university residence. I looked out of the living room window and saw some brown blobs on a distant hill. "Wow, the dots on the hill must be animals. Even though I'm from New York, I know from animals. I lived in rural Blackhole, Virginia for many years. Those must be cows."

"I'm afraid not. You're looking at wildebeest."

"Wildebeest? I'm living with a direct view of wildebeest? Do wildebeest moo and make noise at night? Are wildebeest carnivores? Are wildebeest kosher? These window screens are very flimsy and they contain big holes. There are potential carnivores out there and I have holes in my screens. I knew that when I came to Africa I would encounter Woody Allen's worst nightmare: blades of grass growing far from a subway station. But I never expected to endure having hole-sodden screens serving as the only thing separating me from a carnivore infested hill. Why doesn't the university call the exterminator?

"Calm down Sondra. Wildebeest are not carnivores. Wildebeest are kosher. Wildebeest live peacefully throughout the property adjacent to the university. You won't be able to see them during the rainy season."

"What a relief. Mosquitoes are the only things threatening to eat me I've ever faced. Wildebeest; thus it is. I have to admit that University of Cape Town wildebeest are much more exotic than Blackhole State University cows."

"I must be on my way. There's a food store and a bank located a few blocks from here. Classes start in two weeks. You will be teaching the seminar on Kennedy and Clinton you requested. See you around in the department."

"Will you be free for lunch?" I asked as I thought of the fate people who exit their car in the game preserve meet. Lions would be much more interested than Gavin in lunching with me.

"Maybe towards the end of the term. I'm on sabbatical. I'm using my release time to climb Mount Kilamanjaro."

"I understand that you will be busy. Thanks for inviting me to teach here. Bye Gavin. Don't forget your pith helmet."

I unpacked, thought about Gavin's disinterest, and concluded that I had mistakenly discarded Undress. Unlike death inflicted by wildebeest, what was done in relation to Undress could be undone. I formulated a plan to retrieve him from the cast-off bin, make him a part of my vested interests, and show good will. I phoned South African Airlines. "Hello. This is Professor Sondra Lear, an American scholar teaching at the University of Cape Town. I wonder if you can help me. I was on your flight 108 from Johannesburg to Cape Town today. I sat in seat 7A next to a person named Undress Undressbach. Let me spell it for you. I can't pronounce it properly." (The spelling assuaged the possibility that a women desperately seeking a male plane passenger named Undress might be bent upon terrorizing him.) "I found his gold tie clip after he disembarked. Could you give me his contact information? I would like to return his property to him."

"Thank you for your concern for your fellow passenger. I will get in touch with Mr. Andreasbach and ask if he chooses to make his information available. If so, I will tell you how to reach him. Call back in a few days and ask for reference file zoo911. Thank you for calling South African Airlines. Good day." A few days later, I had Undress's Johannesburg phone number in my hot little hands. I phoned Carrie to tell her that I had arrived.

"Hi. This is Sondra. I'm here in university housing."

"Great. How was your flight? How are you doing so far?"

"Things have been a little hectic. I received a marriage proposal involving scenic hut views, Gavin is not interested in me, and I am stalking Undress. And, oh yes, I'm now calmed down about the potentially chomping wildebeest I can see from my window. Gavin made it clear that they are not interested in chomping on me."

"Due to the fact that you have been here for less than twenty-four hours, I find this report quite extraordinary. I want all the details about your impressions of Gavin. And who is Undress? You can tell me all about everything on the plane to Jo'burg. My husband Garth teaches at the University of Witwatersrand. We have a second house in Jo'burg. I want to invite you to spend the time before classes start living with Garth and me there. We'll have a great time. We can spend a weekend in a game preserve. Do say you'll come."

"Of course I will. What a wonderful opportunity."

During the flight, I filled Carrie in on all the Gavin and Undress details. Her advice: Pursuing Gavin was hopeless; I should concentrate on Undress. I immediately felt at home with her hospitable husband and multitudinous volumes of science fiction literature and criticism. It was a special pleasure to see books I had written shelved in a South African home. However, even as a native New Yorker, I found it hard to adjust to Carrie's multitudinous burglar alarms, the bars covering the doors and windows of her suburban home, and the barbed wired wall which surrounded it. When compared to the rampant crime in Johannesburg, New York resembled Snoopy's bucolic birthplace, the Daisy Hill Puppy Farm. Immediately upon arrival in Carrie's home, I questioned one aspect of her domestic life.

"Who lives in the shack behind your house?"

"Our black gardener."

"You have a live-in gardener? I don't know any American academics who employ live-in gardeners."

"Most suburban white Jo'burg residents have live-in black gardeners."

"Carrie, you are very politically liberal. Don't you feel strange having an impoverished person living substandardly in your backyard?"

"If the gardener did not live there and we did not employ him he would be homeless. I never really thought about this before. This is just how things are here." I decided not to pursue the subject.

At the end of my first day as Carrie's house guest, I was too cold to think about anything. Even though the temperature was hovering close to freezing, Carrie's home -- like the majority of Johannesburg private residences and public buildings -- lacked central heating. My blanket wrapped body stretched on Carrie's living room floor next to the space heater soon became a familiar sight. If, after having a heart attack, I was lying on the floor dead, Carrie and Garth would have treated my corpse as a usual part of the décor and calmly stepped over it. .

"How do you people live without adequate heat and winter clothing? You can afford heat. You can afford winter coats. Why do you live like this?" I vehemently inquired.

"It is only cold for about two or three weeks during the year. Winter accoutrements would be extraneous."

"When I go to the beach for the afternoon I take sun screen, a beach chair, and an umbrella. I do everything I can to make myself comfortable. I just can't understand your mind set." Relegating this subject to the best-not-pursued-further category, I settled down next to the heater while contemplating how to bathe with all of my clothes on. To stay warm, I literally enacted three dog night. Carrie's and Garth's three dogs were happy to sleep in my bed rather than in the backyard. Despite the severity of the cold, I did draw the line at asking the gardener to follow suit.

I was awakened by dog commotion. Two dogs were howling at the top of their lungs and the third was sitting on my head. Carrie peered into my bedroom. "Wake up Sondra. Garth and I are taking you to a game preserve."

"I am already living with three South African animals."

"You know perfectly well that South African dogs do not qualify as big game. Be ready in a half hour." At least I had something appropriate to wear. I reached into my suitcase and pulled out a feminine version of Gavin's Abercrombie & Fitch outfit. The pith helmet suited me especially well. I look good in all hats.

Carrie stood motionless with her mouth agape. "Why are you wearing a parodic hunting costume? Surely this exaggerated outfit is not a routine part of your usual daily wardrobe."

"I love costumes. During a Halloween party at Blackhole State University, I dressed as a Modern Language Association job candidate. I wore a white blouse adorned with a little bow, a really bad suit, and I carried leather briefcase. As a finishing touch, I pinned an MLA Convention name tag over my breast. My colleagues responded in terms of high anxiety, not levity. At the following year's party, I came dressed as a Miss Virginia beauty pageant contestant. I wore a skin-tight red dress, put a tiara on my head, and placed a "Miss Virginia" sash over my shoulder. A few real Miss Virginias did hail from Blackhole State. Unlike me, the authentic Blackhole Miss Virginia's did not author feminist scholarly books -- or scholarly books on any subject. And they are not Jewish. No mere Halloween costume, my exaggerated safari outfit is absolutely relevant to my life in New York; it is perfect for my husband-hunting sojourns. I go husband-hunting about four times a week. You shouldn't know from how much it costs to dry clean my hunting outfit. I need high quality hunting equipment. It isn't easy to track quarry at receptions and diverse singles events. The outfit enables me to stand out from the crowd. I'll be ready as soon as I *spritz* on some *Jungle Gardenia*."

"Don't be so hard on Sondra. She looks cute in her husband-hunting outfit," said Garth.

We entered the game preserve after an uneventful forty-five minute drive.

"Garth and I come here routinely. I do hope you will share our enthusiasm for this place. Oh look Sondra. There's a gray-flecked speckled gnu."

"I don't see anything. I count myself lucky when I can spot André Brink and J. M. Coetzee shuffling papers in the English department copy machine room. I know a celebrity Nobel Prize winner when I see one. Vis-à-vis gnu, though, I don't even know what I should be looking for. Are gnu big animals? Are gnu carnivores? Are gnu kosher? I can only see a lot of rocks."

"Look at that big round rock there. Notice the grazing lily-livered sap-sucking triglyceride. And under that tree I see a red-throated tsorisaurus," Garth chimed in.

"I still just see rocks. Are there any more tsorisaurus? I have encountered a really big tsorisaurus in the Museum of Natural History. Even though they are prehistoric, maybe conditions here are right for their survival."

"No. No more tsorisaurus," Carrie and Garth said in unison.

"It's for the best. A tsorisaurus would cause too much trouble on a game preserve. I can't recognize fauna as well as you. You grew up with gnu, triglycerides, and many a tsorisaurus; I grew up with roaches, pigeons, and subway rat sightings. Wait. Look. I see something. I see a big gray thing over there. It's fatter than I am! I can even identify it. I can't believe it. I'm seeing a wild elephant. I know. I know. I can't leave the car to feed the elephant some of my diet Nestles Crunch Bar. Manhattan does not have everything; Manhattan does not have wild elephants. Thank you so much for bringing me to this game preserve."

"You're so very welcome. You've traveled such a long way to reach South Africa. I want so much for your trip to be memorable," said Carrie.

Despite the excitement the preserve provided, it was somehow good to return to my spot in front of the space heater and go to the dogs. Available resting periods were in short supply. Carrie had more adventures in store for me.

"I've received a call from the University of South Africa in Pretoria. They want you to give a lecture. You're scheduled for tomorrow. Pretoria is about a two hour drive. I'll take you. You've had a lot of excitement lately. Let's just hang around the house today. Later in the afternoon we can go food shopping and to the bank."

We arrived at the bank a few minutes before the five o'clock closing time. I waited outside while Carrie withdrew money. I watched as guards armed with rifles carried bags filled with money to an armored truck. When Carrie rejoined me, she was visibly upset.

"I left my wallet on the counter. It contains my entire salary for the month in cash. The door guard won't let me back inside. He says that the bank closed two minutes ago."

"His decision is ridiculous. Just get his attention and tell him you need to get your wallet."

"It won't work. It 's hopeless. He won't let me in. Let's just go home. I can't believe I've lost so much money."

"Your money is not lost. We know exactly where it is. I have to say what I think. The reticence your culture values is not serving you well. I know that I am a guest and I should shut up and go with the flow. But I can't stand the sight of your dejected face. Stand back. This is a job for an assertive Jewish New York feminist -- as if there is any other kind."

I approached the bank's sliding glass double door and knocked to get the guard's attention. "Excuse me. My friend left her wallet on the counter. Can she please retrieve it?"

"No. I'm sorry. The bank is closed."

"This is ridiculous. There is no reason why you can't let my friend in. Let her in."

"No."

"Let her in or I will stand here kicking the door until you do." I kicked the door with all of my might. Two heavy set black women voiced their encouragement by shouting "Right on, sister." The guard relented. "Tell her to come in quickly," he said as he pushed the glass doors open. Carrie emerged triumphantly with her wallet in hand.

"I can't believe you did that. I've never seen anyone do such a thing. I could never have done it no matter what. Please give me assertiveness training pointers. How did you have the courage to yell and kick the door when you were in the proximity of two men armed with automatic rifles?"

"Oh, in the heat of the moment I forgot about the rifles. My local Citibank and Chase Manhattan branches are devoid of rifles. I was so focused upon retrieving your money, I forgot that I'm not in Manhattan any more. My tactics worked -- and I did not get shot. Let's not talk about it anymore. Tonight I'll turn in with the dogs early. I want to be well rested for the UNISA lecture.

While driving from Johannesburg to Pretoria, I knew that I was not on the Long Island Expressway anymore. Carrie said that it was too dangerous to visit Soweto. She called the Kruger Monument a phallic memorial to patriarchal and racist horror. I compared presenting a lecture at UNISA to visiting Ursula Le Guin's planet Gethen, a.k.a. Winter. The university, like Carrie's house, lacked heat. I was frozen to the extent that I tried to derive warmth from grasping my coffee cup. My hands were so cold, I could hardly turn pages as I read. UNISA, a stark white stone edifice resembling Lincoln Center running rampant, was a refrigerator masquerading as a university. When my lecture concluded, I almost applauded myself to warm my hands. I looked forward to returning to Carrie's warm and welcoming dogs. Her car began to sputter a few miles outside of Soweto.

"I can't restart the car. The car is dead."

"It is very dangerous to be stranded on an American highway. To have one's car act analogously to road kill in South Africa can't be good." Carrie began to cry.

"This is terrible. We're in great danger. Carjackings occur routinely. We're sitting ducks for anyone who wants to rob us -- or worse. I never took my salary out of my wallet."

"*Oy!* Saying "*oy*" made me feel much better. I think we should calmly figure out what to do. Crying is not helpful."

"You're my guest. I'm responsible for you. You're a famous science fiction critic. The entire worldwide science fiction critical community will find out that you were murdered due to my negligence."

"Don't jump the gun. The sun is low in the sly behind that mountain. Will it set fast? How often do police patrol cars come by?"

"The sunset is imminent and the temperature falls rapidly at night. I have never seen a police patrol car on this road."

"Crime aside, it is dangerous to park along a highway without headlights or flashers. I say that we have a better chance if we get out and walk." Carrie continued to cry as we started to walk down the road.

"We have to keep our spirits up. Let's sing. Repeat after me. I love to go a wandering along the mountain track. Val de ree. Val de ra. Val de ra. Val de ra ha ha ha ha ha ha..."

"I can speak Afrikaans and I am familiar with the eleven South African tribal languages. I have never heard the equal of val de ree val de ra ha ha. We're facing serious danger. This is no 'ra ha ha' laughing matter."

"I'll change songs: "Whenever I feel afraid I hold my head erect and whistle a happy tune so no one will suspect I'm afraid.'"

"I'm very obviously afraid. I don't know how to whistle. Anna was much safer in Siam than we are now," said Carrie. We froze in our tracks as we heard a car approach and stop just behind us. Yesterday we were driving in a game preserve; now we were deer in the headlights. We grasped each others' hands and slowly turned to face whatever would befall us. Although it was too dark to see clearly, I discerned that a man was approaching us. There was no way to mistake the sight of the gun which hung from his waist.

Hence, I did not even think about his marital status. Yes, I have routinely experienced teleportation and outer space travel -- and I have met death by initial tenure denial. But please understand that I have led a very sheltered life. The supernatural beings I fraternize with are on-my-side good guys. I could not contact Ilya or the Sondras now. My usual means to communicate with them are not roadside attractions. Red clogs are not appropriate lecture giving attire. The Sondras would not understand that UNISA could substitute for a refrigerator. Ilya and the Sondras are not guardian angels; Jews don't have guardian angels. No supernatural support was available to counter my present reality: a mortal man carrying a gun was approaching along a dark highway embankment. After all of that husband-hunting, I was helpless in the face of a gun-carrying male. I thought of the advertisement which pictures a tornado and says "bad things happen when you leave New York." Close gun encounter of course occurs in New York. Having it happen in Africa seemed to be worse. I took a deep breath and waited for a bullet to pierce my heart. *Oy*, a literal heart break. Carrie screamed.

The man spoke. "Don't be frightened ladies. I'm here to help you. I'm traffic patrol officer Byrnie Byrniebach. I can phone a family member for you." How could I not trust a man named Byrnie? It is embarrassing to be a damsel in distress. When Garth came to the rescue in his car, for once I was not on my feminist high horse.

The next morning, as usual, Carrie cheerfully entered my room and greeted the hungry dogs. "We're safe. It's over. I take my responsibility as a host very seriously. My transgression was egregious to the extent that I never want to think about it."

"Fine. But Garth, 'to the rescue' underscores the importance of having a husband. I still want to find one. I'm going to call Undress."

"I had forgotten about Undress. My curiosity is all agog. I must find out what he is like. Do call him."

"I have his number here in my suitcase compartment." I dialed the number and heard an unmistakable male Afrikaner accent.

"Yeeeeees?"

"Hello. Am I speaking with Undress Undressbach?"

"Yeeeeees."

"This is Sondra Lear. We met a few weeks ago on the flight to Cape Town. I thought it would be fun to get in touch with you. South African Airlines gave me your number. I'm in Johannesburg and I'm staying with a friend who lives on Trafalgar Square Street. Would you be free to have lunch?"

"Yeeeeees, Sondra I do remember you. I never expected you to call. What a coincidence that you would show up on Trafalgar Square Street. I live two blocks away on Charing Cross Road. I'm complimented that you took the trouble to find me. I would like to see you. Before doing so, though, I must tell you the truth. I flirted with you for fun. I do not live alone on Charing Cross Road; my wife lives here too. She might even know your host. But, even though I am married, we can still be friends. I own a diamond factory located downtown on the corner of Piccadilly Circus and Whitehall Road. Please do come, and I'll show you around." Even though I had just found out that diamonds are not always a girl's best friend, I tried to sound cheerful.

"Thank you so much for the lovely invitation. See you soon. Bye."

"What did Undress say?" asked Carrie.

"He talked about diamonds."

"Diamonds? Undress wants to give you an engagement ring? Before the first date?"

"Not exactly. He invited me to visit his diamond factory. His prime inventory is ensconced around his wife's finger."

"I'm so sorry that your husband hunt failed again. Look on the bright side. It will be fun to see a diamond factory. I'll be glad to accompany you. You absolutely can't go downtown alone. I'll try my best to find a parking spot near the factory. We can run inside the building as fast as we can together. I'm up for this."

"You're enthusiasm is contagious. The phone's ringing."

"I'll get it. It's for you. A woman named Herbert says that she's your mother." I put the receiver to my ear and heard the unmistakable piercing voice.

"Why can't you be normal, Sondra? Normal women receive engagement rings. Normal women do not go to the diamond factory the married man they have stalked owns."

"Herbert, you have a point. I'm on my way out. Nelson Mandela is participating in a parade. I must arrive at the parade ground before the parade passes by. Bye."

"Your mother really sounds like a trip."

"Don't ask. Maybe the flight back to Cape Town will divert my mind from having to deal with her call—and the fact that she doesn't know that I'm staying with you."

"We are not up to the return flight yet. There is one more thing on your agenda: *Good Morning South Africa* called to say that they want to interview you. The television studio is located near Undress's diamond factory. We could kill two birds with one stone by visiting the factory and the studio tomorrow."

"Sounds good."

Carrie and I survived going from the car to the factory entrance without violent mishap. Undress was charming. I enjoyed seeing the diamond manufacturing process. I could not resist asking him to appraise the diamond ring I inherited from my grandmother. I have worn it daily since I was seventeen. Teenaged me did have to threaten to sue my mother to acquire the ring. That's another story -- and it dwarfs all the *tsuris* in *The Lord of the Rings*. First ring things first, though. Just in case anyone ever did marry me, I made Undress promise to give me a diamond ring discount. I mean if the man is married I at least deserved to receive a discounted ring. Discount mission accomplished, Carrie and I headed toward the *Good Morning South Africa* studio. I entered the makeup room.

"What kind of makeup to you usually wear?," the makeup artist asked.

"I never wear any."

"I see. This color should go nicely on you." I found myself on stage face to face with a Katie Couric clone interviewer. (This clone bore no relationship to the Sondras.) I was in mid-stock explanation about addressing feminist science fiction's importance to someone who did not know photon torpedoes from zap guns when the director screamed "Cut!" The Katie Couric clone was given a note. After glancing at it, she nervously faced the camera. "Ladies and gentleman, we interrupt this program to bring you a special report bulletin live from Forest Hills, New York." The nearest monitor revealed a big head replete with bleached blonde big hair and a very big mouth. The familiar relentless voice emanated from the big mouth. "Good morning South Africa. This is Herbert, Sondra's mother. I am speaking to you because I know what is best for her. Attention all the single men out there in South African television land. I know there are rich men in South Africa. I know there are Jewish men in South Africa. If you are rich and Jewish and you are a man marry Sondra immediately if not sooner." I excused myself, jumped off of the stage, found Carrie in the audience, and ran out of the studio building.

"Please take me to the airport. I want to fly back to Cape Town immediately. I'm not scheduled to teach for another four days. Maybe my mother will not try to reach me there. I can have four days of peace." Carrie complied. I winged my way back to my apartment and the wildebeest. Wildebeest had never looked so good.

I settled calmly into teaching my Kennedy and Clinton course. The University of Cape Town, one of South Africa's most elite schools, has brilliant students -- the cream of the South African crop. I was pleased that my students were predominantly women. I happened to tell one student that I had recently lost twenty-five pounds. This fact spread like wild fire among all my students and caused them to become uncommonly agitated. "Tell us. We just have to know," a particular feisty student demanded just as I was explaining that Monica Lewinsky was no Marilyn Monroe.

"Sure. I am open to telling you all I know. What do you want to know about? Kennedy's affairs? Hillary's response to Bill's bimbos?"

"We want to know how you lost twenty-five pounds." My class filled with South Africa's most brilliant young women and they were chomping at the bit to learn about calories, not Camelot or Clinton.

"Fair enough. I do know a great deal about diet and nutrition. You can talk to me about it after class. Now please turn to page thirty-five of *It Takes A Village*." All the women remained to find out about my successful weight loss techniques. Dr. Lear had somehow morphed into Dr Atkins. No sweat. A diet doctor and a science fiction doctor are quite similar; both deal with quests to reach unrealistic goals. Luckily, since I hail from Forest Hills rather than Scarsdale, I did not have to worry that I would meet Dr. Herman Tarnower's fate at the hands of Jean Harris.

After spending two hours telling the students about vegetables, exercise, and portion control, I decided to spend the afternoon unwinding in Cape Town's major park. I stopped off in my apartment to change clothes and prepare my usual lunch which consisted of two hard boiled eggs (sans yolks so I do not die from cholesterol poisoning. Seeing all of those triglycerides in the game preserve reminded me that one can never be too careful.) In order to avoid being mugged, I put on my most ratty sweatpants and sweatshirt and removed my grandmother's diamond ring. Recalling my undergraduate days when I tore up my work shirt and frizzed out my hair, I made myself look as poor and disheveled as possible. Upon arrival in the park, I sat on a bench located under an attractive tree and proceeded to eat my hard boiled eggs. Two opulently dressed, obviously married, German tourists saw me and stopped. They looked sad and concerned. "Can we offer you some of our lunch?" the leather suit clad, bejeweled German woman asked. My diet and attempts to dress down to guard against crime were too successful. The Germans thought that they were helping a poor starving destitute South African. For the first time in my life, I successfully lose weight and look thin and now Germans see me as a poster woman for African deprivation. I glared at them and used the stronges? New York accent I could muster: "Naw. Tomorra I'm gonna go on that big boid in the sky flight thoidy-three to be exact back to New Yawk. I'll get lunch on the plane. I ordered a koshaw meal." (Mark Twain never created vernacular like this.) Realizing that they were offering to feed a prosperous American tourist -- and a Jewish one at that -- the Germans quickly extricated themselves from my presence.

My remaining time in Cape Town progressed uneventfully. After handing in my grades, I packed my belongings and, while doing so, located my red clogs. I tapped them together. Smoke, as was to be expected, engulfed the apartment. The wildebeest quizzically scented the air as the smoke went through the big holes in the screens and wafted towards them. "You rang, Dearest S?" asked Ilya.

"I'm so glad to see you. Can we have sex? Gavin isn't interested in me. Undress is married. I need to have sex."

"Happy as ever to comply." Ilya snapped his fingers. "So, now that we are instantaneously undressed, do you want to have bourgeoisie gravitationally routine sex or levitated flying sex?"

"I think I will opt for the routine kind. Please don't turn off the gravity."

"Anything you say. You know I aim to please," said Ilya as he entered me. "What's that noise?"

"The wildebeest must be in heat. I hope they feel as sexually satisfied as I do now. Oh, before you return to your creepy castle, please zap me back to Forest Hills. I just can't face a fourteen hour flight. Especially after dealing with the men I met when I flew here in the usual way."

"Of course. No problem. You know the zap flight procedure by now." I put on the clogs and tapped them together. I found myself sitting naked on the couch located in my parents' apartment with the clogs still firmly on my feet. I smelled a musty, vaguely horse-ish odor. Fearing that the Sondras had decided to reinstate Ms. Ed back into my life, I entered the kitchen to investigate. I saw a wildebeest calmly munching on a head of iceberg lettuce. At least, since wildebeest are not carnivorous, this particular one was not having an *après*-dinner salad to assuage heart burn caused by ingesting Herbert's head. I said hello to the wildebeest. She or he looked at me blankly and chomped on. So this was a real garden variety large hooved animal, not a magic talking one of Ms. Ed's ilk. I could not reason with it -- and it most certainly was not house trained. The wildebeest began to sniff around the refrigerator and paw the linoleum. It grunted, raised its tail, and bent its hind legs. I panicked. I frantically clicked the red clogs together. Smoke appeared. "You miscalculated when you zapped me back. You included an inadvertent stowaway. Ilya, get this wildebeest out of my parents' kitchen this minute. And I mean this minute. The wildebeest is about to excrete."

"Yes Sondra. Certainly." Ilya snapped his fingers. The wildebeest vanished. The kitchen floor was left unscathed. "I'm sorry. I was distracted by having sex with you to the extent that my zap transport sphere of influence became overextended. The wildebeest was accidentally transported to Forest Hills in your wake. All's well that ends well."

Pilgrim Through Space and Time

I am not beginning by alluding to *The Pilgrim's Progress*. I will not say "Call me Christian." I'm Sondra trying to find a husband in Manhattan, not Christian trying to find God in the Celestial City. John Bunyan did not have me in mind.

The phone rang before Ilya had a chance to do his vanish-in-the-smoke-puff routine.

"Professor Lear?"

"Speaking."

"This is D'Elanna Roosevelt, President of the Science Fiction Research Association. We've met before."

"I remember you well. You're a cousin of *Star Trek Voyager* Chief Engineer D'Elanna Torres."

"Yes, that's right. Congratulations! You have won the Science Fiction Research Association's Pilgrim Award for lifetime achievement in science fiction criticism. You're the latest recipient of the science fiction field's highest honor which, as I am sure you know, is named for J. O. Bailey's *Pilgrims Through Space and Time: Trends and Patterns in Scientific and Utopian Fiction*. Please join us at the next SFRA conference in Los Angeles for the awards ceremony taking place aboard the Queen Mary."

"Winning the Pilgrim Award has been my lifelong dream. I wouldn't miss the ceremony for anything. I look forward to seeing you at the conference."

"Ilya, before you go, please move time up to the SFRA conference date, give me a minute to pack, and zap me on board the Queen Mary."

"Congratulations on your award. I'm a SFRA member -- and one of the first Pilgrim Award winners. "Off to the Queen Mary you go," he said as he snapped his fingers and disappeared.

My suitcase and I were now located in a Queen Mary Hotel stateroom. I was thrilled to be on this historic ship. Marlene Dietrich, Clark Gable, and Winston Churchill had all sailed on the Queen Mary. They might have stood on the very spot where I was now standing. This possibility impressed me even though my permanently moored Queen Mary differs from the ocean going one Clark, Marlene, and Winston experienced. The Queen Mary Hotel does not sail. The ship, at once real and unreal, symbolizes my life. I am, after all, the only mortal SFRA Pilgrim (Ilya does not fit the "mortal" category) who has ever traveled via space-time continuum alteration. I can live with restraining from telling my colleagues that I am a literal pilgrim through space and time. But I can't abide having to wait until the end of the conference to reveal that I am the Pilgrim winner. I can't break the tradition stipulating that the Pilgrim's identity must remain secret until the award ceremony. One peep out of me and the word would spread as rapidly as water entering the Titanic. The vicissitudes of this locutionary imperative aside, I am grateful that the moored Queen Mary is not the Titanic. I get sea sick. Even the Queen Mary Hotel makes me feel queasy. Thank God that keeping my mouth shut to avoid the wrath of my tradition-loving colleagues serves as the only life preserver I need while on this particular ship.

Keeping quiet was easier said than done, though. As one of the biggest *yentas* in the world, I literally had to bite my tongue when *kibitzing* with the science fiction critics who had been my friends and colleagues for years. It was particularly hard for me to keep the secret from Jeffrey Blumberger. I am particularly close to Jeffrey -- even though he is one of the few male science fiction critics who never tried to seduce me. Jeffrey, a dead ringer for Steven Spielberg, is warm, humorous, and charming to the extent that he could be a television game show host. He waved and approached across the starboard ("starboard" sounds good -- but, for all I know it could have been the leeward) deck.

"Ahoy, Sondra," Jeffrey said.

"Hi, Jeffrey. Are you sure you haven't changed your mind about marrying me? You're still Jewish and single."

"We have a great friendship and we should just keep it that way." Jeffrey tried abruptly to change the subject. "Any idea who won the Pilgrim Award?" I extricated myself to avoid lying.

"Talk to you later. Gotta go. There are a lot of seagulls overhead. Ya never know when one will decide it's gotta go too. Maybe the sea gull flock flying low over this ship filled with science fiction critics might have heard it said that science fiction is crap. Maybe this association might give them the urge to excrete. So I gotta go immediately. See ya."

I walked to the leeward (or starboard) deck wondering how I would manage to keep my secret. I knew that I had to articulate the information loudly and clearly. The deck was deserted. I walked to the prow, jumped up on the rail, and screamed as loudly as I could. "I am the *yenta* of the world. I have won the Pilgrim Award." Even though the *Titanic*-sodden Leonardo DiCaprio had nothing to fear from me, I felt decidedly better. Somehow I would be able to keep my secret for the next two days -- even if I had to engage with people by acting analogously to an iceberg.

I entered the ship's bar and noticed that Sara Scottywitz, a young Scottish Jewish feminist science fiction critic, was holding court surrounded by a male horde salivating over her very large and very exposed breasts. As she bent to retrieve a fallen napkin, the force of her breasts pulled across her skin-tight shirt almost caused the shirt to rip apart. The man seated closest to her fell off of his bar stool. Sara did not believe in fidelity. To advance her career, she had recently married my friend and former lover Cedric Raymond, the editor of *Science Fiction Endowment* who was twenty-five years her senior. Due in part to the fact that she was so well endowed, Cedric made Sara the subsequent editor of *Endowment*. Cedric was not attending this conference. No middle-aged well published male science fiction scholar who could enhance Sara's career was beyond her manipulative reach. Since she had an open marriage, she could still be on the make. I watched as she whispered sweet nothings into the ear of Pilgrim winner Harry G. Fox while seductively placing her arm around him. Harry, in the manner of his male colleagues, gazed longingly at Sara's breasts.

I halfway expected bisexual Sara to hit on me. I fit the bill *vis-a-vis* her usual professional success quarry criteria. I immediately cast this idea aside. Herbert would fall to her knees in abject misery if

I never defined Sara as appropriate spouse hunt prey—regardless of the fact that Sara is Jewish. Herbert would rather have me marry Ngudu than Sara. Regardless of Herbert's anticipated response, taking up with Sara was out of the question. I could not tolerate occupying the same room with her.

This buxom attractive ambitious loquacious Jewish female science fiction critic was too close to me for comfort -- and I am not just talking location. I already had enough clones. As the first woman to go through the college English teaching profession as a science fiction critic, I was used to being the only show in town. I can deal with being cloned. I like all the Sondra clones. But Sara is something else. Sara is at once me -- and worse than me (as if being worse than me is possible. But, hey, the possible does not hold water as a delimiter on my Queen Mary). Mike Myers' *Goldmember* includes a clone called Mini Me. Sara is Monster Me. I abhor women who use sex to derive career advancement. I sincerely like the multitudinous science fiction critics I slept with. My breasts can stand up to Sara's on any given day of the year; I never wear tight shirts at conferences. (Okay, there was that time in Italy. But I dressed like a tramp to generate sexual attraction, not publication contracts.) As much as I hate to admit it, her method was effective. With breasts exposed and legs apart, she was editing and organizing conferences like a storm. She is a force. She was able to hold her own when I complained about her scathingly negative review of my major scholarly book. I had never met anyone who survived to tell the tale after encountering me in full argument mode. As I approached Sara, a new-fangled next generation Monster Me contraption, I resolved to remain civil.

To remove Harry from his breast-sodden trance, I waved my hand in front of his glazed fixated eyes. Sara removed her lips from Harry's ear and her hand from his God-only-knows-where and put her arm around me. With speed with which I usually ask men to marry me (warp factor six), she articulated exactly what was on her mind.

"What do I have to do to win the Pilgrim Award?" I provided the true answer.

"Spend fourteen years writing books. You're wearing a lovely shirt. But World War Two has been over for years. I didn't know that the British are still rationing fabric." Sensing an impending showdown between the planet's two most buxom Jewish female science fiction critic bigmouthed broads, Jonathan Karl Goodman, one of the men in Sara's thrall, intervened to stop our deployment of weapons of mass destruction -- weapons that would not fail to turn the immobile tranquil Queen Mary into the sinking of the Bismarck.

"I have very much wanted to meet you. I love *Oy Pioneer!*. I think it is one of the great Jewish novels of our generation." Jonathan certainly knew how to get my attention. Nor could I fail to notice his heavy Southern accent.

"You're just saying that to be polite."

"Never! Never under any circumstance would I compromise my professional integrity. I have given y'all my unabashed professional opinion. Thus it is."

"I am thrilled that you think so highly of my novel. I'm writing a sequel."

"Wonderful news. Just keep it up. Create a compelling male protagonist modeled after me. I trust that you will use the phrase 'amazing sexual powers' to describe him. If you fail to do so, I will sue you. When you write your out-of-this-world hotel room tumult scene, don't even think about suggesting that I'm having sex with my horse. If you do, I will hate you as much as some of the other real people who turn up as your protagonists. Let's take a walk on the deck." Desiring to see relic life preservers in the fresh sea air, instead of Sara's breasts in the musty bar, I agreed to accompany Jonathan. This attractive and engaging man who wore a striking white linen suit resembled Tom Wolfe -- that is to say a Tom Wolfe who did not exude a Waspish aura.

"Your Marxist science fiction criticism is very impressive. I am not the only one who thinks you are generating a baby boomer follow up to Ilya Lugosi's eminent work." Discretion was called for. I could not tell Jonathan that I would receive the Pilgrim Award tomorrow. I could also not tell him that Ilya, in addition to being a renowned critic, was an immortal vampire who had had supernatural sex with me the day before yesterday.

"Someone named Jonathan Karl Goodman must be Jewish. But you don't sound Jewish."

"I'm a Southern Jew. I was raised in Mississippi and I teach at the University of Mississippi. I'm divorced and I have twins named Rhett and Scarlett."

"Southern Jews, to my mind, don't count as really being Jewish. When I was teaching in Virginia at Blackhole State, I was desperate to see Jews to the extent that I drove to a temple in Roanoke. There I was standing in the middle of the Roanoke temple surrounded by Roanoke Jews. I asked myself 'where are all the Jews?' To escape Jew-devoid Virginia, I accepted a Fulbright to Germany. I felt more comfortable with Germans than with Southern Jews."

"You're being a New York chauvinist pig. They're not kosher. You were comfortable in Germany because you grew up in an immigrant culture. We Southern Jews are Jews too. New York Jews erroneously think that you have to come from New York to be Jewish."

"You're right. I'll think about what you said. How well do you know Sara?"

"I just met her in the bar. Her breasts are captivating. Like all the men here, I could not take my eyes off of them. She mentioned you to me while she was acting as the center of attention with martini in hand. She warned all the ogling men that if they slept with you, they would end up in one of your novels. I'm willing to take my chances. Can we have sex right now? If you so desire, you can write away right away as soon as it is over. Unlike Sara, you're my age. I've had it with younger women."

In addition to being single and Jewish, Jonathan is brilliant, charming, clever, and trustworthy. I took his hand and led him to my stateroom. We had great sex. Moonlight shone through the porthole and illuminated our entwined naked bodies. Jonathan had amazing sexual powers. "Write on," said Jonathan.

"Okay."

I know from what I am talking about when I say amazing sexual powers. I, after all, have had sex with Ilya the immortal vampire. Ilya can generate fantastic sex. (I refer to "fantastic" to denote "satisfying" as well as -- according to Eric S. Rabkin's *The Fantastic In Literature* -- "unreal.") Maybe Churchill, Dietrich, and Gable had fantastic sex on the Queen Mary. I woke up entangled in Jonathan's arms. A rose adorned our pillow.

"I love you Sondra."

"I love you too."

"Does a hotel ship have a Captain? Do you think the hotel ship Captain could marry us?" Jonathan asked.

"I don't think a hotel ship has a Captain."

"Yeah, you're right. I guess it is premature to marry some-one who you have only known for twenty-four hours. I have a great idea. Why don't you come to Mississippi and live with me? You will love the Goodman ancestral antebellum mansion. It has been in the family for generations. My great-great-great grandfather, Yehuda Goodman, named it Shady Pines. The property includes a beautiful white mansion replete with sweeping porticos and verandahs. An oak-lined drive leads to the front door. You can run your fingers through the sacred red earth of Shady Pines. You can have your very own magnolia tree."

Although I felt certain that Jonathan would not ask his wife to live outside of the mansion in her very own hut, I found it neces-sary to ask this question: "Do you have a black gardener?"

"Of course. How else can I keep up the sweeping verdant landscape and the smell of the sweet verbena wafting across the North portico? The vast south lawn extends all the way down to the Mississippi River."

"I thought that you would have a black gardener. Does the gardener live in the back of your house?"

"As a matter of fact, yes. He bunks in the refurbished serv-ants' quarters which precede the Civil War. I can just see us sitting under your very own magnolia sipping mint juleps while we waiting for the groom (he lives next door to the gardener) to bring my favor-ite black stallion Beauregard Jackson Pickett Burnside over from the barn. I enjoy my daily land surveying ride. We can chat with my fem-inist colleague Penelope the Fat. Penelope the Fat thinks that the right to eat is a feminist political entitlement. She is as wide as the entire Shady Pines plantation and Beauregard Jackson Pickett Burn-side put together. I think that Beauregard Jackson Pickett Burnside is attracted to Penelope. You would like her. She is the biggest *yenta* in Mississippi. And she gossips to the extent that she writes a "Dear Penelope" advice column to mentor young women academics. May-be Sara should write to her. I can imagine her letter: 'Dear Penelope: How much of my breasts do I have to expose and how many science fiction critics do I have to seduce and/or marry in order to win the Pilgrim Award?'"

"I expect that Sara would indeed pen that epistle."

"Please say that you will become the mistress of Shady Pines."

"I love you Jonathan. I love you. You're perfect. Now change."

"Change? Change how?"

"Leave Shady Pines and join me in a Manhattan high-rise."

"I can't leave my ancestral home. Mississippi is where I'd rather stay. I get allergic if I don't smell hay. Hey, I can't tear little Rhett and little Scarlett away from their ancestral roots. Rhett is excelling in bootlegger school and Scarlett loves her cotillion lessons. And where would Beauregard Jackson Pickett Burnside live in Manhattan?"

"On a terrace. My horse Ms. Ed lived on the terrace attached to my parents' Forest Hills apartment."

"What? You had a terrace-dwelling horse? Not bad for a Yankee. Tell me more."

"Don't ask because I can't tell. I have to be direct. No matter how much I love you, and I do love you, Jewish women from Forest Hills do not live with Spanish moss. Mississippi is near Louisiana. What if the Louisiana alligators get confused and invade Mississippi? They can come out of the Mississippi River and eat Beauregard Jackson Picket Burnside -- and us. Is Penelope the Fat too big a mouthful for the invading alligators? I just can't take the alligator risk. I have had enough with the talking horse, the cat/husband, and the last, but not least, errant about to excrete wildebeest. But, again, don't ask."

"I see that we have reached an impasse. Why don't we become great friends?"

"I would love to have such a relationship. This romantic setting -- this ship which transported all of those sexy actors -- gives me an idea. There is a big difference between us and Marlene Dietrich and Clark Gable. We could never be as cool as Marlene and Clark. Let's fantasize that we are. Let's change our names. You could be Juan Carlo and I'll be Sandrine. We can call each other by these *goyish* 'not us' appellations."

"Sounds like fun."

"One last thing. Juan Carlo, would you accompany me to this evening's awards banquet?."

"Sure thing, Sandrine. I'll be back at your stateroom at six to escort you to the main dining room." When Jonathan returned, he was resplendent in a white linen tuxedo and electric red tie. I wore an elegant gold German designer pantsuit. We sat at a round flower-adorned table. This was my night, one of the biggest occasions of my life. I was at once excited, anxious, and overwhelmed by this dining room's historical import. "Juan Carlo, I have held out for two days without breathing a word to anyone. I can't wait another second. I've won the Pilgrim Award."

"What? That's wonderful! I am so proud of you, Sandrine." After a predictable rubber chicken entree, D'Elanna Roosevelt began the award ceremony. "Good evening ladies and gentleman. It is my pleasure to welcome you. We are privileged this year to gather at this lovely hotel ship. I know you are anxious to learn who is receiving this year's Pilgrim Award and the other awards SFRA bestows. I'll begin without further ado. First on the agenda is the Prophylactic Award for a science fiction critic who has never slept with Sondra Lear. Sondra has been single for her entire professional life. She is very attractive. She loves sex. Science fiction critics constitute the preponderance of the men she meets. Hence, this award is very hard to attain. Science fiction is a very small field; science fiction scholars who have not slept with Sondra are an endangered species. Few male colleagues of her generation qualify. I have heard that as of last night Jonathan Karl Goodman is no longer eligible."

Jonathan grasped my hand, smiled at the audience gracious-ly, and stood and bowed as he accepted a round of applause. "With-out further ado, it is my pleasure to present this year's Prophylactic Award to Jeffrey Blumberger," Roosevelt continued. There was fur-ther applause as Jeffrey stepped up to the podium. I was proud that my friend was being recognized for his achievement.

"Thank you so much for this award," said Jeffrey. "I first met Sondra fifteen years ago at a conference in Montpelier. We have subsequently traveled together and even shared hotel rooms. But we never had sex. Unlike the rest of my male science fiction colleagues, I'm not attracted to Sondra. Maybe it is because we are both Jews from Queens of the same cultural ilk. *Shiksas* are more my style. Sex might spoil the great friendship Sondra and I enjoy. I thank you for this award and look forward to my future as Sondra's friend." Jeffrey stepped down from the podium and returned the microphone to President Roosevelt.

"Before proceeding to the Pioneer Award for the best critical essay-length work of the year (which, by the way, has nothing to do with *Oy Pioneer!*), I want to announce that the awards committee is initiating the Pope Award. The Pope Award will be given to all highly regarded middle-aged science fiction scholars who marry Sara Scottywitz. The Award will support their necessity to travel to Rome to seek an annulment. Why will this travel be necessary? Sara's husbands will eventually realize that she has used them to advance her career. Because Sara is so young, we will have to wait a few years for her to rack up enough marriages to make the award sufficiently competitive. But we have no doubt that she will. We look forward to dispersing the Pope Award funds. And now on to the Pioneer Award. I am honored to present the Pioneer to the eminent multitudinous award winning writer and scholar Kirk T. Pistol."

When the whole room rose to give Pistol a standing ovation, I crawled under the table. Jonathan crouched down, moved the table cloth aside, and peered beneath the table. "Sandrine what are you doing under there? You have to accept the Pilgrim Award in about three minutes. You absolutely cannot remain under this table for another second. Come out now. Come out immediately if not sooner."

"No."

"Why not?"

I can't speak immediately after Kirk T. Pistol. He is elegant. He is polished. He is perfect. He is a WASP. He was an adult elegant, polished, and perfect WASP before I was born. He was a university publication relations official. I am a university public relations nightmare. I just can't get up on that stage and follow him. He's an impossible act to follow. No matter what, Juan Carlo, I just can't equal him and speak well in his wake. Juan Carlo, what should I do?" Jonathan only had time to articulate a brief answer. "Sandrine, just get up there and be yourself." I crawled out from under the table as I heard President Roosevelt begin the Pilgrim Award introduction speech.

"The human male," she said, "had no alternative but to apply the brakes, hard, to the runaway locomotive of his own evolution. Confused and frustrated, smoke pouring from his ears, he gazed pitifully in the direction of his mate. Of course, she had problems of her own. The identity of the female had been closely tied to her biological role of procreation, creating family and community for the male to enjoy and protect. "Be fruitful and multiply" had been the guiding principle, intended to provide safety in numbers. The larger the community, the more secure were its individual members understood to be. The second shock of the twentieth century, however, was the collision, now clearly predictable, between unlimited population growth and limited material resources. Technology was perfected to help control the runaway fertility of human reproduction. Suddenly, the primary element in the traditional definition of womanhood was radically altered. The female of the species returned the pitiful gaze of her male counterpart with affection. When the smoke cleared, a completely new dialogue between the sexes began.

SFRA's Pilgrim for this year has been a major contributor to this dialogue. She has published three feminist criticism books: *Alien to Femininity*, *Feminist Fabulation* and *Lost in Space*. In these works, as well as in numerous shorter publications and editorial projects, she has explicated the work of renowned fiction writers. Science fiction written by women is seen by this year's Pilgrim as occupying a ghetto of its own within the more general ghetto of science fiction. Consequently, she has argued for placing it within the larger context of feminist fabulation. In her book by the same title, she writes, '[s]tructural fabulation addresses man's place within the system of the universe; feminist fabulation addresses woman's place within the system of patriarchy.' She then argues for the appreciation of feminist fabulation within more inclusive canons of postmodern literature. This year's Pilgrim has devoted herself with remarkable courage and energy to her work. She is a controversial figure who would rather create real dialogue than go along with the status quo. She has become an international statesperson representing women and the science fiction community. Most recently, she has been a Visiting Professor at the University of Cape Town in South Africa. She has just completed another book-length manuscript of criticism called *Genre Fission*. In conclusion, let's quote one more passage from *Feminist Fabulation*. 'The contemporary world needs new words,' our Pilgrim writes, 'new versions of patriarchal stories. Creating space for women's words, stories, and interpretations facilitates such narrative replenishment. Patriarchy might understand that opening its narrative walls to admit women's discourse is analogous to accepting a gift, not becoming vulnerable to a surprise attack.' Friends and colleagues, we are proud to present our new Science Fiction Research Association Pilgrim, Professor Sondra Lear."

When I heard the descriptions of the mate and the clearing smoke, I wondered how the audience would respond if they knew that I had mated with Ilya after he arrived ensconced within a magic smoke cloud. I was not going to tell them that I was a Pilgrim who lives in a fantastic novel, a Pilgrim who routinely experiences altered space and time. I, after all, had enough trouble speaking immediately after Kirk T. Pistol. Pistol looked at me approvingly. Damn the torpedoes. Full speed ahead to accept my award on the Queen Mary. I follow Jonathan's advice about being myself. I could never be Pistol -- and, luckily for him, he could never be me.

"You like me. You like me," I effervesced into the microphone. All the men in the room who I had slept with removed their clothes, ran up to the stage, and stood behind me.

"*Oy*, streakers at the Pilgrim Awards."

"Yes, Sondra we really like you" the men said in unison to imitate a Broadway musical production number. They formed a Rockettes chorus line, kicked their hairy legs in unison, swung their penises, and sang: "We love you Sondra. Oh yes we do. When you're not near to us, we're blue. Oh Sondra we love you." Sara Scottywitz lost control and jumped on the table. "You will all end up in one of Sondra's novels. The same thing could happen to me. But she wouldn't dare. Sondra, now hear this: if you put me in your novel, I will spend every day disparaging you to the entire science fiction community," she shouted.

I tried to save the situation and re-establish an aura of decorum befitting an awards ceremony. "We have streakers in our midst. They're trying to enact the worst musical comedy that a producer could possibly produce: 'Sex Time for Sondra'." The naked men, who knew all about the sexual adventures I enjoyed during my German Fulbrights, responded to this cue by changing their tune. "Sex time for Sondra in Germany," they crooned. Jonathan took the microphone and began to serenade me.

"You make my cotton easy to pick. You give my old mint juleps a kick. Whoever thought a Yankee could put a little British slut to shame? I think you're just sensational. I think you're inspirational." Ilya, another Sondra seductee, took it upon himself to appear -- without being summoned -- and use his smoke cloud to provide special effects. And someone else suddenly materialized to cloud the occasion. I looked up. I saw a big bleached blonde talking head silhouetted against a plastic covered couch. The talking head was pictured on the two huge viewing screens located on each side of the dining room. "Hello, Herbert. Well hello, Herbert. It's so nice to see you back home where you belong," I sang into the microphone Jonathan had handed to me.

"Don't you 'Hello, Herbert' me, Sondra. All the naked men dancing around you lack substance because not one of them has proposed to you. Grab one that is circumcised and marry him. Get married."

"But I'm on stage because I have worked all of my life to win the Pilgrim Award. And I just did."

"The Pilgrims were not Jewish. Marry someone Jewish." The ever helpful Jeffrey pulled the viewing screen plugs. I continued to gush because I couldn't figure out how to ignore Herbert's histrionics and Ilya's pyrotechnics -- and restore the ordered atmosphere predominant during the Prophylactic Award ceremony. "You like me. You really like me. The streakers even like me. Unlike Marlin Brando's refusal personally to accept his Oscar, I'm here at the Pilgrim Awards in the flesh. I didn't ask a Native American to substitute for me. The streakers have vacated the stage. I'll proceed with my remarks."

Jonathan flashed a thumbs up sign as he returned to his seat, gathered his strewn white linen suit, and zipped his fly. Kirk T. Pistol, who had of course remained completely zipped throughout the entire proceedings, was engaged in his version of thankfully kissing the ground because even the slightest flirtation between us was out of the question. I was too afraid even to speak to him, much less flirt with him. Pistol, a perfectionist who I imagined wore ironed socks, would never ever appear naked at an awards ceremony. The audience -- all readers of Anne McCaffrey's "The Ship Who Sang" -- could cope with shipboard streaking science fiction singers sufficiently enough to compose themselves and listen effectively to my acceptance speech.

"Although I am being given an award for producing a large amount of writerly verbiage, I do not have the words to express how grateful I am to receive this honor and how meaningful it is to me. I am overwhelmed as I contemplate the achievements of past recipients. During the past two days, I found it exceedingly difficult to be secretive about being the award winner. I so much wanted to run up to everyone, jump up and down, and scream, 'I won the Pilgrim Award!' Although I must defer to Hardon Ellidaughter in regard to having the most locutionary force in the world, I do have a very big mouth. So, I was placed in a difficult situation: I have a very big mouth and I could not scream that I won the Pilgrim Award. I am so relieved that the need for secrecy is over and I am free to express just how honored and happy I feel.

I'm standing on the Queen Mary and this is no ordinary venue. Think of all the luminaries who have traveled on this ship. Marlene Dietrich or Clark Gable or Winston Churchill could have occupied this very room. But, despite their considerable achievements, Marlene and Clark and Winston did not win the Pilgrim Award. I did not want to be an actor. I did not want to be a Prime Minister. I did want to be a Pilgrim Award winner -- and now I am. I am thrilled to have accomplished my objective. It must be obvious to anyone who knows me that I have also accomplished another objective: during the past year, while serving as a guest professor at the University of Cape Town, I managed to lose twenty-five pounds. Throughout the long return flight from Cape Town, while contemplating this banquet speech, it became clear that the occasion would present me with my worst nightmare. I mean I sat in a Cape Town restaurant considering the fat gram content of the *maphunga-phunga* worm club sandwich. This discipline (unlike being a feminist science fiction critic) was no sweat. But to stand behind a podium at dessert time competing for attention with an entire room full of cheese cake slices -- well, this is just the limit.

Let me switch abruptly from my worst nightmare to my most heartfelt dream. All humor aside, I have often dreamed about winning the Pilgrim Award. I want to thank this community for your recognition -- for making my dream come true. There is just one appropriate utterance: thank you."

So I told a little white lie. So I made believe that I returned from South Africa like a normal person in an airplane instead of in an immortal vampire induced smoke cloud. And there is now an entire cadre of science fiction scholars who believe that *maphunga-phunga* worms are real and fattening. I returned to my seat as enthusiastic applause resounded. Colleagues who had worked with me for years -- the science fiction critical community which I considered to be my wide extended family (with a little incest thrown in for good measure) -- congratulated me. The dining room was soon empty --with the exception of Jonathan and myself. I began to cry my eyes out.

"Sandrine, why are you crying? You were great. You just needed a little help to garner the courage to come out from under the table. But you were really something once you got going. Everyone was enthralled. Even Kirk T. Pistol. Why are you so upset?"

"Everything that was said about me is true. But it is hard to be a courageous groundbreaker. I wanted to win the Pilgrim Award. And now it is over. What do I do now? What will become of me? Where will I go? What will I do?"

"Frankly my dear I do give a damn," said Jonathan as he picked me up and carried me back to his stateroom. As he struggled to support my weight (I failed to count calories during the awards dinner), my cell phone rang. It rang even though I am not sure if cell phones were invented at the time.

"Hello Sondra. This is Marie Schirer of the University of Outsbruck in Austria. Since your guest lecture here was such a resounding success, we want to invite you to be a Visiting Professor. Would you like to come?"

"Yes."

"When will you arrive?"

"Tomorrow."

"Fine. See you tomorrow. *Auf wiedersehen.*"

"Wait. Don't hang up. Just one point of information. I want to make it absolutely clear that I am Jewish. Am I still welcome?"

"Most certainly."

"Juan Carlo, tomorrow is another day."

The Heidi Chronicles or How Do You Solve a Problem Like Sondra?

After a thankfully uneventful flight (a rare occurrence in my life), I made my way to the furnished apartment in central Outsbruck which would serve as my new home. Marie had thoughtfully placed a Sacher-torte slice and a *dirndl* on my bed. Her explanatory note stated that she thought the *dirndl* would help me to acculturate fit to Outsbruck. Since I was too tired to unpack, I put on the *dirndl* and set out to explore my new temporary home. Wall to wall Alps surround Outsbruck. Regaining my usual energy, without bothering to climb ev'ry mountain and ford ev'ry stream, I climbed the nearest and shortest Alp and found myself in a grassy field. I struck out my hands, twirled in a circle, and sang: "The hills are alive." I stopped abruptly. The scene I was enacting could not work. It was too much of an imaginative leap -- even for me. A Jewish woman cannot be Maria von Trapp -- not even in my wildest imagination. How could I possibly qualify as a nun? I couldn't survive in a convent for five minutes. If Jews named their daughters Maria, suddenly that name would never be the same again. To me, "doe" is not a deer, a female deer. "Dough" is a calorie laden food stuff which can go awry to form matzo. Mucho dough is what is needed to afford to live in the Five Towns of Long Island or Scarsdale. "Fa" is more akin to "feh" then to "so." The nondenominational enough rain drops on roses and whiskers on kittens are not my favorite things. (I like sex and book contracts better.) I am neurotic to the extent that simply remembering my favorite things does not make me feel less bad. I can't do the Maria von Trapp thing in the usual sense. Some metafictional re-creation is called for.

I climbed down from the Alp and walked around downtown Outsbruck. No one thought that my *dirndl* looked out of place; in fact, many Outsbruckians were wearing *dirndls*. Where to go to imitate Maria in my own way? I remembered that the guide book to Austria I read on the plane included a description of a small Outsbruck synagogue. I made my way there and knocked on the door. A kindly looking elderly woman answered.

"*Kann iche helfen sie?*"

"I'm not sure. Do you speak English?"

"Yes."

I'm an American Jew. In order to assimilate here, I just climbed a short Alp and tried to re-create myself as Maria von Trapp. It didn't work. You have to be not Jewish to be Maria. I mean, I can't possibly go to a convent. I came to this synagogue instead."

"My English is not that good. Your meaning escapes me. But you are welcome to come inside. I'm Nessa Cohen."

"My name is Sondra Lear."

"Why do you want to re-cast yourself as Maria von Trapp?"

"I'm trying to establish a rapport with the local customs. You know when in Rome do as the Romans do. Furthermore, Maria found a husband and lived happily ever after. I'm single and I would like to do the same."

"You're single? How old are you?"

"I am definitely not sixteen going on seventeen. You must know the entire Jewish population in Outsbruck. Are there any local single Jewish men?"

"Our Jewish population is quite small. I don't know any single Jewish men. This is a problem. I would like to help you. I wonder how do you solve a problem like Sondra?"

"Both my mother and Blackhole State University have been contemplating the same question for a very long time."

"Why don't you become a Jewish version of Maria von Trapp? Her method worked for her. Maybe it can work for you."

"No, I don't that's a good idea. Child care is not my thing. Maria was a governess. Even contemporary American culture's version of governesses don't coincide with my life style. I've read *The Nanny Diaries*. It was written by thin, young *shiksas*. I have no more in common with them than I do with Maria. I can relate more closely to Fran Drescher's *The Nanny* than to *The Nanny Diaries*. *Oy*, do I know from protagonist Fran Fine's blonde big haired Jewish mother Sylvia's obsession with her daughter getting married. Sylvia's plastic covered Flushing apartment mirrors the home I hail from. But Fran Fine/Drescher is just as thin as the *shiksa Nanny Diaries* authors. Fran Drescher is smarter and more talented than Fran Fine -- and so am I. I would rather focus my energy upon writing feminist science fiction criticism than strategizing to convince a man to marry me."

"This is all very interesting. Please excuse me. There seems to be someone at the front door. I'll be right back." Nessa returned escorting a very attractive and very well dressed man.

"This person came to the synagogue to ask for you," she said.

"Are you Professor Sondra Lear?" he asked in a high class British accent.

"Yes. I'm Professor Lear."

"I'm so glad. I wasn't sure how to locate you. I ended up deciding that a synagogue is a logical place to locate a Jew. My name is Maxwell Sheffield. I'm from Manhattan and I'm a Broadway producer. I heard about the "Sex Time for Sondra" performance at the Science Fiction Research Association Conference. I want to stage it. May I have your permission to do so?"

"Please talk to my agent, Curtis Richards. He represents such eminent science fiction writers as Hardon Ellidaughter and Kirk T. Pistol. I am sure that Richards will work something out. I have one condition of my own."

"What may I ask is that?"

"I want the star of the show to sing 'Climb Ev'ry Mountain'."

"No problem. But may I ask why?"

"I am trying to act like Maria von Trapp on my own terms."

"Really? Well, I have three children. You have style. You have class. Even though Fran is much thinner than you, would you like to return to Manhattan and become the nanny? You can live in my sumptuous townhouse. You can spend all day caring for the children, buying clothes, polishing your nails, and looking sexy to attract my attention. The job's major requirement: you must sit on my desk attired in a short tight skirt and cross your legs."

"I am not comfortable with crosses."

"Sondra, your problem is solved. By eschewing a convent and coming to a synagogue, you have fallen into a viable means to live as a Jewish Maria von Trapp. You can work as a nanny. You will be able to live in New York. Mr. Sheffield will marry you. This is a perfect solution," said Nessa.

"No, it isn't. I am the world's most prolific scholar of feminist separatist lesbian planets. I live to polish my prose, not my nails. I must be going now. Goodbye, Nessa. Thank you for your hospitality. Good luck producing 'Sex Time for Sondra,' Mr. Sheffield. Goodbye, Mr. Sheffield. Goodbye. So long. *Auf wiedersehn*. Goodbye."

It was time forever to shut my trap regarding finding a husband according to the Maria von Trapp method. In other words: whiskers on kittens got me nowhere other than marriage to my cat Norris. I am a feminist theorist and a professor, not a nanny. It was time to tackle the brown paper packages tied up with strings: i.e., to unpack, change out of my dirndl, and venture to the University of Outsbruck American Studies Department.

Outsbruck most certainly possesses one of the world's most beautifully situated universities. The campus is surrounded by Alps and located next to a river. I entered the building which houses the American Studies Department and found Marie sitting in the department's office with two women eating Sacher-torte.

"Hello Sondra. I'm so glad that you arrived safely," she said. Let me introduce you to your new colleagues. This is our department head Ursula Schwarzenegger, our assistant professor Johanna Dehlerenegger, and our secretary Maria Guggenegger."

"I'm very happy to meet you all."

"Welcome," said Ursula. "We gather every day at three to chat and eat Sacher-torte. Have some."

"Definitely no thank you. If I ate Sacher-torte every day, the department would have to pay for me to use five seats during my return flight. Rule number one for my stay: No Sacher-torte -- not ever. What lovely china. American faculty members use Styrofoam during their department functions. Your office china is more beautiful than any china I've ever owned." While I thought it was appropriate to comment on the china, the same did not hold true for Ursula's attire. Her skin-tight floor length red gown was set off by a diamond choker. She resembled Julia Roberts in *Pretty Woman* watching an opera with Richard Gere -- or Fran Fine, wearing an outrageously expensive and flamboyant gown, traipsing down Mr. Sheffield's townhouse staircase. I could no longer restrain from inquiring about Ursula's clothing choice. "What a beautiful dress. Are you going to the opera?"

"No. I'm teaching my afternoon seminar. We are starting a new novel today. I decided to dress up a little, but not too much, to mark the occasion." Marie, noticing that my jaw dropped, tried to change the subject.

"Funny you should mention the opera. It just so happens that I am going to the opera tonight accompanied by my boyfriend Count Axel von Trachtenegerstein. We have an extra ticket. Would you like to join us?"

"I would love to. But I don't have anything to wear."

"No problem. I can lend you something. I was just on my way home. Come with me and we can search my closets. One of my graduate students is writing a dissertation on late twentieth century evening gowns. She spent a year indexing all of my gowns. I am sure I can find one to lend you."

Marie and I entered her Porsche and proceeded to her apartment. It was cavernous and furnished with priceless antiques to the extent that it made the domiciles featured in *House Beautiful* appear to be so many mud huts. Marie peered into a closet the size of a Manhattan studio apartment and halfheartedly regarded an amount of clothing that could substitute for an entire Bonwit Teller boutique inventory. "Absolutely nothing in here is right. But I do have just the thing for you in my country house. We have enough time to take a few minutes to drive there and dress before we meet Axel at the theater." Marie's "country house" resembled a Newport "summer cottage." I could not refrain from commenting.

"Why do you maintain two opulent residences in such close proximity? And how do you afford them on a professor's salary."

"I like having both an apartment and a house. Austrian professors are paid very well."

"Oh. Okay. I understand." Marie entered another enormous closet. She emerged holding a long white gown inlaid with pearls.

"Perfect. You can shower and change into this."

"Okay."

I did as I was told. "Let's go. I'm anxious to meet Axel. He will be my first count close encounter."

Marie looked at me, gasped, put her hand to her chest, and collapsed upon slipcover-free couch.

"Is something wrong?"

"Es ist völlig unmöglich, ein weißes Kleid mit braunen Holzschlapfen und ohne Make-Up zu tragen."

Marie was stating her firm conviction that it is improper to wear a white gown with brown clogs -- and to be devoid of makeup. All of my foreign travel had taught me that, when people spontaneously speak their native tongue, they mean business. As Marie's guest, I was willing to try to comply with her requirements.

"Oh. Okay. I see. I'll be happy to wear matching white clogs. I planned to save them for my wedding. But, at the rate I'm going, that occasion may never present itself. So, yes, I will be glad to wear white clogs right now. You probably don't have any. You don't strike me as the white clogs owning type."

"Shoes, Sondra. I'm talking about normal shoes." I recalled how I uncomfortable I felt while wearing the high heeled glass slippers my fairy godmother Barbara Bush had once conjured up for me."

"Okay. Normal shoes. May I please wear flats?"

"Flats will be fine. And you must wear makeup."

"Makeup?"

"Yes. Makeup."

"Oy, not makeup too."

"Makeup too." It was impossible to argue with Marie. After I put on the normal flat shoes and applied makeup, she scrutinized the opera-ready Sondra she had created.

"Something is missing."

"I'm afraid to ask what."

"Jewelry."

"Jewelry I can deal with." She handed me an emerald necklace encrusted with diamonds.

"Put this on and you will be perfect." I appeared as a cross between Henry Higgins' re-made Eliza Doolittle and the transformed Sandra Bullock in *Miss Congeniality*. We drove to the Opera House. Marie was right about the House dress code. None of the gown-clad Austrian women were wearing clogs. A man attired in a top hat and tails smiled when he saw Marie and approached us. I knew that he had to be none other than Count Axel von Trachtenegerstein.

"Marie, darling, I am so glad to see you," he said as he kissed her on each check. And who is your lovely companion?"

"Count Axel von Trachtenegerstein, please meet our American Visiting Professor Frau Dr. Sondra Lear," Marie said.

"My dear, for an American, you have a wonderful style sense," he said as he reached for my hand to kiss it. I panicked. Not only had I never meet a count, I had never coped with a man who was about to kiss my hand. Before I knew it, my hand was embarked upon a nonreturnable trajectory to his lips. What to do?

"How kind of you to let me come," I said with a distinct hint of a parodic elite British accent as his lips brushed against my hand. With not the slightest tinge of mirth, acting as if I had articulated the most normal phrase in the world, he replied: "I am very happy to have you." Dress code and count meeting traumas behind me, I settled into box seats with Marie and Axel to see *Die Fledermaus*. The extremely fat *Fledermaus* endlessly singing in German was excruciating. I committed a large faux pas when I tried to alleviate my boredom. I told the fat *Fledermaus* what to do. "Move your bloomin' arse," I shouted.

"What did you say, my dear?" asked Axel incredulously.

Marie answered for me. "Sondra thinks the *Fledermaus* has pizzazz."

When I came to the department the next morning, I was dying to discuss my experience. I stuck my head into the main office and encountered Maria the secretary.

"Good morning, Sondra."

"Maria, I have one question. Are Marie's residences normal for Austrians?"

"No."

"Thank you so much for the clarification. Now I can go on with my life." This conversation was unsatisfying, though. I needed to discuss what happened with a friend. Because Johanna was young and seemed to be more open than Ursula, I knocked on her office door and entered.

"I'm so glad to see you, Sondra. I was an undergraduate when you first came to Outsbruck. I had a question and I wrote to you. You answered my letter. I was thrilled that you would take the time to do that."

"I don't remember writing the letter. But if it serves to make you like me now, I will be very glad. I don't know anyone here and I need a friend."

"You came to the right place for friendship. I had a Fulbright to Oklahoma. I taught at the University of Tulsa for a year and fell in love with Michael from Long Island. I'm familiar with American culture. Hey, I heard that you went to the opera with Marie and Count von Trachtenegerstein last night. I'm dying to know what happened."

"My night at the opera is just what I am chomping at the bit to talk about. Maria just told me that Marie's homes are abnormal. But the clothes, and the count, and the hand kissing. I have never experienced the like of it."

"How did you get through the evening?"

"I survived by thinking Eliza Doolittle. When Count von Trachtenegerstein kissed my hand, I said 'how kind of you to let me come.'"

"No. Tell me that you didn't really say that."

"I truthfully and absolutely did." One newly minted assistant professor and a mature visiting scholar were cracking up to the extent that they were trying not to pee. Leg crossing was again ensuing.

"I have to compose myself so that I can teach my first class," I said.

"What are you teaching?"

"I'm team teaching ethnic women with Marie and I'm doing a seminar on blacks and Jews."

"Blacks and Jews. How interesting. Why did you choose that subject?"

"It never failed to aggravate the conservative geezers at Blackhole State University. Great talking to you, Johanna. I can see that I will be making frequent trips to this office to clue you in on what's transpiring. Talk to you soon." I made my way down the hall to meet my class. All of the students were attractive blonde-haired, blue-eyed young women.

"I'm Dr. Sondra Lear. I have been looking forward to teaching black and Jewish literature. I hope that we have an interesting time together." One student immediately raised her hand.

"Dr. Lear, how do you know so much about blacks and Jews?" The question stunned me. For this student, I was no more Jewish than black. She had probably never seen a Jew; she envisioned Jews in terms of stereotypes. Since she was encountering an attractive woman who had blue eyes and a normal sized nose, she could not imagine that I could be Jewish. Although I made the fact that I am Jewish clear to the faculty, I did not want to share this information with students. I did not expect them to discriminate against me; quite the contrary. In order to compensate for their history, I imagined that these sweet, naïve, and sheltered young women, to welcome me, would wave Israeli flags and bring recorded *klezmer* music to class. I wanted the students to treat me as a garden variety person, not as someone who evoked guilt feelings. There were already enough cultural differences between me and these skiing Alp dwellers. I struggled to gain my composure and buy time.

"What an interesting question. By the way, what's your name?"

"Heidi." She was no Heidi Abramowitz.

"Well, Heidi, I know a lot about Jews and blacks because I come from New York." My answer satisfied Heidi and her classmates. Another student raised her hand.

"Yes. And what is your name?"

"Heidi.

"Your name is Heidi too?"

"Yes. You can call me Heidi Two. It will be very easy for you to remember our names. We're all named Heidi." The name repetition situation was perfectly sensible. All my American students answer to Jennifer. And, as you are aware, all my clones answer to Sondra. I could simply add the multitudinous Heidis to the Jennifers and Sondras.

"What is your question, Heidi Two?"

"I'm so glad you told Heidi One that you're from New York. I have never been there and I am curious about it. I am particularly interested in Harlem. Can you tell us from personal experience what daily life in Harlem is like?" This time I decided to be truthful.

"As a matter of fact, I can't. Although I'm a native New Yorker, my only direct experiences of Harlem consist of trips to the Schomburg Center Library and attending the Harlem Book Fair. In addition, when I heard Toni Morrison read at the Abyssinian Baptist Church, I publicly asked her if *Paradise* is a feminist science fiction utopia. She said no. I disagree. But what do I know? The northern United States is segregated. I did not have a black classmate until I was a senior in high school. To compensate for my lack of experience, I will add some Spike Lee films to the syllabus." I spent a pleasant hour engaging with Heidi One through Heidi Twelve and met with Marie when class ended. Her spacious office, replete with Alp and river views, was appointed with an antique desk and a Persian rug. Fresh flowers adorned her desk. I thought that I had died and gone to feminist academic heaven. Feminist utopia may or may not be located in Morrison's *Paradise*; feminist utopia is definitely located in the University of Outsbruck's American Studies Department, an academic space under women's complete local control.

Team teaching with Marie was just at surreal as the night at the opera. Although I was anxious to bring my American perspective to the class, Marie was a control freak to the extent that she would not let me say a word. She did not even ask me to contribute to the class on Jewish fiction. Silence is not my style. At the conclusion of every solo, supposedly team taught seminar, I barged into Johanna's office and screamed. At least I could not complain about being over worked.

Lacking male company, I devoted the first weekend of my stay to jogging along the river. I dressed in the *schmata* sweatshirt and sweatpants that constituted my usual running attire. This was the exact outfit I wore when the German tourists thought I was a destitute Cape Town denizen. Since Outsbruck is devoid of starvation victims, I did not expect anyone to mistake me for a homeless person. After my run, I decided to do some research in the American Studies Department library. During work hours, I would never go to the department dressed so informally. But I expected that the building would be deserted on a Sunday afternoon. My reading was interrupted by a blinding light flash. Light rays bounced from the Alp, to the river, to Ursula's diamond encrusted tiara, to my eyes. I should have known. Even though it was Sunday and the building was deserted, Ursula was a dead ringer for Jackie Kennedy dressed to impress President De Gaulle at that famous state dinner. Ursula was as surprised by my attire as I was by hers. We stared at each other in horror. I broke the silence. "Ursula, it is true that no matter how hard I try, I could never look as elegant and as out of place as you. And it is also true that no matter how hard you try, you could never look as ragged and as out of place as me." She nodded in assent and hugged me.

"I have a great idea, Sondra. We can go shopping together. I know this great antique auction house in Vienna. It is my favorite place to shop. One can never have enough chandeliers and priceless porcelains, you know. You just have to see it." I thought about how multitudinous chandeliers and porcelains would set off my mother's plastic covered apartment.

"Does a mid-twentieth century couch qualify as an antique? The one I have in mind is very well preserved; it has spent its entire life covered in plastic."

"I'm not sure. Plastic covered furniture is not my style. On second thought, maybe we should go clothes shopping."

"I can relate to clothes shopping. Clothes shopping it is."

"And I am going to give a party in your honor for the department at my house."

"I'll look forward to it. One more thing. Just out of curiosity, because I want to learn more about Austrian culture, I would like to know how your over-the-top attire coincides with your afternoon plans. What are you doing today?"

"I'm going grocery shopping and running some errands. I might work on my book later."

"See you Monday, Ursula."

On Monday morning, ready to regale the Heidis with another episode of Blacks and Jews 101, I entered the elevator A gorgeous gray haired Cary Grant clone also entered. Okay, he wasn't a real clone. He merely resembled my cat Norris after the Sondras turned him into his human husband form. How to attract this man's attention in an elevator crowded with German speakers? He could exit at any moment. I could possibly never see this gorgeous Norris-as-human replica again. I made an instant decision about how to get his attention. I didn't know enough German to mention his resemblance to the cat/husband. My appropriate German vocabulary was limited to *katze* and *raumschiff* (i.e., cat and spaceship). Someone located in a German university building elevator could be expected to understand English. I articulated a pick up line: "Excuse me. Are you Norris Katz?"

"No. I'm not. I'm sorry." Discerning that I was a sex-starved American visitor, and that the mere sight of him caused me to swoon, he brilliantly let me know how he could be found. "I'm Hans Hanskraut and I teach in the German Department." Hans flashed a seductive parting look while vacating the elevator. I resolved to track him down. Finding one man in a particular academic department would be much easier than trying to locate Undress in all of South Africa. I also resolved to ask the Sondras about Hans' resemblance to Norris. Teaching was first on my agenda, though. On my way to class, I heard horrific shrieks emanating from Ursula's office. Running to her rescue, I saw her screaming while staring at the floor.

"What's wrong?" I asked as I prepared to call paramedics.

"The situation is just too terrible for words."

"Whatever it is you can tell me and I will be as helpful as I can."

"I somehow have to cope with what has happened. I might as well tell you." I steeled myself to hear her explanation.

"A button has fallen off of my suit jacket and I can't find it. I can't teach or write or function because my button is missing. My entire day is ruined. I have to go home immediately and change. I have to cancel all my classes, meetings, and appointments."

Knowing that privation is relative to a particular individual, I tried to comfort Ursula.

"*Oy*, such a catastrophe ya shouldn't know from. You're not alone. Think of all the starving people in Africa who are traumatized because their jacket buttons have fallen off."

"That's true. I will think of them as I muster the courage to face the tragedy which has befallen me. Thank you for understanding. I have to leave immediately because my maid departs at noon and I need her to change all the jacket's buttons. I could never harbor an imperfect garment in my home."

"I understand. I will be thinking about you somehow managing to cope. Bye."

I barged into to Johanna's office -- again. She tried to help me make sense of the situation.

"Marie and Ursula are very privileged and very high strung. They're great women who work very hard. I just ignore their eccentricities. For instance, Marie routinely leaves her parrot Tweety in my office whenever she travels. Parrot care is certainly not in my job description. Because she is so enamored of Tweety and he is, after all, a very nice parrot, I'm glad to look after him. Further, Marie, who is unable to type, asks the secretary to type all of her handwritten messages into the computer. Marie and Ursula are certainly better than all the sexist patriarchal male professors who infest this place. Sexist men run rampant here. I'm sure you know the type."

"I know them better than I care to say. Sexist patriarchal male professors are the bane of my existence. Marie and Ursula provide a wonderful respite from them. I'm off to teach and then I have to attend to a pressing matter at home. See you."

Class went smoothly. Even though Heidi One through Heidi Twelve looked exactly alike, I was finally discerning the subtle personality differences which differentiated one Heidi from another. The extent of the students' privilege continued to boggle my mind, though. All of the Heidis' mothers -- that is to say the senior Heidis of my generation -- do their children's laundry. The state pays the Heidis' tuition. Their academic life is far from arduous: Classes are not held on Catholic holidays. A Catholic holiday occurs at least once a week. I thought that the university closed every time that Jesus sneezed. Austrian college students called for a strike after the state considered rescinding the policy of paying for students' train tickets home during Catholic holidays.

"Your assignment for next week is to read Susan Jane Gilman's *Kiss My Tiara: How to Rule the World as a Smart-mouthed Goddess* and after that we will turn to *Oy Pioneer!*," I said to signal that class was over. I made a mental not to recommend *Kiss My Tiara* to Ursula.

I ventured swiftly over hill and dale -- or, more accurately, over Alp and river -- to get home quickly. I could not wait to ask the Sondras about the resemblance between Hans and Norris. I put a note in the refrigerator. Although Austrian refrigerators are exceedingly small, at least they have sufficient space to post notes to one's extraterrestrial clones. "Attention Sondras. Attention Sondras," my note read. "This is Sondra. I need some of you. Can some of you please come quickly? Thank you in advance. Love, Sondra." I closed the refrigerator door. Three Sondras appeared immediately.

"Thanks for coming. You all look a little thinner."

"You have lost some weight. We are all exact replicas of you, after all."

"My slight weight loss must be due to from climbing ev'ry mountain and fording ev'ry stream. I am also refusing to touch the Sacher-torte which appears daily in the department."

"What can we do for you, Sondra?"

"Sondras, I'm flummoxed. I met an exact replica of human form Norris. He says that he is Hans Hanskraut, not Norris. How can this be?"

"Elementary my dear Sondra," said a Sondra. As we explained when we first met in the Hayden Planetarium, each individual human is derived from a planet whose entire population exactly biologically coincides with her. As you are aware, we are from the planet of the Sondras. We will not forget your stipulated rule that we can never under any circumstance send you to the planet of the Herberts. When we created the supernatural entity who was Norris transformed into a human, we used the planet of the Hanses as a model. Hans is from central casting in regard to the type of man who most attracts you -- that is, the tall, thin, urbane, elegant, gray-haired, sophisticated type. Hence, we modeled Norris after Hans. We knew that you could not fail to be attracted to him. How nice that you have met him."

"This is indeed good news. You will recall that I left your spaceship and rejected the Fulbright to the feminist planet because, although Norris the cat/husband was wonderful, I became dissatisfied being married to a man who was once a cat. Norris meant well. He just lacked worldly experience. Despite the great sex I had with him, I could not continue a relationship with a man who claws the starship Captain's chair, jumps on the table when I open the tuna fish cans the food synthesizer provides, and spends his spare time hunting extraterrestrial mice. The human Hans is a professor, not a former cat. I fell in love with him at first sight. "

"He's German. Be careful Sondra."

"I will take my chances with Hans the German. Remember that I have held Fulbrights to Germany. Some of my best friends are German."

"We wish you well. You know how to reach us if you need us. The Chief Engineer Sondra will beam us up. Our transporter works over vast distances."

The Sondras dematerialized. I ran back over Alp and river to return to campus. Immediate agenda: hunt down Hans the German.

I adopted this nickname for private obnoxious emphasis. Because Germans are so supercharged for Jews, it is impossible for Jews to think of Germany and Germans out of context of the Holocaust. Husband-hunting with a German as my quarry could never be business as usual for me. Hans the German's national origin aside, finding him would not be too troublesome. It would not be necessary for me to wear khaki shorts and a pith helmet during this husband hunt: scanning the lobby's faculty directory was the only effort needed.

I knocked on Hans' office door and entered immediately. He flashed his charm sodden smile. I was so relieved when I saw his devoid of claw marks upholstered desk chair. I felt completely at ease with him. Even though he and Norris had different brains, their brains were housed in the exact same body. I had had sex with Hans' body many times. Thoroughly physically familiar with him, I merely had to experience his personality. A Dr. Frankenstein brain transfer chair replete with two skull caps and protruding electrical wires would not be needed. Relationship lightening was striking.

"I'm Sondra Lear. I was very attracted to you in the elevator. I'm a feminist American Visiting Professor in the American Studies department. Are you single?"

"Yes. I'm divorced. From a woman named Sondra as a matter of fact. I find you attractive too. I'm glad you sought me out. I'm also a guest professor from America."

"What about your German accent?"

"I immigrated to California from Northern Germany twenty-five years ago. I now teach in the German Department at the University of California at Beverly Hills. I came to Outsbruck because my colleagues make me sick. I especially hate my department head Leonardo Lehr."

"I hate the patriarchal pricks at Blackhole State. Your former wife has the same first name as me and your despised chair's last name sounds like mine."

"We have a lot in common. Feminist theory is crap, though."

"If I can look away from the fact that you're German, I can also look away from your opinion of feminist theory."

"I think I know why you are bothered by my national origin."

"Yes, I'm Jewish."

"Not a problem. Some of my best friends are Jewish. The German Jewish thing will not pose a problem between us. There's a lecture at the university tonight. Would you like to join me?" I was enraptured with Hans to the extent that I would go to the ends of the Earth to share his company. I could even arrange things to have a spaceship at my disposal to take us to the lecture hall. But I did not want to appear to be too anxious."

"Who is speaking?"

"Kurt Waldheim."

"Kurt Waldheim? How can you expect me to listen to Kurt Waldheim! I, of course, do not think that all Germans and Austrians are Nazis. Waldheim really was a Nazi."

"Have you ever come face to face with a real Nazi?"

"No. Not that I know of."

"The experience will be good for you. Meet me in Lecture Hall Four at six." Hans the German took my hand as we entered Lecture Hall Four. All the Heidis and all my Austrian colleagues were present. I could not believe that they sat and listened to a Nazi as if he were a normal person.

"What do you think of his talk?" whispered Hans.

"I have no clue. I do not know enough German to understand what he's saying."

"I'll be glad to translate."

"No thank you. Listening to an old Nazi for five minutes is a sufficient time expenditure. My failure to understand him aside, he strikes me as a very boring speaker. I have seen this one Nazi and I have seen enough. This is no reflection on your company, but I want to leave." Wearing my trusty clogs, I stomp out loudly. Although small, this particular revenge tactic was very meaningful to me. My accepting attitude toward Germans and Austrians notwithstanding, there is something unkosher about having a first date with a German which involves a lecturing Nazi.

Hans showed up at my office the next morning.

"I hope Waldheim didn't upset you."

"I'm not really upset. I'm just surprised that the Austrians accepted him as a normal person. A Nazi just does not fit my definition of a garden variety individual. Jews in Germany or Austria can never stop thinking about the Holocaust. When I go about my business here, the Holocaust often reappears. For example, I went to a flea market last weekend. I came across a photo of a World War Two soldier wearing a Nazi uniform. The picture shocked me."

"I was an infant during the war. Yet, as a German living in America, the war permeates my life. Enough of war, Jews, and Nazis. Would you like to have some lunch?"

"Great. By the way, do you like tuna fish?"

"No. I much prefer bratwurst. Why do you ask?"

"No reason, really. Norris Katz, the man you remind me off, went berserk every time he smelled tuna fish."

"Were you involved with Norris?"

"Well, yes. He accompanied me during my Fulbright to Germany. Then he changed a lot and we got married. But all of that is in the past."

"Why did you divorce Norris?"

"Even though he is very attractive and he looks exactly like you, I had nothing in common with a man who wants to be an exterminator."

"An exterminator?"

"Let's not pursue this subject. Extermination is not a great topic for a Jew and a German. Most importantly, I do not think all Germans are exterminators."

"I thought we were done with Nazis. I really need to divert your attention. Let's take a long drive to the Bodensee." I felt completely happy as I stood in Hans' arms looking at a gorgeous lake surrounded by snow-capped Alps. I was enjoying a fairy tale European romance in a story book setting with the man of my dreams. Hence, it was time for real world sex. Upon arrival at my apartment, I asked Hans in. He took me in his arms and kissed me. "I would bet anything that you have a scar on your stomach," I said.

"How do you know?"

"I just do," I answered as I removed Hans' clothes and began to recall every aspect of Norris's body. Unlike Norris, Hans never had a tail and he had a human penis for his entire life. Hence, having sex with the Norris body containing the Hans completely human brain was much better than having sex with the Norris body containing the Norris partially cat and partially human brain. (Only a feminist science fiction scholar can write a sentence like that. Be grateful that I stuck to the brains without mentioning the penises.) "All good things come to those who wait," I thought while enjoying a terrific orgasm.

The telephone rang as I was purring while lying entangled with Hans. "This is Ursula. I would like to have the party for you in my house next Saturday. Can you come?"

"Most definitely. May I bring a guest?"

"Of course. Saturday it is."

"Bye Ursula. Hans, we're going to a party."

"Fine. I love parties."

The week progressed pleasantly enough. I taught the Heidis, sat silently while team teaching with Marie, and enjoyed pleasant excursions and great sex with Hans. Ursula's party altered this comfortable routine. When Hans appeared at my door to accompany me, I was shocked by his attire.

"Why are you wearing a tuxedo?"

"I brought one to Austria. A party constitutes an occasion to wear it."

"Who brings a tuxedo for a year abroad as a guest professor? Who wears a tuxedo to a department party?"

"A German."

"Of course. I should have known. I'm wearing normal attire. Now we will look weird together."

"Now is a good time to tell you that I wish you wore tight bras instead of no bras and normal shoes instead of clogs. Outsbruck is replete with bra stores and shoe stores. I think you would do well to patronize them."

"You sound just like my colleague Marie. I went through the Eliza Doolittle thing with her. I enjoy being the way I am. Outsbruck is replete with women who wear tight bras and normal shoes. If you want a woman who wears tight bras and normal shoes, then I suggest you go out into Outsbruck and find one. I am unique. Take me as I am or leave me."

"You're right . You're unique. Okay clog wiggle fish. Stay as you are."

"Clog wiggle fish?"

"That is what you are. A clog wiggle fish."

"I think this phrase should be filed in our don't ask don't pursue category." We made our way to Ursula's house, which was almost as over-the-top as Marie's houses. Her floors were covered with thick white carpet which required daily cleaning. It appeared as though she resided in an antique store. I introduced Hans to the other guests and between Hans and Johanna at the dinner table. I tried to facilitate the conversation.

"Ursula, this is the most beautiful china I've ever seen."

"Thank you. It belonged to the Shah of Iran."

This information ruined my appetite. I was afraid to eat. What if I dropped my plate? What if I even chipped it? I continued the conversation to mask my discomfort.

"This dinner looks lovely. What exactly is it?" I asked knowing perfectly well that answer would not be "dorm mystery meat."

"Duck breast stuffed with truffles," Ursula nonchalantly answered.

"What a treat. No American has ever served me duck breast stuffed with truffles."

"What is a typical menu at American department parties?"

"Hot dogs and hamburgers. Chicken is sometimes served at fancy occasions."

Ursula and Marie turned pale. I clenched my plate to make sure that I did not inadvertently drop it. Hans surreptitiously touched my knee to convey moral support. "The dinner and the apartment are very opulent," he whispered.

"I've gotten used to it. At this point, I would not be surprised if either Marie or Ursula casually mention that they own Versailles or the Taj Mahal. I have made up categories for these women. I call Marie the empress, Ursula the princess, and Johanna the lady in waiting. To assuage the social discomfort the royal trio caused me to feel, I excused myself and headed to the bathroom. I interrupted Marie's similar trajectory as I made my way back to the table.

"I'm dying to get your opinion. You're the world's expert on manners, presentation, and men. What do you think of Hans? Does he merit the Marie Seal of Approval? I know that the Marie Seal of Approval is as hard to come by as a Michelin star."

"Actually, you give me too much credit. I'm not the world's highest authority on those categories. I am the world's second highest authority. Ursula's mother is the world's highest authority. She has even given me advice."

"Even though I have a very big imagination, I cannot begin to fathom the force of Ursula's mother."

"Don't even try. Hans is a very nice man. As a German he is, of course, perfect in regard to appearance and propriety. But even I would say that wearing a tuxedo to a department dinner party is just a tad too much."

We rejoined the group and the dinner progressed without incident. As Hans and I expressed our thanks and departed, I was thanking god that I had not dropped a plate, bumped against an antique, or stained the white carpet.

The minute I next set foot in the department, I ran to Johanna's office.

"I couldn't believe that dinner." I said.

Yes, the duck breast was something else. Do you know that Ursula has not come to school for the last three days?"

"Why not?"

"She has been washing the Shah of Iran's dishes. She doesn't trust the maid to do it. People here seldom give parties in their homes. The preparation and clean up is just too onerous."

"I vote for American informality. It makes it easier for people to interact." Ursula knocked and entered the office. I noticed that she had dish pan hands.

"Thank you for that stupendous dinner."

"You're very welcome. I have good news. Sondra, your friend Jeffrey Blumberger is coming to campus to lecture on *Schindler's List* next week."

"How nice. I will enjoy seeing Jeffrey. He is such a pleasant fellow." Before I knew it, Jeffrey was knocking on my apartment door.

"Here I am, Sondra. Since I am a Prophylactic Award winner, I've invited myself to sleep on your floor. You can rest assured that I am still not attracted to you. Since we are such good friends, I thought it would be fun to camp out *chez* your place rather than in some lonely hotel."

"Fine. American friends don't knock on my Austrian door every day. I'll enjoy having you." That night I watched Jeffrey's six foot snoring body plunked down in the middle of my living room floor. I was incredulous that a male science fiction critic who did not want to have sex with me existed. I tried to enjoy the oddity of the situation and refrain from thinking of myself as unattractive. After spending the next day sightseeing around Outsbruck, Jeffrey and I

made our way to the university in time for his lecture. Ursula introduced him. "We are honored to welcome the distinguished American
science fiction film critic Jeffrey Blumberger. Professor Blumberger
will tell us about *Schindler's List*."

The atmosphere became strained when Jeffrey deviated
from his prepared text. "I can't continue to read my paper as if this
were a normal venue. I'm talking about Steven Spielberg's depiction
of the atrocities you people committed. How can you just sit there
without manifesting any guilt or remorse? What happened to my
people is the fault of people like you." The audience was stunned.
Marie put her head in her hands. Jeffrey continued with his prepared
text. Both he and the audience acted as if nothing unusual had occurred. Jeffrey and the Outsbruck American Studies community politely bid each other *adieu*. The faculty members, unable to contain
their responses to Jeffrey's comments, continued to discuss them
throughout the duration of my stay. I talked about what had ensued
with Marie.

"Of course he has a reason to be angry," she said. "But the
people he was addressing are not Nazi perpetrators. The students are
two generations removed from the Nazi era and I was an infant at
the time. Let me tell you something that I do not often discuss. As
you know, I have spent a great deal of time in America. I will never
forget what happened when I was invited to an academic dinner party in a Jewish home in New Jersey about five years ago. When the
host's wife found out that I am Austrian, she screamed at me and
ordered me to leave her home. That hurt will remain with me for the
rest of my life."

"I can understand the emotions on both sides. I was am-
bivalent about accepting my Fulbright to Germany. I only garnered
the courage to go because my former professor Leonardo D'Antona,
an Italian Jew who escaped the Nazis when he came to America at
age six, told me that I should. I only did so because I trust Leonardo
implicitly. It seems to me that while European Jews like Leonardo
understand that not all Austrians and Germans are Nazis, American
Jews have a stereotypical attitude toward them. Even my very liberal
American friends and family members have chastised me for living in
Austria and Germany. I'm glad that I came to garner firsthand experiences. Austrians and Germans have been lovely to me. I experienced intense anti-Semitism when I was a faculty member in Virgin-

ia. I would rather be in Austria or Germany than in Virginia any day. We enjoy a great friendship. If you were an anti-Semite, you would not choose to be my friend. In addition, hordes of non-Jewish American professors would welcome a chance to teach at Outsbruck. Yet, you invited me. I can convey these facts to my family and friends until I am blue in the face and they will still feel a great antipathy to Austrians and Germans. I'm so glad that I was open to coming. I'm very attached to you, Ursula, and Johanna. You put flowers on my desk; the Virginians did everything in their power to make me miserable. All I can do is to explain my experiences and hope that I can motivate people to overcome their prejudices."

"I'm glad we had this conversation, Sondra. Time for us to team teach. I have my remarks on Ozick's *The Shawl* prepared." I knew that, as ever, I would not be expected to say anything. When I, according to my usual ritual, entered Johanna's office to vent about being unable to talk during a two hour seminar, she looked exceedingly crestfallen.

"What's wrong?"

"It's about Heidi, one of your students." Sparing her the details about my not being able to tell the difference between Heidi One through Heidi Twelve, I pressed for more details."

"What's Heidi's problem?"

"She wants to go to New York and she needs to cut housing costs." After Johanna completed her sentence, she looked directly at me with the saddest face she could muster.

"Tell Heidi that she can stay with me in Forest Hills as soon as I return home."

"You're the best."

"You befriended me and listen to me complain. It's the least I can do." I wondered what would happen when Heidi traded the Alps for Forest Hills' hills. Pushing all speculative disaster scenes from my mind, I hurried to keep my lunch date with Hans. I stopped at my apartment to change into the real shoes and tight bra I had recently purchased.

"Now, like all the other women in Outsbruck, I'm wearing a tight bra and real shoes. Does my acquisition of these contraptions make you happy."

"Yes. Clog Wiggle Fish has joined the rest of humanity. This is a change for the better. But there is still something that I wish you could do."

"What? Haven't I done enough by drastically altering my attire?"

"I wish that you could cook *Apfelstrudel* and *Leberknödelsuppe*. I would love to come home and to a tight bra normal shoe wearing woman who has spent her entire day cooking *Apfelstrudel* and *Leberknödelsuppe* for me. I applaud all your academic achievements and feminist publications. When push comes to shove, though, I really want homemade *Apfelstrudel* and *Leberknödelsuppe*. Feminist theorists have their place in the world. And so do *hausfrauen* who serve men."

Spending all my time cooking for a man was beyond beyond me. Hans the German now resembled someone other than Norris the Cat: Ngudu the African. I in no uncertain terms had told Ngudu that I could not under any circumstance become one of his multiple wives and live in my own hut. I did not love Ngudu. I did love Hans. I would just have to consult with Marie, the expert in all things -- especially *Apfelstrudel* and *Leberknödelsuppe*.

"Marie, I need your advice."

"I will be glad to help you. By the way, you look terrific in that bra. Your real shoes are fetching."

"The advice I need sort of relates to the bra and the shoes. Hans the German wants me to learn to cook homemade *Apfelstrudel* and *Leberknödelsuppe*."

"Some things are just impossible to achieve, Sondra. I was able to make you shine for our night at the opera. I cannot repeat this resounding success in regard to teaching you how to cook superb *Apfelstrudel* and *Leberknödelsuppe*. Doing so requires spending your entire life in a Germanic family. Face the fact that you can never be a *hausfrau*. Hans is not right for you."

I could not acknowledge the fact that Marie was correct. When I met Hans for our last walk along the river before his return to California, I hoped for the best as I strapped myself into the bra and shoes.

"Clog Wiggle Fish, there is no easy way to say what I have to say so I might as well be direct and get it over with. I don't love you. I don't want to continue our relationship."

"I can't believe what I am hearing. I really really love you."

"I'm sorry Sondra. I'm marrying someone else."

"Who?"

"Brunhilde. My old girlfriend Brunhilde the Austrian has come back into my life. She is a recently divorced housewife who has five children. My first marriage to an American was a disaster. I want to marry a native European Germanic woman. My decision stands. There is no procedural irregularity."

"Did you make this decision because I am Jewish?"

"No. That has nothing to do with it."

"Can Brunhilde the Austrian cook homemade *Apfelstrudel* and *Leberknödelsuppe*?".

"Of course. Everyone named Brunhilde the Austrian can do so. Don't look so sad, Clog Wiggle Fish. I promise to remain your friend. As you know, a German friend is a dependable entity." Now I knew exactly how Norris and Ms. Ed felt when I left the the the starship and deserted them. .

"I feel terrible. I see that there is nothing I can do. I had a great time with you. I will be glad to be your friend. I wish you the best of everything." Hans walked over the bridge across the river and disappeared into the sunset. I was very proud of the way I handled the situation. Hans never knew that I cried every day that I remained in Outsbruck and it took me more than a year to get over him. For the moment, though, I had to act according to *Sondra Gets Dumped Rule Book*. I picked up the well-thumbed tome and turned to Rule Number 101. This rule reads as follows: "Rule Number 101: If you get dumped out of the blue and there is no hope that you can get the man back, distract yourself by going to a conference. Corollary One to Rule Number 101: you never fail to meet men at conferences. Corollary Two to Rule Number 101: if you are hurt beyond repair, attend two conferences." Getting dumped by Hans was definitely a two conference situation.

During my return trip to the States, I arranged to go to England to attend a utopian studies conference at the University of Exeter. Immediately after the Exeter conference, I planned to stop in New York before flying on to Kirk T. Pistol's science fiction conference in Kansas. Pistol was concerned that I was cutting things a little too close. "You must promise that you will arrive no later than when the clock strikes three," he stipulated in an e-mail message. This blunt statement struck me as being rather ominous. I mean what if

Pistol was yet another member of my supernatural creature friendship circle? Since one can never be too careful, I asked for further clarification.

"What will happen if I arrive after three?"

"All hell will break loose. I am a perfectionist. My conference must run smoothly. You must arrive at three, not one minute later."

"I give you my word of honor that I will arrive exactly on time."

Pistol's response, although he would never use these particular words, clearly constituted a case of "*oy*, don't ask." If "all hell will break loose" meant that my lateness would function as a Pandora's box in which monsters would really appear and terrorize Kansas, he would never tell me so directly. I had to be aware of the possibility that my tardiness could cause Kansas not to be Kansas anymore. Myriad magical catastrophes could ensue. What if I arrived at one minute after three and the Wicked Witch of the East decided to drop her house on the conference venue? Simply resolving to be on time, I forced myself to stop imagining potential supernatural *tsuris* (the worst kind -- as I know well).

Before departing from Outsbruck, the last item on my agenda was to attend the department's goodbye party for me. I was very sad to leave these wonderful women who would remain my friends for life. Marie, Ursula, and Johanna expressed their gratitude for my willingness to welcome a Heidi into my home. It was hardest to leave Johanna. I threw myself into her arms.

"Cheer up, Sondra. You're not leaving me. I'm marrying Michael. We're moving to Forest Hills, to Yellowstone Boulevard and Sixty Eighth Drive. Are you familiar with the area?"

"Yes. I grew up in the apartment building located at those exact quadrants. Yellowstone Boulevard is situated below steep hills that lead to Queens Boulevard. Those hills, located in a very Jewish neighborhood, are alive with the sound of *oying*, a song Jews have song for a thousand years. The Forest Hills hills are no Alps. I will help you to adapt.

Second to Last Fling –Unflung

I arrived at the University of Exeter science fiction conference and waited for my roommate Lara Smorkaloff, my peer who
had published a lot of good criticism. I amused myself by watching
rabbits cavort outside my dorm room window. When I saw them go
down their rabbit holes, I hoped that I would not be joining them.
Because I was too *zaftig* to fit in the holes, the chances of my doing
so were slim. When Lara entered the room she seemed very agitated.

"Hi Sondra. I can't talk to you now. I have to call my mother immediately."

"Just briefly tell me why."

"I'm not sure you will understand. I have a very difficult
mother. She doesn't know that I am in England and she wants me to
attend to matters at home involving my husband. I don't want to
cause an upheaval by telling her I'm abroad. She won't approve of
me leaving my husband alone to take care of our house and our
twenty cats. I have to call her now and pretend that I am in New
York. Does this make sense to you?"

"Absolutely. I'm not at all competitive with my friends. But
I'm sure that my mother is more difficult than your mother."

"Can't be."

"Call your mother. We can have a mother difficulty contest." I listened to Lara calmly explain to her mother that she was
having fun in the Whitney Museum and she hoped to beat the afternoon traffic. They hung up after exchanging pleasantries.

"Now I'll call my mother. Take cover."

"Hello Herbert."

"Where are you?"

"At a conference in England."

"Don't waste your time listening to those stupid academic papers. Devote every ounce of your strength to finding a husband. Find one now. Find one immediately if not sooner." I held out the phone so that Lara could hear my mother screaming at a decibel level intolerable to the human ear.

"Can't you just end the conversation?" she asked as her eyes widened with incredulity.

"There's no such thing as politely ending a conversation with my mother. I just have to hang up. She can't call back because she does not know where I am." Lara, overwhelmed by my mother's excessive locutionary ferocity, had to compose herself.

"I've never heard the like of that screaming. You win the mother difficulty contest. You win hands down."

"You can't get off that easily. I won fair and square. I deserve a prize."

"What prize do you want?"

"Thurston Howell is coming to the conference. I want you to protect me if he attempts to murder me."

"Why should Thurston murder you? He's a very civilized and sophisticated science fiction scholar."

"I published a novel called *Oy Pioneer!* which is about how I was in love with him for years and pursued him on three continents. I revealed that his orgasms were loud enough to compete with building demolition sights. True, Thurston's orgasms are not at loud as my mother's screaming. But, in terms of noise pollution, they're right up there with Herbert."

"I'm not sure that you were right to write about someone's personal life. I disapprove."

"F. Scott Fitzgerald wrote about Zelda. Whose life is it anyway? It's my life. I have the right creatively to mine what is mine."

"What you have done cannot be undone. I lost the impossible mother contest; I promise to protect you from murder by death at the hands of Thurston. Let's just go to the conference's opening reception and enjoy ourselves."

Thurston was at the reception. He nodded hello and seemed to scowl at me. After so many years of pursuing him to no avail, he suddenly did not interest me. I nodded -- and scowled back. Thurston is an American New England WASP who imitates patrician Englishmen. An authentic exemplar of what Thurston emulated was showing interest in me. Reginald Rarrington, a scion of an aristocratic English family and a highly respected Philip K. Dick scholar, was following me around the room. I was both surprised and flattered. Reginald had never before given me the time of day. I enjoyed his attention and returned it. He asked if I would sit next to him at dinner.

He ordered beef and I chose fish. He eyed my plate.

"Your fish looks so good. I'm sorry that I didn't order it. May I taste your fish?"

"You mean that you want to pierce my food with your fork and eat it?"

"Yes. That's exactly the action I propose to take."

"Fine. I enjoy eating out of my dinner companions' plates. But I'm not you. You're an aristocratic Englishman. I'm a New York Jew. New York Jews routinely eat out of each other's plates. As far as I am aware, such is not the case with people of your ilk. To what can I attribute this behavioral deviance?"

"I feel very comfortable with you, Sondra. Furthermore, I've enjoyed eating out of the plates of other New York Jews."

"I'm complimented. Go right ahead. Have some fish." Reginald speared a fish piece with the alacrity of Jacques Costeau undertaking a fish-finding mission. Once eating out of someone else's plate starts, I find it impossible to stop. I stared with intense desire at the juicy pickle ensconced upon a bed of organic mescaline greens positioned smack in the middle of Reginald's salad plate.

"May I have your pickle?"

"My pickle is your pickle. Take it. Take it off my salad plate. Take it all off."

I picked up the pickle and an adjoining peck of pickled peppers and placed them on my plate. (Is a peck is too large to comprise one portion?) I wrapped my lips around Reginald's former pickle, sucked its succulent pickle juice, and moved it laterally between my lips.

"Bravo Sondra. I just taught *Tom Jones*. Fielding's lascivious sex scenes can't hold a candle to your behavior."

"I can accomplish the same with a candle as with a pickle."

"How sad that this is not a candlelit dinner. I look forward to hearing your paper tomorrow. And by the way, I own a family beach house located about an hour from here. Would you and Lara like to accompany me there at the end of the afternoon sessions?"

"What a nice invitation. I accept. I'll ask Lara if she wants to join us."

I returned to the dorm and told Lara how much I enjoyed gossiping with her. "Sondra, tell me what happened with Thurston. Did he murder you? If so, I'm sorry that I did not keep my promise to protect you. Tell all. Let's dish."

"There's nothing to say about Thurston. All the dishing in this conversation concerns Rupert Rarrington's unexpected strong desire to eat out of my plate."

"Rupert ate your food at a formal dinner? That's very weird. He's usually so proper. He has impeccable manners."

"Weird or not, that's what happened. And I have an invitation for you. Would you like to come with me to Rupert's beach house tomorrow afternoon?"

"Sorry, no. I have to call my mother at six sharp. I'm telling her that I spent the day at Bloomingdale's. And I've already made dinner plans. But you should go. I am sure that Rupert has a beautiful beach house."

"I can't go to a man's house alone. What will he think?"

"If he wanted to seduce you, he certainly would not have invited me along."

"True. I will tell him exactly how I feel. There is only one problem. I don't know how I feel."

"You have to decide if you want to have sex with him or not. If you do, he will surely comply. If you don't, he will act like a gentleman."

"At least I don't have to make this decision until tomorrow."

Rupert joined me as soon as the last conference session ended. "Lara is unable to come. We have to have an honest talk."

"Talk away."

"Are you available to engage in a serious long term relationship? This is a ludicrous question because I'm returning to the States in two days. I've just been dumped by a man that I loved and there is a man here who has rejected my efforts to marry him for years. Enough is enough. I've had it. I've reached my limit with men who won't commit to me. If I can't be the number one woman in your life, I don't want to sleep with you."

"I'm sorry that you feel this way and you don't want to enjoy a casual fling. I'm in a serious relationship."

"Thank you for being truthful. My fling days are over. I can't believe I said that. You're so cute and so nice. I agree to visit your beach house as your friend."

"I'm very disappointed. Especially after I saw you devour that pickle. But I'll look on the bright side. Your decision puts me in serious contention for the Prophylactic Award. The Prophylactic Award would look great on my twenty page vitae."

During the drive to Rupert's beach house, he entertained me with the history of hedge groves. The house was very comfortable and replete with science fiction novels. I was intrigued by a winding staircase that led to a small attic room.

"What's up there?"

"My telescope. I use it for bird watching."

"I'd like to look through it. I'm not that good at sighting wildlife. When I came face to face with a lily-livered sap sucking antelope during my sojourn at a South African game preserve, I thought I was looking at a rock. Maybe I will do better this time."

Rupert put his arm around me as he helped me to focus the lens. "If you look straight ahead to the end of the beach you might see some interesting birds."

"I see some things. I don't think they're birds."

"What do you see?"

"These big things with four feet, tails, and horns. I don't know about hedge groves. But I'm sure that wildebeest do not inhabit English beaches. And believe me when I say that I know from wildebeest. Those animal things are definitely mammals, not birds."

"You're looking at cows grazing in the grassland above the sand line."

"Cows? What are cows doing at the beach? American obesity problems aside, there are no bovines at American beaches. I know from cows too. I spent years teaching at the cow college in Virginia. When my beloved dissertation director Norman N. Holland wrote me a reference letter emphasizing my commitment to diversity he said -- and this is a direct quote: 'This young woman from Queens has learned to live with cows.' Yes, I can live with cows. And I even coped with a wildebeest who showed up in my mother's kitchen. (Don't ask. Are wildebeest kosher? I don't think they are. Good. If wildebeest were kosher my mother would tell me to marry one. But that is another story.) I didn't expect to look through a telescope and see cows. I expected birds."

"You never know what can happen. Because you trusted me and agreed to accompany me here, you've become England's first bona fide cow watcher."

"This credential will not serve me well. When I return to New York, can you imagine me trying to husband hunt via establishing a cow watching interest group on the Meetup web site? No one would come. I can just hear my mother saying that being the world's sole cow watcher will get me nowhere. She would tell me to stop aiming my telescope at cows and to start focusing upon men. You're wonderful. I'm very attracted to you. I really want to have sex with you. But it is the wrong thing for me to do at this point in my life. I want a man I can keep. Why can't I meet an uninvolved man who is just like you?"

"To do so, you will just have to keep looking. I would give you my telescope to enhance your chances. But it is a family heirloom and my sister owns half of all the property in the house. Don't give up your search. I suspect that one day you will be as successful regarding love as you are regarding feminist science fiction scholarship. "

"What you say is true. I can't give up my husband hunt. But, after all these years, I'm starting to think that my quest is akin to science fiction -- or to mission impossible. More accurately, my husband finding methods are becoming a horror story. I know from genre fiction. I can just see myself married to an alien. It could happen; I've traveled in a spaceship my alien clones provided. Don't ask about this either."

Upon returning to campus, Rupert opened the car door for me, took me in his arms, and kissed me passionately.

"I want the best for you. I hope you find the man that you deserve. And no more talk about mission impossible, horror stories, and finding a husband who is an alien."

"Although this is not an appropriate moment to comment about our profession, you make me think that all the effort I directed toward being a science fiction scholar was worth it."

When the Exeter conference concluded, I said goodbye to my friends -- and snarled at Thurston. I felt very sad as I watched people depart. I had had a wonderful distraction from the Hans the German fiasco. Exeter was in the past. Onward to flying across the planet to attend Kirk T. Pistol's conference in Kansas.

I made my way to London and boarded my flight to New York. I planned to pick up clean clothes and my conference paper in Forest Hills before continuing on to Kansas. The flight progressed smoothly until the Captain made the following announcement. "We are immediately returning to the London airport because a passenger's luggage has been misplaced. There is no problem." While everyone calmly accepted the Captain's comments, I knew that he was not telling the truth. Planes do not turn around due to misplaced luggage. I hoped for the best. The plane landed on the first available runaway. I had a full view of what was ensuing on the tarmac. I saw people in white spacesuits converging on the luggage compartment and hysterically screaming "Get it. Get it." I kept this information to myself; alarming people would serve no purpose. I knew that I was watching a bomb search. Even though I have feared death by wildebeest invasion, this time I remained absolutely calm. How I don't know.

A space suited figure emerged from the luggage compartment with a suitcase in hand. S/he threw it into an armored vehicle. The Captain instructed passengers to vacate the plane. Upon reaching the gate lounge, passengers were told to take another flight in the morning. All of my aforementioned composure was now nowhere in evidence. I began to cry; the full import of the situation became apparent. It seemed impossible for me to keep my promptness promise to Pistol. I phoned the University of Kansas English Department. I was still sobbing when the secretary answered.

"Hello. This is Sondra Lear. I wish to leave a message for Kirk T. Pistol. Please understand that I am very upset because I am in the London airport and I have just been flying in a plane involved in a bomb scare. I have to let Professor Pistol know that, due to this unforeseen circumstance, I may not be able to arrive at his conference before three. Tell him I will try my best to make it. Thank you so much for taking my message. 'Bye."

Next, I explained my situation to an airline official. "I have to be at a conference in Kansas at three sharp the day after tomorrow and it is necessary for me to stop in New York to pick up my scholarly paper. It is imperative that I arrive on time; I gave my word to an eminent member of my field. If I break my promise, all hell might really break loose. Since I can't fly out until the morning, it will be impossible for me to follow my schedule."

"We will do all we can to help you. If there is someone available to give your paper to a courier, we can deliver it to the Kansas airport in time for your arrival. The courier will make it unnecessary for you to stop in New York. Feel free to use our phone to make a free call."

"What a wonderful idea. I'll phone and make the necessary arrangements. I so much appreciate your help." Luckily, my parents had not yet left for Florida. My mother's familiar knife piercing screaming voice soon assaulted my ears.

"Where are you, Sondra?"

"The London airport."

"Did you look for a husband during your flight? Are you looking for a husband in the airport lounge?"

"My plane had to return to London due to a bomb scare. I knew about the bomb throughout the entire return flight. I'm very upset. Please. I can't cope with the husband thing now. For once in your life, desist with the husband thing. I need you to locate one of my papers so that a courier can pick it up. If the courier receives my paper, I will be able to arrive at the Kansas conference on schedule."

"You and your papers and your conferences. Your papers and your conferences are the ruination of your life. All of the women sitting at the beach club watching their cute little babies are not involved with papers and conferences. Why can't you be normal? I have no idea how to find one of your papers in all of your things. The bomb scare is no excuse. The bomb did not go off. You're alive. Instead of wasting time being frightened for nothing, you should use your energy to find a husband. Maybe there was a rabbi on the plane who could have married you. If worse came to worse and the plane exploded, at least you could have been married in the afterlife. At least your death certificate would say that you were married. Because you didn't bother to look for a husband during your flight, you're still in the same situation: You're still alive and you're still single. What good was accomplished?"

"I can't cope with this conversation. Put my father on." Herbert screamed to the extent that I had to move the receiver away from my ear. The airline representative heard and looked at me with incredulous sympathy. Lacking the ability to take a chair to a lion on a transatlantic phone line, I mustered my most serious and icy tone.

"I said put my father on." Herbert complied.

"Hello Sondra dear. How can I help you?"

"I need you to find one of my papers filed in a red folder. The folder is on top of the book pile on the left side of the living room window. A courier will arrive early this evening. Please give my paper to the courier."

"I see the paper right now. No problem. Rest assured that it will be safely placed in the courier's hands. Have a safe trip. And listen to your mother." Imbued with thankfulness that at least one of my parents was reasonable, I made my way to an airport hotel. When I boarded my morning flight, I was relieved that I would arrive in Kansas on time.

When I heard a commotion emanating from the front of the plane, I looked up from my reading material. I heard a woman screaming. Brandishing a plastic knife, she ran down the aisle shouting "kill, kill." Unlike all the other visibly agitated passengers, I was able to cope with the screaming. My experience as the daughter of an incessantly screaming woman inured me to this situation. A plastic knife is no weapon of mass destruction. So there was screaming in the cabin. Screaming I am used to. At least this screaming mouth was not telling me to get married. I helped the frazzled flight attendants serve drinks. A male attendant subdued the woman.

The Captain announced that the plane was returning to the airport. This announcement made me more unhinged than the entire knife wielding scenario. I did not know if the next available flight would enable me to arrive in Kansas by three. When the plane landed, two men entered and put the woman in a straitjacket before removing her. Due to the two unusual inflight incidents, Herbert's usual behavior, and the stress regarding my scheduled arrival in Kansas, I thought that I might also need a straitjacket. If I were put in a straitjacket, Herbert would insist that I was still free to open my mouth to inquire about the most probably male straitjacket deployer's marital status. I knew that if I did not discontinue this thought, I would become the screaming woman's roommate in the nearest London mental hospital.

I was told that the next available transatlantic flight and domestic connections would enable me to land in Kansas at one thirty.

No longer thinking about Herbert, I considered phoning Phileas Fogg. If he could travel around the world in eighty days, I could fly from London to the University of Kansas in accordance with my time parameters. I called the department secretary to let her know about my revised schedule. When she expressed surprise, I used my tried and true "don't ask" refrain. Luckily, it works just as well for real events as for supernatural ones.

"Hello. This is Sondra Lear -- again. Due to further unforeseen flight circumstances (don't ask and ya shouldn't know from them), I'm still in the London airport. Please tell Professor Pistol that I am now scheduled to land at one thirty. I expect to arrive at the conference by three. I appreciate your help."

I flew over the Atlantic Ocean, changed planes in New York, and landed in the middle of America. During the flights, I was obsessed with one thought: the courier could fail to transport my paper. After the plane landed at one thirty sharp, I ran to the ticket counter. "Do you have a package for Sondra Lear?" I asked the agent.

"Just a moment please. I will look in the package storage area." I died a thousand deaths until I saw her return with the package. I hailed a cab and asked to be taken to the dorm in which I had reserved a room. I arrived at two fifteen, jumped into the shower, put on professional attire, grabbed my paper, and attempted to find the conference venue. This was no easy task. There are few available people to provide directions during intersession. And it was ninety nine degrees in the shade on the four-mile-wide campus. Sweating, exhausted, and bedraggled to the max -- but present nonetheless -- I arrived at the conference at exactly two fifty eight. An exceedingly perturbed Pistol -- who was steeling himself against the possibility of all hell literally breaking loose -- was at the podium explaining that I was delayed by unexpected flight changes.

Pistol's face lit up when he saw me. He mopped his brow. "Sondra Lear has arrived just in time to present her paper," he said to the audience. He smiled and flashed an a-okay sign at me. I translated this sign as dignified male Midwestern WASP for "*oy* I was so worried about you and what you had to go through and I thought you wouldn't make it and if you didn't how would I fill the time you were scheduled to use but now I don't have to know from this problem because you're here -- and last but not least all hell did not break loose." I omitted the myriad potential supernatural tsuris possibilities from this translation. Instead of using the minute I had to spare to approach Pistol and say "*oy* you should never know from what I had to go through to get here such a trip I had," I cut to the WASP chase. I nonchalantly returned his smile, calmly approached the podium, took a sip of water, and read my paper. It was one of the best paper presentations I had ever delivered.

Pistol, fully aware of the effort I had made to keep my promptness promise, became my friend. Once upon a time (no fairy tale intended), his reputation and demeanor intimidated me to the extent that I was afraid to speak to him. But, in contrast, an enormous change had happened during this last minute. Pistol told me that he wished to contribute to my anthologies and co-edit one with me. He explained that, because co-editors have to get along over a lengthy time period, co-editing is akin to marriage. I was honored that he thought that I could live up to his high co-editing standards.

Pistol's proposal would never satisfy Herbert, however. She would never buy the idea that co-editing is analogous to marriage. Continuing husband-hunting failures aside, I flew to New York while basking in the glow of my new friendship with Pistol. I felt honored beyond words. I arrived at Kennedy Airport in time to welcome Austria back into my life. One of the Heidis (probably Heidi Five, but I'm not sure) from Outsbruck was coming to live with me in Forest Hills. While waiting for her plane to land, I felt grateful that my parents were once again on their way to Florida.

Heidi was impressed with Forest Hills. "You live in a seventeen-story building? Your building is as tall as an Alp."

"My home is most certainly not an Alp. Heidi, you aren't in Outsbruck anymore. I suggest that we do some grocery shopping."

"I can't believe all the varieties of available merchandise. Are there any differences between all this toothpaste, paper towels, and toilet paper?"

"They're really the same."

"Then why have different brands?"

"Americans like to think that they have choices. We are, in fact, encountering the same product packaged differently." I did not tell her that I placed all the multitudinous Heidis in the same category as her observation about the at once multitudinous and similar toothpaste, paper towel, and toilet paper brands.

"Another question. The food labels say "low fat" and "fat free." If the food is fatless, why are Americans so fat?"

"Great question. Americans love to forget that "fat free" does not mean "calorie free." If you ingest too much fat free yogurt, cookies, and granola, you will get fat. Let's go home and I will explain how to take the subway to the 42nd Street library."

"You mean that I have to travel on the subway alone? I am used to gathering alpine field edelweiss. I have never been on a subway."

"There's no time like the present." Heidi returned from the library triumphant that she had successfully conducted her research and returned to tell the tale.

"What are you going to do tonight, Sondra? May I join you? I don't want to sit in the apartment alone."

"I'm going with my lifelong friend Carol to an Elizabeth Taylor festival to see *Cleopatra*."

"*Cleopatra*?"

"Yes. Carol and I think that Rex Harrison and Richard Burton are very sexy. We also derive hope from the fact that Elizabeth Taylor, the most gorgeous woman in the world, suffered from middle-aged spread. Joan Rivers would describe the presently *zaftig* Ms. Taylor less politely."

Rex Harrison and Richard Burton? Oh yes they are old actors. In addition to being old, they are dead. I'm a long way from middle-aged spread. Seeing *Cleopatra* is not my idea of fun. I would rather go to a noisy club and party until dawn.

"Heidi, you would have a much better time fraternizing with people who are your age. I have an idea. The 92nd Street Y houses international students. You should live there. I will e-mail Ursula to ask her if she can find funding for your rent." Ursula sold her least favorite antique to raise money to cover Heidi's housing costs.

"Your rent will be covered. I will help you move to the Y tomorrow." Heidi began to cry.

"I know that you mean well for me. But I'm afraid to live alone in New York. I will watch *Cleopatra* and contemplate middle-age spread even though I eat fat free food." She cried harder. Not knowing what to do, I phoned Hans the German.

"An hysterically crying Heidi is residing in my apartment. I think that she would be better off living in a dorm for international students. She is afraid to do it. I don't know how best to handle this situation. You have a daughter who is her age. You know from Austrians. You married one. What should I do about the crying Heidi?"

"Motivate her to leave. Tell her she can return if she is unhappy."

"Heidi, my German friend suggests that you go to the dorm. If you agree, I will grant you the right of return."

"Sounds good," Heidi sniveled. Two days later, she phoned to say that she was having a great time carousing in noisy smoke-sodden clubs with other international students. She clearly did not want to exchange club carousing for watching an old movie. Heidi's last report to me: "I met a cute boy named Peter. My grandfather will approve of him."

Some Enchanted Evening You Will Meet a Stranger

Heidi returned to Austria. I had no more conferences to attend. It was time to address the pressing matters at hand: finding a job and a husband. To accomplish the former, I phoned a fellow Blackhole State University refugee, Dean Rachel Fromkiss of SUNY-GV. In regard to the latter marital goal, success was about to be attained. The husband was on the horizon.

"Nice to hear from you, Sondra. I can arrange for you to teach at SUNY-GV. Your multitudinous publications have always impressed me. How exciting that you have published a novel called *Oy Pioneer!* SUNY-GV will be privileged to have you."

If only my husband hunt could be this easy. Even though I had been husband-hunting for twenty years (but who is counting?), there is no time like the present to begin again. A Municipal Art Society lecture smacked of being a potentially happy husband-hunting ground. The Society is located in a Madison Avenue Italianate palazzo. A sign saying "The Palace" adorns the palazzo's front façade. "The Palace" is the perfect place to meet Prince Charming -- especially in my life which oozes with fairy tale, fantasy, and science fiction scenarios. Juxtaposed real world and fairy tale venue aside, I had nothing to lose by attending the free Society lecture.

"Five dollars, please," said the woman posted at the door.

"Five dollars?" I really thought that the lecture is free."

"No. Sorry."

"Then I guess I can't attend," I said as I looked crestfallen and made my way out. I had only five dollars in hand. If I spent it to attend the lecture, I would have to go to a cash machine to obtain subway fare. I stood rooted in mid-palazzo courtyard. I could not make a decision between whether to spend the five dollars for the lecture or for the subway. I went so far as to say "enough already, make up your mind" out loud. I could not understand why such a trivial matter uncharacteristically caused me to fail to act. I didn't even care about the lecture. Art lectures are not my thing. I hunt husbands at an endless array of lectures, readings, and conferences. Even if this boring art lecture was located in a building clearly labeled "The Palace," the odds of meeting a Prince Charming husband within were nine billion godzillion to one. After six minutes had elapsed, I gave myself exactly two more seconds to make a decision. As I was in the midst of shifting my recently five-ounce-less weight (I had cut down on fat free yogurt portions) to turn on my heel and depart, the ticket taker entered the courtyard.

"I'm so glad you're here. I didn't expect to find you. You looked so sad when I told you about the five dollar admission price. I believe you truly did think that the lecture was free. Please feel welcome to attend gratis. Come on in and join us." I could not believe that a Manhattan ticket seller was thinking of me, going out of her way to locate me, and inviting me to attend an event free of charge.

"Thanks so much. I've had the weirdest experience. It was like I lost control of my trajectory. I was standing here for all this time unable to decide whether to stay or to leave. I am usually very decisive. I never act like this."

"You must be fated to attend. Enjoy yourself."

As an unabashed reception lover, I happily made my way toward a cheese and grape-laden table. I concentrated on the food, not the men in the room. I was surprised to hear an accented male voice addressing me.

"Excuse me. I forgot my glasses. Could you please help me read my program?" The accented voice emanated from a very attractive man. I stopped in mid cheese and cracker chomp to shift my attention to him. He was Captain Picard attractive rather than Cary Grant attractive. Fine. I needed a change from Norris the cat/husband and his clone Hans the German. Partial baldness suited him. I liked his perfectly cut jacket and cool black tee shirt. His accented English and foreign allure intrigued me.

"I'm glad to help you. Your program says 'this art lecture concerns the history of the pre-Raphaelite flying buttress and its influence on rococo terracotta Renaissance façades'."

"Very interesting. Thank you so much. You're so nice and helpful. What do you think of the lecture subject?"

"Sounds Byzantine to me. Art is not my main interest. But I sometimes go to lectures outside my field. Do you know about art?" I left out the part about how I attend lectures to meet men. Ditto for drowning myself in cheese and crackers when my efforts fail.

"Yes. A little. I'm a professional art historian. I teach Art History at the City University of New York."

I was puzzled. Despite my international travel experience, I could not identify his foreign accent. He seemed to be some sort of European. I decided to use his national origin as a conversation catalyst.

"I'm trying to figure out where you come from? Are you European? I'm Sondra Lear, by the way."

"You are not the first person to be puzzled about my origins. I'm from Canada. I'm a French Canadian, a *Quebeçois*." *Quebeçois* were definitely off my radar screen. Because I went into mental overdrive while trying to compute how a Canadian -- and a French one at that -- could fit into my life, I let down my guard and spoke my natural language.

"*Oy*."

"Well, Sondra, I'm not confused about your origins. Although I chose not to become an American citizen, I've lived in America for thirty years. You're definitely a New York Jew."

"Correct. And you're a noncitizen, an alien. Your field is art. My field is aliens."

"Aliens? Are you a sociologist specializing in immigration?"

"No. I'm a feminist science fiction scholar. I know from aliens. I feel a special affinity for them." An alien husband would be especially perfect for me. Still, since I had yet to learn this man's name, it was a tad too soon for The *Science Fiction Research Association Newsletter* to resemble a supermarket tabloid and run this headline: "Sondra Lear Marries Alien."

"I have never met a feminist science fiction scholar. I like facts, not fiction. I'm intrigued. I would like to know more about your field."

"Before I describe my professional interests, why don't you tell me further details about yourself? Do you like to travel?"

"I have lived all over the world. South Africa was particularly exciting."

"You've been to South Africa? Me too. You're the first fellow traveler to South Africa I've spoken to in America. What did you like most about your stay?"

"The South African National Gallery in Cape Town."

"I've been there." Our shared South African connection was drawing us closer. His specific Cape Town reference made me trust his veracity. One could not be too careful when meeting men in Manhattan. A pathological rapist/killer would probably not know from the South African National Gallery. I had already imagined myself marrying this alien. It was definitely time to escalate the relationship. "What's your name?"

"The name is Le Pew. Pepe Le Pew."

"Pepe Le Pew? Are you a skunk? Have you ever been a skunk?" Echoing McCarthy-era inquisition, although less than sexy, was unavoidable.

"Why do you ask?" I certainly couldn't tell him the truth: since I had married a former cat, it could be possible for me to marry a former skunk.

"Pepe Le Pew is a Warner Brothers cartoon skunk."

"So I've been told. I'm not that familiar with American popular culture. I was never interested in the cartoon character named Pepe Le Pew. Rest assured that I am not now nor have I ever been a skunk. I take two showers a day. I stand in front of the mirror for ten minutes whenever I leave my apartment -- trips to the incinerator and the laundry room included. I'm a member of the proud French Le Pew family. The founder emigrated to Canada from Burgundy during the sixteenth century. Never having seen a Warner Brothers cartoon, my mother named me Pepe. There's nothing skunkish about me. I'm more akin to a metrosexual than to a skunk. Just out of curiosity, since you're a popular culture scholar, do you like my cartoon character namesake?"

"Yes. Pepe the skunk is very direct when he pursues the opposite sex. He's always horny and incessantly tries to seduce female skunks. If he met an attractive female skunk, what would he most likely say in French?"

"Something like *'je desire avoir votre queue.'* Sondra, *je desire avoir votre cul.*"

"Your native-speaker French sounds so much better than my 'graduate school foreign language requirement test failure' French. Are you asking me out?"

"Oui. Absolument."

The generous ticket taker had altered my life. I was fated to marry Pepe Le Pew.

Chair of the Apartment

I phoned my B.F.F. Carol to convey all the Pepe details.

"I met a really cute and sexy French Canadian. He invited me to have dinner with him in his apartment."

"What? You're going alone to a man's apartment on a first date? That's dangerous. I strongly advise against it."

"I trust him. He's an academic."

"Bring mace."

I ventured to Twenty-ninth Street between Second and Third Avenue and entered Pepe's thirty-story apartment building. A doorman straight out of central casting as a Rhoda Morgenstern confidant house phoned the news that I had arrived. Pepe's living room window framed a spectacular World Trade Center view. Before I had a chance to put down my backpack, he grabbed my arm and ushered me into his bathroom. I panicked. Carol was right. I should have brought mace. What if Pepe was a homicidal maniac about to hurl me out of his twenty-fourth floor bathroom window? What if he was a *Sopranos* fan who knew that hacked-apart dead bodies could end up in bathtubs? This *Sopranos* scenario was coming true. Pepe ordered me to step into the bathtub and look out of the window.

"Look. You can see the Empire State Building when you take a shower," he excitedly said. Relieved that Pepe had nothing to do with *Psycho*, I enjoyed seeing the landmark in all its colorful nightly glory.

"Your apartment certainly has gorgeous views," I said while trying to avoid bathtub slip-induced concussion. "Is being immediately herded into your bathroom a usual component of being on a first date with you?"

"I love my bathroom window's Empire State Building panorama. Being an art historian involves looking at beautiful objects. I must be able to see the sky. I chose this apartment because of its spectacular views. I love to look at you. I see, though, that we should not spend the evening in my bathroom. Come sit on the sofa. We can enjoy the World Trade Center view while we get to know each other."

"Tell me about yourself and your family."

"I suppose I'm a self-made man. I arrived in America with no money. I worked my way through art history graduate school at SUNY-GV by being a *maitre d'* at expensive Manhattan restaurants. It was easy for me to get the job by capitalizing on my Frenchness, good looks, and sense of order. I'm a perfectionist. I excelled as a Canadian army officer. I ran some of New York's most expensive restaurants with military precision. When I was working at the Tavern on the Green in Central Park, Jackie Kennedy rode up on her horse. It's unusual to encounter celebrities on horseback in Manhattan."

"I have some experience with SUNY-GV, Manhattan, and horses myself," I said as I appreciated Pepe's plastic slipcoverless couch and thought of how I used to routinely park Ms. Ed with police horses in Washington Square Park.

"Really?"

"Don't ask. Tell me more about yourself."

"I come from a large family and I grew up in a small town located near Montreal called Joliette. I have seven sisters and two brothers."

"Wow. I'm an only child. Large families intrigue me. Describe your siblings."

My sisters are drop dead gorgeous and exceedingly sexy. They're named Annette, Claudette, Georgette, Lynette, Nanette, Pierrette, Suzette -- and Hadassah."

"Hadassah?"

"Yes, Hadassah. My mother met a Jewish woman in Montreal called Hadassah and she liked the name. By the time Hadassah was born, mother had used up all the "ette" names she could think of. She discerned it was time for a change. Hadassah, my most feisty sister, looks as if she could be my twin. It was really something to grow up surrounded by gorgeous sisters. I was always horny. I wanted to sleep with all of them."

"How old were you when your sisters first made you feel horny?"

"I was horny from the time I was born. Very sexy people comprise my family. Even my mother's brother's wife was gorgeous. After my uncle died in the 1960's, I wanted to have sex with her. She's now eighty. I told her about my youthful feelings when I saw her two years ago."

"How did she react?"

"She was pleased."

"Are your brothers also attracted to your sisters?"

"I don't know and I don't want to know. My older brother is named Michel and the younger one is named Marcel."

"What a relief. After hearing about Hadassah, I was worried that your mother named your brothers Yehuda and Mordecai."

"Michel is a moose hunter and Marcel is a Mountie. Marcel, who always gets his man, is very attached to his horse named Fung Whoa."

"I have a very good friend who is an intrepid husband hunter. She's always in dire need of Marcel's man-getting alacrity. 'Fung Whoa,' by the way, is as weird a name for a French Canadian horse as 'Hadassah' is for a French Canadian sister."

"Marcel traveled to China and named his beloved horse in terms of remembering things past in relation to his trip. Marcel and Fung Whoa are inseparable. He built a stall for him in his yard. I think his wife Carol is jealous."

"I understand. Marcel's wife suffers from Mr. Ed syndrome."

"Mr. Ed?"

"Of course, of course. *Mr. Ed* is a sixties sitcom. Wilbur Post, the protagonist, spends more time talking to his talking horse than being hitched to his wife."

"'I'm an alien. As I mentioned, I don't know a great deal about American popular culture. A talking horse is impossible."

"I wouldn't bet on that."

"Why?"

"Don't ask."

We sat down to a candlelit dinner consisting of delicious homemade vegetable soup and chilled pineapple for dessert. I enjoyed the World Trade Center view. Pepe's taste in music was the only fault I could find with him. His background New Age music, an acoustical assault, sounded like a *maharishi* who had mistakenly ingested too much Kaopectate.

"I love this soup. It's very healthy. Are you a good cook?"

"You might say that. I qualify as a gourmet cook."

"Your apartment is so orderly."

"I must live in order. I routinely circumnavigate the apartment to pick up specks from the floor. To ensure that I am doing a thorough job, I conduct an inspection using a magnifying glass. No speck escapes me."

"You don't think that your magnifying glass method is a little extreme? Sherlock Holmes is not a *Quebeçois*."

"I've gotten a little more sloppy. I now examine the floor with a magnifying glass instead of a microscope. Even I could see that my microscope follow through was a little too compulsive. I graduated to the magnifying glass. This change is as disorderly as I can get. Are you a neat person?"

"No." I left unsaid the fact that I keep my clothing in piles whose heights rival the Austrian Alps. If I need to locate, say, a particular shirt, I have to begin to excavate it a day in advance. I usually keep shirts on mountain four level six, an estimated location which could not be fully depended upon. Trying to avoid discussing my nonexistent relationship with neatness, I signaled that the evening should come to a close.

"I enjoyed dinner and the chance to get to know you better. Healthful eating is important to me. A man who served me fried pork rinds and pie *á la mode* would turn me off."

"The pleasure was all mine," Pepe said as he kissed my hand.

"It is now much colder outside than when I first arrived. May I borrow a jacket? Do you have a jeans jacket, *schmata*?"

"I'm very attached to my jeans jacket. If I let you wear it, how do I know that I will ever see it again?"

"I'm very trustworthy. If I promise to return your jacket, you can be assured that I will. I hope that you like me well enough to want to see me again."

"I do." Pepe's phone rang. I cringed.

"Don't pick it up. It's a wrong number."

"How do you know?"

"Don't ask."

"Le Pew residence," said Pepe, failing to heed my warning.

"This is Herbert, Sondra's mother. I heard you say 'I do' to her. I've been disappointed before. Sondra's cat taught me to look before I leap and jump for joy *vis-à-vis* a man, or a purported man, saying 'I do' to her. Are you human? Have you ever been anything other than a human?"

"Why do you ask?"

"Don't ask. Put Sondra on."

"There's a woman on the phone named Herbert who claims to be your mother. How could someone who has a mother named Herbert question why my mother named my sister Hadassah and why my brother named his horse Fung Whoa?"

"It's a wrong number," I desperately said.

"As I told you, I have lived in America for thirty years. I have dated American women who have Jewish mothers. Herbert is authentic. Speak to her."

I held my nose and spoke with the best nasal accent I could muster. "This is the overseas operator who handles calls placed between Manhattan and Florida. I regret to inform you that your call has been terminated. Goodbye."

Pepe, despite his familiarity with Jewish mothers, was not yet ready for a Herbertian phone call.

"Overseas operator?"

"Don't ask."

Pepe put the phone receiver back in its place and opened his hall closet. I noticed that everything in it was flawlessly folded and hung according to color and season.

"Please take this jacket. I would very much like you to return it next Saturday at seven. I do mean seven, not six fifty-nine. Propriety dictates that you can arrive after seven but not a minute before. We can have another soup dinner."

Pepe's punctuality demand reminded me of my experience with Kirk T. Pistol. "Does the smoke alarm in here go off a lot?"

"No. It has never done so."

Great. At least, unlike Ilya, Pepe was not a smoke puff-creating vampire. The Saturday soup dinners ensued for five months. I would arrive on Saturday nights at precisely one minute after seven and leave at nine forty-five. We ate our soup and engaged in extensive conversations while cuddling on the couch. I felt more satisfied sitting entwined in Pepe's arms with my head resting against his stomach than I did after having full-blown sex with all the other men I had ever known (Prophylactic Award winners excluded, of course.) I intuited that Pepe could not be rushed with regard to having sex. But, then again, he did say that he was horny when he was one minute old.

Sometime near the end of month five, Saturday night soup became Saturday night soup and sex -- *la soup du Samedi et un cul*. We went as far as to name our soup and sex interactions "S and S." When the latter S was added to the soup, Pepe extended my permitted hours in his apartment. I was now scheduled to arrive on Saturday night at one minute after seven and to depart at precisely nine thirty on Sunday morning. Pepe's appointment book reflected our new "S" activity. Before "S" became "S and S," his Saturday notations read as follows: "9:04 AM: Purchase ingredients for soup: 5 and a quarter large carrots, 2 medium potatoes, 7 fennel stalks, 235 barley pieces, 694 rice kernels, and 367 and a half kidney beans." The notation entry was expanded *après* the new "S" addition: "9:04 PM: Have sex with Sondra." After our third sexual encounter, Pepe asked me exactly what he could do to enhance my pleasure. A week later, I found that he had listed all my suggestions on an index card and propped it up against his night table lamp. This is not to imply that Pepe is completely inflexible. I noticed that he had added something new to his soup ingredients list: "4 and a half fluffy matzo balls." A *Quebeçois* could no more make fluffy matzo balls than I could produce *Leberknödelsuppe* and *Apfelstrudel*.

I can adjust to someone's peculiar sexual proclivities. I have had fantastic sex -- and I use "fantastic" to denote both "superb" and "supernatural." I adjusted when Ilya and I defied gravity and experienced sky-high floating sex. I also accustomed myself to having spaceship sex with my cat/husband Norris. Yet, I could not get used to having perfectionist sex with Pepe. At precisely one minute after nine P.M., his alarm clock and kitchen cooking timer would ring simultaneously.

"Ah ha. It's just after nine. Time for our sex appointment," he would never fail to say. In the beginning, I was taken aback and attempted to protest.

"Don't you think it is a little extreme to call sex an 'appointment,' write said appointment in your calendar, and file my desires on index cards?"

"Not at all. My methods guarantee that we will be organized and everything will be in order."

Although Pepe could neither defy gravity like Ilya nor enjoy an "appointment" in a spaceship like Norris, he was as sexually unprecedented as his mortal terrestrial limitations allowed. Pepe required that our sex appointments always began with me standing on a chair while he kissed and caressed my body. He requested that I remain silent and pretend to be a statue.

"I demand the right not to remain silent. Posing as a non-interactive statue is not my style."

"I visualize you as my private sex goddess. The chair represents a pedestal which allows me to worship your body."

"This is a Madonna Whore Complex manifestation. I'm a human, not a sex goddess." Since I'm straight, a sex goddess -- Aphrodite, for example -- was not among my supernatural sex partners. At least Aphrodite never materialized in the Forest Hills apartment. I had had my hands full with the wildebeest.

"You are my sex goddess. Having you stand on a chair means so much to me and so little to you. Can't you just comply?"

"Okay. If you put it that way, I suppose I can. I'm teaching a feminist mythology course at SUNY-GV. What would my students do if they knew I was your sex goddess?"

"Never tell them. Keep your sex goddesshood *entre nous*."

"Fine. The chair it is. But you have to give up having appointments to the background tune of that blasting horrific *mahareshi* suffering from diarrhea music. Appointments, *oui*. Chair, *oui*. Index cards, *oui*. *Maharishi* music, *non*."

I won on the music front. The chair goddess appointment scenario never desisted. Complying was not as easy as Pepe had indicated. As our relationship progressed to include traveling together, I felt like a circus acrobat who had to confront myriad hotel room chairs: high and low, plush and hard. I almost did not survive the hotel room furnished with a wobbly soft swivel chair and an inordinately high four poster bed. I nearly lost my bearings as I jumped off the chair and tried to negotiate the bed climb. Despite such difficulties, I eventually learned to interpret "appointment" as a synonym for "sex." This idiosyncratic denotation proved to be disastrous during my conversation with three Prophylactic Award winners. My schedule called for me to meet them in a New York Hilton hotel room during a Modern Language Association Conference to discuss the following year's MLA science fiction panel.

"Welcome, Sondra. You're exactly on time for our appointment," said one Prophylactic Award winner.

"Appointment?" I queried as I removed all my clothes and stood on the nearest chair. One Prophylactic Award winner forfeited his right to possess the award.

Alien/Aliens/Alien 3

I was soon moving some of my possessions into Pepe's small one-bedroom Manhattan apartment. He panicked when he noticed my proclivity for accumulating material things.

"Before our relationship can proceed, we must have an understanding. You abhor empty spaces. When you see an empty space, you must fill it with material. I, on the other hand, revel in spaciousness. There is a limit to the amount of things you may bring into my apartment. When you reach what I define as the saturation point, you must remove something before acquiring its equivalent. I consider this stipulation to be a contract between us."

Always one to circumvent rules, I began to pile clothes that I didn't care too much about outside the apartment in the vestibule fuse closet. I would use this outside space as a way station storage area. When Pepe wasn't looking, I would sneak *des vêtements* into his apartment. One day, though, I brought home an amount that was even too large for the secret closet. I returned from a neighborhood thrift shop sale with twelve clothes-filled plastic bags. I rang Pepe's door bell, lined up the bags outside his apartment door, and used the direct honest approach.

"I've done something that will make you faint. I have twelve clothes-filled bags out here. I love these clothes. I can't part with them. Can I please bring them in?"

"Okay. Fine. But don't tell me about it. *Fin du sujet.*"

When Pepe granted me permission to invade his apartment with myriad plastic bags filled with thrift shop clothes, I knew that he was beginning to fall in love with me. It was time to bring a particular personal possession I could not possibly live without into the apartment -- i.e. my magic red clogs. After all, one never knows when a supernatural vampire literary critic's immediate presence might be necessary. The sight of the red clogs raised Pepe's ire.

"Red clogs? Why do you need red clogs? You have brown clogs, white clogs, and black clogs. Red clogs are decidedly uncool. I do not even approve of the American sneaker wearing penchant. Wear your red clogs by yourself, not with me. There's no room in here for another pair of clogs. I'm throwing them all down the incinerator."

Before I could stop him, Pepe picked up the red clogs. Not knowing what would happen if a mortal other than myself touched them, I tried to grab them out of his hands. When doing so, I accidentally knocked them together. A puff of smoke appeared. Ilya Lugosi stood in the middle of Pepe's living room. At least I did not own blue clogs. If I possessed both red clogs and blue clogs, Pepe's apartment could become a *Matrix* movie set.

"You rang, Sondra? What can I do for you? What a nice apartment. Can we have antigravity sex in here?"

"Definitely not. This apartment belongs to an attractive human man—the one laying stunned on the sofa. I'm trying to have a relationship with him. I could never explain you to him."

"Did you tell him about your mother? He doesn't look Jewish. If you can explain your impossible Jewish mother to a Gentile man, then you can also explain that you're friends with a vampire who enjoys having sex with you. I'll just turn him into a skunk and then we can have sex."

"Don't turn him into anything -- especially a skunk. Skunks are a sore subject with him. Ilya, you have got to make him forget that you materialized in his apartment. Do you have one of those *Men In Black* forget-zapper contraptions?"

"As a matter of fact, I do. I'll forget-zap him. Would you like me to change him? No problem to throw in an extra zap or two to alter anything about him."

"I'm tempted to ask for big changes. Can you transform him from Felix into Oscar?"

"Felix? Felix the cat? Didn't you have enough trouble with your cat Norris?"

"On second thought, since I am exceedingly sloppy, two Oscar types can't live in the same small apartment. It wouldn't be fair to change Pepe. I felt badly enough about neutering Norris before he was transformed into a human. I elect to leave Pepe as he is. On second thought, maybe not exactly as he is. It really couldn't hurt if you programmed him not to explode upon noticing the difference between his meticulous closet and my disaster area closet. Before you use the zapper thing on Pepe, give me a chance to hide my red clogs. What Pepe doesn't know about them won't hurt him."

"Done," said Ilya as he waved the forget-zapper contraption in front of Pepe's eyes and disappeared in his usual smoke cloud.

"I smell smoke. The smoke alarm is going off. What is that smoke smell?"

"Oh nothing. The neighbor across the hall is probably burning dinner."

Pepe will remain forever oblivious to his close encounter with the supernatural. I, however, was not entirely convinced that Pepe was truly human. As a science fiction scholar par excellence, I know an alien when I see one. And I don't mean aliens hailing from Canada. Anyone as meticulous as Pepe could not be completely human. Anyone who has sex by appointment and files his partner's suggestions for enhanced sexual techniques on alphabetized index cards has to be either an android or a planet Vulcan denizen. Due to Pepe's ignorance of American popular culture and his exaggerated sense of propriety, *Star Trek's* Mr. Spock and Lieutenant Data were more adept than he at enacting human proclivities.

Late one night, I awoke from a deep sleep to closely encounter evidence to support my theory that Pepe was an extraterrestrial. Located on his bookshelf, precisely between his well-worn copies of the *Joy of Cooking* and the *Joy of Sex,* I saw a green blinking light emanating from an unrecognizable object. Although it occurred to me that my response might result from having read too much science fiction, I was absolutely convinced that I was seeing the communication device which enabled Pepe to keep in touch with an extraterrestrial controller called the Big Giant Head. Why not? Ilya had recently used his forget-zapper implement in the apartment. Maybe fantastic devices in New York apartments were analogous to roaches: if you see one you can be sure that others are lurking somewhere. As you are aware, the stuff of science fiction routinely shows up in my life. Discovering that Pepe is an alien could be more akin to Sigourney Weaver playing Ellen Ripley than to Ripley's believe-it-or-not. I tried to convince myself that a horrific outer space monster would not momentarily jump out of Pepe's stomach. So I was in bed with an extraterrestrial alien rather than a Canadian alien. I had to remain calm. There was little else I could do. Pepe's rule number 109.5A stipulated that, unless an emergency was ensuing, I could not disturb his sleep. I was not sure if he had filed "potential space monster" under "emergency." Furthermore (as Ripley knows well), in space no one can hear you scream. Searching for more evidence of Pepe's off-planet origins, I ran my hand over the side of his head while hoping to find a panel which would open to reveal mechanistic components.

"Why are you touching my head and waking me up? I no longer smell smoke. There's no fire, no emergency. You know perfectly well that, according to rule number 109.5A, you are forbidden to wake me unless there's an emergency."

"I saw the device you use to communicate with an extraterrestrial Big Giant Head. I'm trying to find the on and off switch which must be located on the side of your cranium. You're too efficient to be human. You're either an extraterrestrial or an android. There's the proof," I said while pointing to the device from which the green blinking light emanated.

"Where? What are you talking about?"

"There. The green blinking light is coming from the communication mechanism which enables you to contact your home planet. Don't worry. Even if you are an extraterrestrial or an android, my feelings for you won't change. Some of my best friends are extraterrestrials who look exactly like me. Don't ask. I don't know how my mother will react to this news, though. I guess that if she can accept the fact that you're not Jewish, she can deal with the fact that you're not human."

"Although I usually would not express myself in this fashion, I will draw upon my thirty-year residence in New York and my foreign language felicity to use a word which precisely describes you. Sondra, you are an absolute *meshuganeh*. The green blinking light comes from my electric shaver. I think I need to have my head examined for becoming involved with a *meshuganeh*. There's no reason for you to examine my head. No switches are to be found there. Go back to sleep."

As soon as Pepe's talking head began to snore, I retrieved my red clogs and tapped them together.

"What now?" asked Ilya.

"I just need you to execute one more little forget contraption zap aimed at Pepe. My future credibility depends upon its effectiveness."

Last Fling

I received an unexpected phone call from Dudley Wrong, a science fiction critic and professor of Science and Technology Studies at Meshuconsinois State University, one of those Midwestern university monstrosities replete with billions of students and miles-long campuses. I had a rather serious relationship with Dudley about a decade ago. On paper, he was great: smart, affable, reliable, and honest. We were in the same academic field and shared the same intellectual interests. Dudley made it clear that he wanted to marry me. Considering his many attributes, I contemplated marrying him. After two years, I realized that it I couldn't bring myself to do it -- a decision I attribute to Dudley's *goyish kup*. He could not see outside of his rule box. I was too much of a maverick to tie myself to someone who refused to understand that (1) the letter of the law is always subject to interpretation and (2) anyone failing to comply with my wishes is always subject to demise via being nudged to death. We remained on cordial speaking terms as the relationship petered out. When I heard his voice on the answering machine, I was resolved not to mention our past.

"I'm calling with an offer you can't refuse. There is a job available in my department and I am the head of the hiring committee. Meshuconsinois State is a much better school than SUNY-GV. As the committee head, I will be able to hire you. I can immediately offer you a job which starts next semester. If you come now and meet everyone, you will be a shoe-in for the position."

Dudley knew me well enough to discern that he absolutely was describing a unrefusable offer. My relationship with Pepe had not progressed during the two years I had been living with him. More specifically, he had not proposed. Quite aware that Pepe would equate nudging with the kiss of death, I seriously considered Dudley's offer. As someone who had always placed my career before my personal life, I concluded that potential career advancement was more advantageous than endless soup and sex.

"Count me in, Dudley. I accept your offer." I hung up and turned to Pepe.

"I'm going to take a leave of absence from SUNY-GV and teach at Meshuconsinois State. I'm not your wife. Goodbye city life. Midwestern Green Acres here I come."

"I would never stand in your way. But what about us?"

"I have enough energy to commute and spend every other weekend with you. At the height of my miserable treatment at Blackhole State University, I lived in Forest Hills and traveled to Virginia. I subwayed to La Guardia, changed planes in Baltimore, took a forty-five minute limousine ride down the interstate, arrived in time for my four o'clock class, taught until ten, slept in the student union hotel, and left at eight in the morning. I kept this up for an entire semester and received excellent teaching evaluations. Trust me when I say commuting will work."

"I have no choice. People must be free to do as they choose. Follow your star. The soup will be on the stove when you return. I will reschedule our sex appointments on my calendar. Tell me your flight schedules as soon as you know them. The sooner I record the sex appointments the better."

Dudley met my plane when I arrived in Meshuconsinois. I was not at all excited to see him. He threw himself into my arms.

"You've arrived at last. My dream has come true. You're finally here with me. We can now get married and live happily ever after. We can spend every day of our lives sitting on my front porch watching squirrels eat acorns."

I was surprised to the extent that only Dudley's arms kept me from keeling over. How could someone who I had talked to only intermittently during the last ten years expect me to disembark from a plane and marry him on sight. I had to buy time to figure out how best to handle the situation.

"Are acorns kosher?"

"I have an encyclopedic mind and I know the answer to everything. This question stumps me, though. Which reference book do you suggest I use to find the definitive answer?"

"Try crossing a horticulture text with a *The Haggadah*. Maybe a dietary law stems from the fact that the acorn does not fall far from the tree. Jews do not eat squirrels. It is not kosher to combine milk and meat. Maybe there's a dispensation in regard to acorns and squirrels."

Contrary to Jewish beliefs, an angel appeared on my right shoulder and a devil appeared on my left shoulder. Luckily, they were invisible to everyone except me. On the one hand, sex with Dudley was pleasant enough; if I led him on, I could live in his comfortable house and eventually get the job. On the other hand, I had never used sex to advance my career. I slept with hordes of male science fiction scholars simply because I liked them. Regardless of their influence, I relegated unattractive or boring male science fiction critics to Prophylactic Award eligibility. As I shifted my gaze from the angel to the devil, another vision overshadowed them. I saw a large-breasted woman wearing a much-too-tight shirt whispering into the ear of the influential male   science fiction scholar she married to advance her career. No. No matter how much I wanted the Meshuconsinois State job, I would not stoop to Sara Scottywitz's level. I looked into Dudley's languid and trusting cow eyes; I knew that I could never hurt him. Devastating Dudley and cheating on Pepe were too terrible to contemplate. My lips mouthed the right thing to do.

"I have come here to do a job. I will be your colleague and your friend. Nothing more. My decision stands. There is no procedural irregularity." Dudley's cell phone rang. "There's a woman screaming in a New York accent who says she wants to talk you," Dudley said as he handed me his phone.

"This is your mother, Herbert. You're making a terrible mistake. Dudley is nice. Dudley is your age. Dudley is a man. Marry him. Marry him immediately or not sooner. That's an order. I don't care if he's a *sheygetz*."

"It's a wrong number," I said as Dudley calmly and emphatically articulated his response.

"If you will not marry me, I no longer want to have anything to do with you. I will drive you to the university faculty housing complex. After that, you're on your own."

"I don't have a car. I thought that you would help me with things like grocery shopping. How will I manage to *schlep* home groceries in blizzards? The faculty housing complex is seven miles from the department. How will I get there? What will become of me here? How will I survive?"

"Your choice is either to marry me or to survive on your own. If you choose the latter, regarding what becomes of you, frankly, my dear, I don't give a damn."

"I'm a survivor. Just take me to faculty housing and then you can abandon me. I will be abandoned and not seduced by your offer of a job and a cushy existence in your house. Mary Tyler Moore played a single woman who was going to make it after all in Minneapolis. Minneapolis is not colder than Meshuconsinois. Sondra Lear has as much true grit as *shiksa* incarnate Mary Richards," I defiantly said as I threw my hat high in the air. "Mary Richards had to contend with Mr. Grant. I have the talent to get a grant -- and I don't have to sleep with or marry any man to do it."

"You have made your bed and now you can sleep in it -- alone."

"So be it. Goodbye," I said as I slammed Dudley's car door and faced a faculty housing complex which resembled a prison. I entered a stark room with bare cinder-block walls and a stained brown linoleum floor. I threw myself on the bed and cried as I contemplated spending two semesters living in an ugly room located in a boring beyond-endurance college town. Post football game tail gate parties were the place's biggest events. What can one say about people who guzzle bear and stuff themselves with corn chips which emanate from car asses? Crying jag over, I unpacked and named my new abode The Hovel. I really used this name as a synonym for my address. When people asked where I lived, I matter-of-factly replied "in The Hovel." My manner of setting up a household in The Hovel was slightly eccentric. Resorting to my own inimical creativity, I used the Frisbees which were given to students as free promotional advertising material as plates. Dinner guests at The Hovel never failed to *plotz* (nonJewish Meshuconsinoisites *plotzed* nonetheless) when their food was presented on Frisbees. The guests did concur with my argument that it is both logical and efficient to use Frisbees as plates.

My approach to transportational needs was a little more normal than my table setting. I used a bicycle and roller blades to negotiate the seven-mile distance separating my home from my workplace. The students were impressed. "Cool. My mother would never roller blade to work," one student approvingly said. I was soon in great physical shape and able to walk to class through blizzards.

Imagining hungry wolves salivating at the thought of ingesting a physically fit albeit still pleasantly plump Jewish New Yorker, I was resolved to return home to Manhattan. I phoned the SUNY-GV English department chair. "Take me back. I want to come home. Please please take me back."

"I want what is best for you. I have to advise against your immediately leaving Meshuconsinois State. You cannot under any circumstance break your contract. For your own good, I will not let you return to SUNY-GV until you have fulfilled your contract at Meshuconsinois." I knew that the chair was right. There was nothing to do other than grit my teeth and live for my bi-weekly flights home to Manhattan and Pepe. Soup, sex, and skyscrapers had never looked so good.

Dudley's colleagues had even less appeal than he. The department was headed by Clarice Birdslaw, a dullard botanist who dressed like a refugee from 1960s' Height Asbury. This botanist worshipped flower power to the extent that she saw nothing wrong with dressing for success attired in Birkenstocks (with sweat socks), tie-dyed tee shirts, and floor length wrap around skirts made in India. She was very happy to underpay me. So much for expecting to be treated well by a female department head. This woman who saw nothing wrong with going off on a Caribbean vacation in the middle of the winter term was compassionate only to herself. The two female assistant professors offered no better possibility for establishing friendships. Heated competitors, they hated each other to the extent that they had no time to interact constructively with anyone else. Even if they did something other than plotting to do each other in, I would not be interested in spending time with either of them. One was an expert on East Germany who comported herself in the manner of a central casting reject from a grade-B Gestapo movie. The other cast herself as a Ms. Perfect Tenure Candidate who kissed up to Dudley to ensure that he would vote in her favor. They exuded mutual hate which made everyone they encountered uncomfortable. These women physically assaulted each other during a department meeting. Dudley and I, momentarily forgetting our own animosities, separated them before they could commit murder. In short, the science and technology department was not filled with happy campers.

The place did include one breath of fresh air, though: Diane, another exploited temporary faculty member, who was exactly my age. She was blonde, well-dressed, beautiful, and married to a Viet Nam era Army Special Forces Agent. Good taste and cool style characterized her entire bearing and all of her possessions -- with one exception I inspired. When she invited me to her well-appointed home for dinner, she served scallops flambé presented on Frisbees. She commented that Frisbees did indeed make useful plates; she intended to make them her permanent tableware. Diane later landed a permanent job at Southern Meshuconsinois University. There is justice in this world.

My unhappy Meshuconsinois sojourn had another bright spot. My M.A. degree was from the University of Meshuconsinois at Orville Orchard, located about an hour south of Meshuconsinois State. Orville Orchard was one of my favorite towns. I still had friends there. Or, more accurately, Orville Orchard was the home of my first love Leonardo D'Antona, the forty-one year-old married professor I seduced when I was his twenty-one year-old graduate student. My experience from Leonardo was far from a one night stand. He was there to advise me as I faced surviving Ph.D. school, finding an academic job, fighting a tenure battle, and failing to find a husband. Leonardo had shaped my life in that he told me that the SUNY Buffalo Ph.D. program would be the most appropriate one for me. This Austrian-born Jew who fled the Nazis motivated me to embark on my international travels. He assured me that it would be fine to accept a Fulbright to Germany. I loved him -- and I was never able to keep him.

I was obviously attracted to Hans the German because he reminded me of Leonardo. Ditto for Pepe, a Leonardo in *Quebeçois* form. Both men are meticulous, charming, slightly foreign without being too foreign, and not fat. Or should I say that they do not have the stereotypically American male hunk body. Typical American males, Bill Clinton and Al Gore for instance, are rather analogous to the Incredible Hulk. Sleeping with men of this type evokes fear of being injured by unintentional smush mode. More specifically, I refer to what a normal size woman feels like when she is in a swimming pool lap lane and she fears being mowed down by large speed-demon men executing racing turns. The difference between an American and a European male body is analogous to the difference between a race horse and a Clydesdale, a Mack truck and a Ferrari, the Incredible Hulk and Spiderman. You get the picture.

When I was twenty-one, I reasoned that it would be decidedly uncute to still be in love with Leonardo when I reached thirty. Well, here I am, never to see thirty again, and I love him still. My feelings will never change. Neither will Leonardo's. No matter how old I become or what I will accomplish, Leonardo will always see me as the frizzed out green-army-pants-clad graduate student who had the courage to seduce him. Masters and Johnson's son was my classmate in the small seminar Leonardo taught. How does someone accomplish seducing the teacher of seminar which includes Masters and Johnson's son? I managed. The scene is forever emblazoned in my memory. I entered Leonardo's office with the paper it took me fifteen minutes to write in hand.

"Professor D'Antona, I'm having trouble with my paper. Would you please help me?"

"Of course. Let me see it. This paper is far below the quality of your usual work. Is there something on your mind?"

"Yes."

"What is it?"

"I am being driven to distraction and I'm really suffering because I am so attracted to you. Telling you this takes all of my courage. You're my most important professor. I don't want you to think that I am saying this to improve my grade. You did give me an 'A' on everything so far. I sincerely have strong feelings for you. Even if I have made a fool of myself, at least I will receive a definite answer. Can I sleep with you?"

"Maybe."

"Maybe? How can you say 'maybe?' 'Maybe' is worse than my not saying anything and not knowing how you feel. I would prefer 'no' to 'maybe.' How will I ever face you again? I will have to come to class with a paper back over my head."

"The paper bag will not be necessary."

"So what is your answer? I need an answer."

"This is a big decision. Come back to my office tomorrow at three. (When I heard this stipulation, I of course did not know that the Kirk T. Pistol temporal proviso would be in my future.) I will give you my answer then."

117

I returned at the designated time and happened to notice the entry in Leonardo's open appointment book: "3PM: Tell Sondra my decision about sex." Android men are a part of my history. How do I manage to find them? I am not sure that I was familiar with the word "android" during my MA degree days. Be that as it may, Pepe and Leonardo clearly emanate from the same android planet. Back to the past story.

"My answer is yes." Leonardo stood up, emerged from behind his desk, took me in his arms, and kissed me passionately. A lot of kisses from Leonardo had existed between that first one and the one I was presently experiencing. Having sex with Leonardo in Orville Orchard constituted an ongoing campus homecoming ritual never described in the University of Meshuconsinois alumni magazine. No matter how much time elapsed, Leonardo continued to love me and to love having sex with me. And, *après* sex, he never failed to say that he had to get home to his wife in time for dinner. I don't resent his consistency. He at once guided and nurtured fledgling me and did not hurt his wife. I hold Leonardo in very high esteem. You only get one first love in life, after all. Oh yes, Leonardo is also consistent about another thing: he continues vociferously to proclaim that science fiction is crap and that I am not a meat and potatoes scholar. His unrelenting diatribes against science fiction inspired me to co-edit the first science fiction issue of *Publications of the Modern Language Association*.

Although Leonardo's literary taste does not encompass celebrating science fiction, our story adroitly defies the stereotypical narrative of the older married man exploiting the victimized young woman. Even my parents approved of our relationship.

"I'm having an affair with a married man who is twenty years my senior," twenty-one year old me directly informed them.

"What does he do?" asked Herbert.

"He's my professor."

"Is he Jewish?"

"Yes."

"We'll look away."

"How come you're not upset?"

"You are alone and away from home. An older Jewish professor is a responsible person. He can be a good influence on you and help you if something happens to you." This is the most reasonable thing that Herbert ever said to me. I suppose my being twenty-one predated her hysteria about my getting married. Little did she know that Leonardo would play such a big role in my attitude toward marriage. Leonardo was the model Jewish husband -- and he was sleeping with me. Young savvy Sondra knew very well that having a husband is not worth scarifying oneself. Get married and settle down? "Hell no, I won't go," I once insisted. Young savvy Sondra was backed by a supporting cast of wonderful men: the best father in the galaxy; a consistent, undemanding and supportive lover; and a famous dissertation director who applauded his female graduate students and was loyal to his wife. Young savvy Sondra resolved to earn a PhD, write books, travel the world, and have sexual adventures. This was all well and good until young savvy Sondra became middle-aged savvy Sondra. Middle-aged savvy Sondra had traveled to every country of interest to her, written enough books to say everything she wanted to say, and slept with every attractive male science fiction scholar on planet Earth. Hence, it came to pass the middle-aged savvy Sondra finally decided to listen to her mother's incessant unrelenting imperative to get married.

Back to young savvy Sondra. My parents' decision to accept my relationship with Leonardo culminated in their willingness to meet him in his office. He knew that they knew and they knew that he knew. No observer would ever know that anyone knew.

"Leonardo D'Antona, I would like you to meet my parents, Roslyn and George Lear. I call them Herbert and Egor."

"Nice to meet you," they all said in unison.

I was grateful that Herbert realized that meeting her daughter's graduate school professor/lover differed from elementary school Open School Day. She thankfully did not ask Leonardo if I was doing well in class. After twenty minutes of polite and restrained chatting, all three middle-aged adults were glad to terminate the meeting. Young savvy Sondra, obnoxious to the core, enjoyed the entire spectacle.

My father, an unfailingly rational and rather conservative person, was surprisingly open to facilitating my efforts to fraternize with Leonardo.

"Egor, I need a favor. Can you drive me to Kennedy Airport and wait for me for an hour in a separate terminal building before driving me back home?"

"Why?"

" Leonardo is coming home from his Fulbright to Germany. He has a short stopover, and I want to talk to him. Please say yes. Talking to Leonardo is very important to me."

"Okay."

When we reached the Jewel Avenue exit of the Grand Central Parkway, Egor articulated his gut feeling about the situation. "If my father could see me driving my daughter to rendezvous with a married man -- even the harmless rendezvous that this particular one constitutes -- he would turn over in his grave."

Egor dutifully waited in a terminal separate from Leonardo's arrival location. He seized the opportunity to eat a hot dog for lunch without the health-conscious Herbert being the wiser. I relished the opportunity to see Leonardo.

Orville Orchard will always be the beloved place of my youth. I will never belong there. I will never belong with Leonardo. Leonardo drove me to the bus station for my trip back to Meshuconsinois State. I clutched his hand for as long as I could before boarding the bus. I looked at him from the bus window until I could no longer see him. I knew that I had to look ahead. I belonged in New York -- and I belonged with Pepe.

The time to leave Meshuconsinois State with my contract fulfilled thankfully arrived. I packed all of my Hovel possessions and boarded a New York bound Amtrak train. Hours later, Pepe was present at Penn Station to retrieve my bedraggled body. He gathered me in his arms and kissed me. After years of searching, I had finally found someone who I loved just as much as I loved Leonardo.

"I'm so tired. Please take me home. There is no place like home. I will never leave home again."

"I saw other women while you were gone. I did not like any of them. They made me appreciate you. I missed you. I'm so glad you're back. Being with other women showed me just how great you are."

"I learned that I now care more about my personal life than my career. If Meshuconsinois State offered to pay me thirty billion dollars, I would turn them down and choose to live in Manhattan. Life is short. No amount of money could motivate me to spend my life watching squirrels eating acorns and fat people eating fried pork rinds out of car asses. Subway fare: a dollar-fifty. A real bagel: seven-ty-five cents. The Sunday *New York Times*: four dollars and fifty cents. Rent for a one bedroom Manhattan apartment: one thousand five hundred dollars a month. Living in that apartment with a wonderful man: priceless."

"Unpack and settle back in. What are those round plastic things you're putting in the kitchen cabinets?"

"Plastic?" My intonation differed from the one Dustin Hoffman heard in relation to this word. These are my Frisbees -- and our new plastic dishes."

"*Jamais*. We will never use Frisbees as dishes in this *maison*. *Les Frisbees sont pas pour moi*. We cannot use Frisbees during our candlelit dinners. We have no room for Frisbees. I'm throwing all your Frisbees down the incinerator."

"Wait. Don't throw out my Frisbees. I'll mail them to my friend Diane. You wanted me back and I'm back. I bet that not one of those other women you dated, women who you do not like as much as you like me, use Frisbees as plates."

"True. Let's go for a walk." We ended up in the sculpture garden adjacent to the United Nations complex.

"Look at that neat life-sized elephant statue. He's anatomically correct."

"His balls are very big -- just like mine."

"Let's go and stand directly under his tail. Here we are situated beneath an elephant *cul*. It's a good thing that this elephant isn't real. I once came face to face with impending wildebeest excretion."

"Stop talking, Sondra." Pepe took me in his arms and looked into my eyes. "I'm not going anywhere. *Jamais*."

"Are you saying that you have enough room in the apartment to keep me forever?"

"*Oui*."

"I need further clarification. Even though I'm Jewish, I am thoroughly familiar with the under the mistletoe kissing imperative. Do *goyish Quebeçois* have a custom which dictates that when a man and a woman find themselves standing beneath an elephant *cul* (especially an elephant who has big balls), the man automatically proposes marriage to the woman?"

"*Non*. Not that I know of. We have just started a new custom."

"Let me get this straight. Does your appointment book contain an entry for today which says "6:33 PM: propose to Sondra."

"*Oui.*"

"*Oui?* Really?"

"*Oui.*"

Oui. We at last. We at last. After years of fruitless husband-hunting, I was a "we" at last. While standing beneath an elephant which would do Teddy Roosevelt proud, I had been notified that my incessant hunt was over.

My Small Thin Non-Jewish Wedding

I phoned my mother with the news she had waited twenty-five years to hear.

"Hello."

"Get married."

"I am getting married. That's what I called to tell you."

"Get married."

"You're not listening. You're so used to telling me to get married, you're telling me to get married even though I am getting married. Let me be clear: I'm getting married in the morning. 'Ding dong, the bells are going to chime.'"

"What? What bells? *Oy*, my daughter is getting married in a church. Your father and I are not going to a church. We can look away from the *shaygetz* groom because you are now so old our only requirement is that you marry a man who is human; but a church wedding is out of the question. Jews from Forest Hills do not go to church. Your father and I are no exception. Remember that Tevye never again spoke to his third daughter."

"No. No church. I'm getting married in the morning in Queens Borough Hall on Queens Boulevard. Pepe and I will come by to pick up you and Egor at 10:30."

After completing the marriage announcement call to my mother and spending exactly three minutes on the wedding plans (devoting attention to ceremonial detail is not my style), I returned to the evening's scholarly writing work at hand. Writing was easier than planning what to wear to my wedding. My task was to write a blurb for a critical essay collection called *Taking The Red Pill: Science, Philosophy and Religion in The Matrix*. I came up with something which (if I must say so myself) is exceedingly clever and exemplifies my playful, unorthodox academic prose style: "Dr. Lear enthusiastically pre-scribes *Taking The Red Pill* for all readers who wish to enhance their understanding of science, philosophy, and religion in *The Matrix*. *Taking the Red Pill* acts as a wonder drug, a miracle cure for all the cognitive complications *The Matrix* generates. The volume, after all, is replete with doctors who are not physicians... This plethora of Ph.D.'s concocts brilliantly articulated interpretive medication which goes down in a most delightful way." Blurb written, I returned to a reality in which choosing what to wear to my wedding was making me gag. Wedding attire choice was absolutely alien to me. Better I should go back to the familiar world of *The Matrix*: "Blue Pill -- the key to a lifetime of ignorant bliss... Take this pill, and there's no need to worry about the desolate world of the real... Red Pill -- take this and be plunged into the depths of shocking reality." I know. I know. I'm supposed to be writing a novel and not a piece of science fiction criticism. Have patience. There's a reason for this divergence.

Instead of facing the mess in my closet -- the imminent threat of having clothing mountain six fall on my head and cause concussion induced death on the eve of my wedding -- I turned back to *The Matrix*. Red pill, reality; blue pill, the fantastic. Eureka! My problem about finding appropriate wedding attire was solved. *Modern Bride's Magazine*, which I would gladly face death by closet avalanche rather than read, eat your heart out. I thought of my wardrobe. Red clogs. White clogs. By getting married, I was choosing white clogs, that is to say matrimonial commitment to a mortal Gentile man. I had, after all, decided to give up the world of the red clogs, the world where I can tap them together and summon a magical creature who transcends the limits of space and time. I got off the spaceship and got out of the marriage to the wonderful husband who used to be my cat. (Admittedly a little far-fetched, this clog scenario -- a stretch-er to be sure -- is no more extreme than the *Matrix* scenario. Re-member: I have read a great deal of science fiction. I can have my unreality cake and eat it, too. I can at once live in the real white clog world and keep the red clogs in the back of the closet -- just in case I ever need supernatural assistance. My white clogs can serve as per-fect wedding shoes. They go well with one of the designer jumpsuits I had purchased during my Fulbright to Germany. Relieved that I had decided to get married in typical Sondra attire rather than adhere to predetermined style dictum (which, of course, reflects patriarchal imperatives), I closed *Taking the Red Pill* and called it a night.

The Lear nuclear family (which was about to include Pepe) entered the Queens Municipal Building and seated themselves in the holding area reserved for about-to-be-married couples and those who accompany them. Herbert surveyed the terrain with the marry-a-straight-guy eye she had used for my entire adult life.

"Look at all of these women who are about to be married. Why can't you get married? Why can't you be like all of these women? Why can't you be normal, Sondra?" Because Pepe was not used to Jewish mothers -- especially Herbert, who was over-the-intolerable-scale-top -- I tried to remain calm.

"Mother dear, please recognize that I am here for the purpose of getting married."

"All these men are already taken. But check out the clerk who is performing the marriage ceremonies. Maybe he's single. Ask him if he's single. If he's not single, I will ask these grooms-to-be if they have single friends or brothers." And so ended my cool resolve.

"Your comments are beyond beyond. Here I am, finally waiting to get married, and you are so used to telling me to get married that even when the event is imminent, you still can't stop nudging me and making me miserable. Are you still going to tell me to get married when the ceremony is over? And if you do decide to desist in the face of the indisputable evidence that your haranguing is no longer necessary, what new thing will you fixate upon? I'm sure that there will be a new thing. You can't start the grandchild thing because I am too old to have a baby. Egor, please do something. Please tell Herbert to stop telling me to get married and find a husband when I am getting married in fifteen minutes and the husband I have found is right here."

"Do what your mother says. Listen to your mother," said Egor calmly.

"Aaaaaargh," I said.

"Please excuse me. I'm going to use the restroom," said Pepe. Five minutes passed and Pepe still had not returned. I panicked. I imagined that Pepe, after seeing Herbert in action, had decided not to go through with the wedding. I thought that Pepe was heading for the hills in Forest Hills. Although the hills in Forest Hills are paved, they are hills nonetheless. After being exposed to Herbert, it was perfectly possible that Pepe thought it best to head for them. I re-solved to keep my fears to myself. I could not fathom how miserable Herbert could make me if she were privy to my sense that Pepe had flown the coop.

"Next. Lear-Le Pew marriage," said a municipal employee.

"My fiancée is not here,"

"Where is he?"

"I have no idea. He left the room, and he has not returned." All of the waiting couples and their entourages fell silent and looked at me sympathetically. Herbert broke the silence.

"Sondra, find your about-at-any-moment-to-be husband. Find him immediately if not sooner." Herbert was telling me to find my husband at my wedding -- and she was now making sense.

I entered the bowels of the labyrinthine Queens Municipal Building doubting that I would ever locate my origination point. I had just escaped the monstrous Herbert and now I was lost in a laby-rinth. Luck was with me. Having taught Mythology 101, I knew ex-actly what to do. What worked for Theseus could work for Sondra. I would simply tie a thread to a door handle and follow it back. Back to the drawing board. I didn't have any thread. I, instead, had a cook-ie in my pocket. So long Theseus. Hello Hansel and Gretel. I could make a cookie crumb trail and use it as a direction finder. Frantically searching for Pepe while dropping cookie crumbs, I knew that, if I came back without him, Herbert would shove me into an oven and turn me into gingerbread. On second thought, Herbert could not bake gingerbread if her life depended upon it. Unlike fairy tale wick-ed witches, Jewish mothers do not turn their daughters into ginger-bread. They simply nudge them to death.

I reached a second floor indoor terrace parapet which over-looked the lobby. "Pepe, Pepe," I frantically shouted as my voice reverberated off the lobby walls. My repeated locution was no less desperate than Dustin Hoffman's repeated "Elaine" wedding cere-mony articulation. It reverberated throughout the entire first and second floor public areas -- and failed to elicit a response from Pepe. Investigating the restrooms was the only thing left to do. I stuck my head in every men's bathroom I could find while yelling "Pepe, Pe-pe" at the top of my lungs. Luckily, "Pepe" sounds like "pee pee." Maybe I could avoid being arrested if my "Pepe, Pepe" inquiries were seen as those of a strangely accented deranged person who felt an urgent need to urinate. I could just see the charge: littering a municipal building with bread crumbs and soliciting in men's bathrooms. The verdict: incarceration in Bellevue Psychiatric Hospital. Bellevue was preferable to my fate at Herbert's hands if I returned to my wedding ceremony sans a husband.

I tried to calm myself and rationally think my way out of the situation. The *Sex and the City* episode in which Carrie Bradshaw's boyfriend uses a Post-It note to communicate his intention to break up with her came to mind. The always socially decorous Pepe would not leave forever without saying goodbye. He could, at the very least, be counted upon to use a Post-It which said *"au revoir."* My fear that Pepe had headed for the Forest Hills hills had to be unjustified. Pepe had to be located somewhere in the Municipal Building. Since I had spent so many years husband-hunting, it made sense that I should have the ability to find my husband located within a specifically demarcated space. These logical thoughts became extraneous as soon as I saw Pepe nonchalantly walking down the hall.

"Where were you? I thought that Herbert appalled you to the extent that you decided to desert me forever. The clerk called our name to no avail. Despite my usual ability to circumvent rules, I couldn't get married without you. Herbert ordered me to hunt for a husband at my wedding. Due to your absence, she was finally being logical."

"Don't make a major story out of this scenario. You found me when we met and you found me now. All is well. I will never leave you, Herbert or no Herbert -- although I must say that she is a little much. Let's get married." When I entered the Municipal Building marriage ceremony location with Pepe in tow, all the people in the room breathed a sigh of relief. Herbert and Egor looked on proudly as I heard the clichéd ceremony words finally being addressed to me. When the clerk reached the part about people having objections Herbert, as ever, did not keep silent and did not hold her peace.

"The purpose of my life for the last quarter century has been to tell Sondra to get married. Now that she is finally and better late than never getting married even if it is to a *goy* -- and at this point I am willing to look away -- what will be my purpose now? I can't imagine not telling Sondra to get married. What will I do?" For once in my life, I was speechless. I was embarrassed to the extent that I wished I was wearing my red clogs instead of my white ones. The red clogs would enable me to call upon Ilya to beam me up from this untenable situation. The ever-trustworthy Egor, who never failed to help when I really needed him, came to the rescue.

"Rozie, this is not about you. This is not about you saying 'what will I do?' This is about Sondra saying 'I do' -- finally. Ask not what your daughter's 'I do' can do for you; ask what you can do for your daughter's 'I do.'"

The clerk continued without blinking an eye. Since he had probably seen everything, he took Herbert in stride.

"I do," I said.

"I do," Pepe said. The clerk did his pronouncing thing. I was married -- finally. As I kissed Pepe, and Herbert and Egor kissed each other, the moment was absolutely magical. Or, in terms of my life experience, it was magical but nonetheless real. The mundane white clogs, not the supernatural red clogs, were the most appropriate attire for my particular small thin non-Jewish wedding.

Since Pepe and I had lived together for two years prior to the wedding, our return home *après* marriage ceremony was very routine. Pepe scheduled our usual sex appointments. Between appointments, he sat incessantly in front of his computer researching the latest electronic innovations. When an appointment was not ensuing, I used Pepe's desk chair wheels as means to move him bodily away from his computer screen. Since he did not share my Jewish cultural proclivity for verbally rehashing every aspect of a particular event, it was clear that he most often preferred his computer screen to engaging with me. I was at a loss about how to compete with his interest in electronics. I imagined trying to attract his attention by dressing up as either a woofer or a tweeter -- even though, not being sure of exactly what woofers and tweeters are, I didn't know how to devise a woofer or a tweeter costume.

Our next sex appointment was scheduled for 6:07 PM -- sharp. At exactly 6:06, I entered our bedroom stark naked and seductively swinging an electrical cord to the tune of Gypsy Rose Lee's refrain "Let me entertain you; let me make you smile." Pepe was not amused. He was not entertained; he was not smiling.

"You know that I take appointments very seriously. You know that I don't believe that levity should be a part of appointments. You meant well. My arousal mood is now spoiled. We will have to reschedule for tomorrow. Are you doing anything in the late afternoon? Check your calendar and tell me the exact time that you plan to leave the house so I can reschedule accordingly."

And you ask why, electric shaver interplanetary communication device misconception to the contrary, I still often really believe that I am married to an android? I had resolved to keep the marital peace by treating Pepe's perfectionism peculiarities as if they were normal.

"That's fine and for the best. Now I will not have to worry about tripping on the electric cord when I climb up or down from the chair."

"Don't think that you are competing with my computer screen. Yesterday, I read my barber's *Playboy*. The bunnies don't excite me. They are posed and artificial. I would rather have you than a Playboy bunny."

"That's some statement. I could be the bunny's mother. Thanks for the compliment."

"Don't say anything more. Quit while you're ahead."

"I was worried that you would rather have me be the Energizer battery rabbit instead of a *Playboy* bunny."

"Not at all. I like *Playboy* bunnies better than Energizer rabbits. Maybe for appointments you can dress up in a *Playboy* bunny costume. On second thought, maybe not. Scratch the bunny costume from the record."

"Thank god. *Playboy* bunny costumes are not my style. I can't even cope with bras -- and shoes that are other than clogs. Regarding the *Playboy* bunny -- tricks are for kids." Pepe turned on his computer and settled in for the afternoon. I tried to be interested in the subject matter he perused.

"What new electronic component are you investigating?" I asked, feigning enthusiasm. Pepe was annoyed.

"I'm in the middle of something. I'm busy." Obviously, if I couldn't beat the woofers and tweeters, I had to join them.

"Wooooof. Wooooof. Tweet. Tweet," I said plaintively. Much to my surprise, this sexualized verbalization of woofers and tweeters worked. It really turned Pepe on. By him, I was sounding a mating call relating to his love for electronics. He removed his eyes from the computer screen (a miracle in itself) and caressed my leg. What if I had to spend the rest of my life countering the seductive appeal of Pepe's computer screen by woofing and tweeting? As my luck would have it, Sylvester the cat -- Tweetie Bird predator incarnate -- would appear and desire to eat me. Didn't I have enough trouble with Norris? Effectiveness as a mating call aside, I needed to nip this woofing and tweeting attention method contrivance in the bud. I pulled out the computer's plug -- that is the usual tried and true method.

"We neglected to reschedule the next appointment."

"Let's reschedule for tomorrow now. While I have my calendar in hand, it occurs to me that we should also schedule a honeymoon. I suggest driving to the Grand Canyon."

"What? You think that it is too far to drive to the Upper West Side. How could someone who thinks that the Upper West Side is a galaxy far far away contemplate driving from Manhattan to Arizona?"

"Highway driving differs from city driving. Let's go for it."

"Okay."

After many days of driving, to celebrate our honeymoon, we checked into a hotel on the Las Vegas strip. Pepe was investigating the chair situation for our first scheduled appointment. I went into the bathroom and was greeted by a very large puddle located under the sink. "Pepe there is a flood in here. It isn't my fault. It isn't caused by my being sloppy with the shower curtain or anything." After we complained to the front desk, two burly plumbers appeared, announced that they had to spend six hours replacing the sink pipe, and settled in for the duration. Pepe and I sat on the bed with our heads hanging. "I wonder what the plumbers would think of me standing naked on the chair," I said to cheer him up.

"They would be thrilled," he answered.

"My purpose on this honeymoon is to thrill *you*, not two strange plumbers. Our honeymoon is being ruined. I'm going to complain to the manager." I made my way to the lobby and entered complaint mode, a stance which is not foreign to me. "Excuse me. I'm on my honeymoon and two plumbers are spending six hours in my bathroom. May I please have another room?" I said to the male manager.

"No other room is available. The entire strip is booked due to a very large convention."

"Can we get a discount?"

"No. I can't accommodate your request." I countered by asking him a familiar question -- a question which I no longer had to pose to potential husbands.

"Are you married?" Out of long habit, the question came naturally to me. The reason why it was sensible for me to ask about a man's marital status during my honeymoon will momentarily become apparent.

"Yes. I'm married."

"Good. If you're married you must have had a honeymoon. How would you feel if you had to spend your honeymoon with two humongous plumbers inhabiting your bathroom? And I am paying for this yet. I'm not a young bride. It took me years to find a husband. My one and only honeymoon is being ruined. Either give me another room or give me a discount." I was bullshitting. I was not at all sentimental about my honeymoon.

"I can't accommodate your request. Your choice is either to remain in the room or vacate and try your luck finding another room elsewhere." Knowing that I was beaten, I skulked back to the room, said hello to the plumbers, and informed Pepe that I had been defeated. I spent the duration of my honeymoon night fully clothed while sitting on a chair -- in the manner that a normal person uses a chair. We checked out of the hotel in the morning and made our way to the Grand Canyon.

We stayed at one of the cabins in the Grand Canyon National Park and marveled at the stars and the sounds of coyotes. Pepe is afraid of heights. Close proximity to the canyon rim did not sit well with him. He greeted me with surprise news when I awoke on our first Grand Canyon morning: "I've booked a mule trip to the bottom of the canyon."

"What does a mule trip to the bottom of the canyon entail?'"

"Mules."

"Mules?" I was in denial about the fact that Pepe referred to large four-footed animals. Riding a mule to the bottom of the Grand Canyon struck me as a worse fate than encountering a wildebeest in a Forest Hills apartment kitchen."

"The mule trip is a once-in-a-lifetime experience. It's perfectly safe. We're going. We're about to ride a mule into the canyon on a trail that is seven feet wide."

"You want me to put my life in the hands of a mule who doesn't even have hands? Anything can happen. What if my mule gets stung by a bee, panics, and makes an eight-foot side step?"

"This has never happened. Mules are not suicidal. Enough with the Jewish neuroticism and penchant for making much ado about nothing." I found myself standing by the mule corral making friends with the mule assigned to me, a tan-colored female named Buttermilk.

"Hi Buttermilk. It's not your fault that, in addition to my being scared to death to ride you into the canyon, your name makes me think of calories and cholesterol. Buttermilk is kosher; I'm not sure if the same holds true for my canyon sojourn with you." Buttermilk moved her ears back in response. Our conversation was interrupted by returning mule riders. Clearly, although they were bedraggled, they had survived to tell their tale. I listened to their responses. My ears went back in response to a couple's discernible New York accents.

"Wow, Myron. What an experience."

"It was certainly unforgettable, Sylvia." New York Jews! I had found *compadres*. Slightly exaggerating to make my ethnicity clear, I approached Myron and Sylvia to receive moral support.

"Excuse me. I'm Golda Goldfarb from Manhattan. I'm about to go on the mule trip and, *oy*, I'm a little leery, to say the least. Would you recommend it?"

"Absolutely," said Sylvia and Myron in unison. Their certainty was not reassuring.

"This is my exact question: can people like us survive this experience unscathed?" They immediately discerned what I was really asking: can New York Jews successfully fraternize with mules and non-Jewish mule-ride-guide cowboys. Also: can New York Jewish *tushies* survive being *schlepped* into the Grand Canyon via mule?

"The answers are definitely yes. Enjoy your trip, Golda."

"I mounted up on Buttermilk. Pepe followed aboard Meesekite. (The name choice makes sense. Hadassah Le Pew's mother knew a Montreal Jew. Perhaps Meesekite's owner knew a Tucson Jew.) Poor Meesekite was not as attractive as her fellow mules. Since mule riding is not a typical metrosexual undertaking, Pepe was woefully deficient in this area ("whoafully," too; he didn't know how to tell Meesekite to stop).

As Ms. Ed could attest, because of my years spent at summer camp, I was an accomplished equestrian. I was at ease in the saddle; Pepe suffered from big time ass laceration. He was grateful when the mule ride guide asked us to rest our mules and maneuver them so that their heads faced the canyon. The thinking behind this request: mules who are able to see the canyon bottom's distance from the trail are less likely to risk taking a misstep. Meesekite got it into her head to put her front hooves directly on the trail edge. She wanted to position her mouth over the side in order better to accomplish succulent bush chomping (Attention literary critics: do not read a slur directed at George W. Bush into the preceding sentence). Pepe, nearly passing out from fright, began to speak my language -- better late than never.

"*Oy*," he gasped.

"*Oy*, indeed. You must be the first *goyish Quebeçois* to say '*oy*.' Use the reins to pick up Meesekite's head -- gently. You don't want to upset Meesekite. You don't want to risk making her feel that she is going over the edge." Pepe was much more confident when we reached Mule Trek's halfway point and stopped for lunch (Mule trek? Due to my meeting with Myron and Sylvia, I can't claim that, when venturing to the Grand Canyon bottom aboard a mule, I was boldly going where no New York Jew had gone before). Not so for me. I felt dizzy and nauseated.

"I don't feel well."

"Nonsense. You're just acting Jewish -- again. There's nothing wrong with you. Stop complaining. Enjoy the view."

"No, really. I'm not just *kvetching*. I'm very sick. I'm going to tell the guide."

"You have the classic symptoms of electrolyte imbalance," the guide matter-of-factly said.

"What does this imbalance cause?"

"Death."

"*Oy!*"

"Don't worry, little lady. Drink this electrolyte imbalance medication and you should be fine."

"'Should' sounds spurious. What happens if I am not fine and I can't make it back to the top of the canyon?"

"I will have to radio for a helicopter to get you. Helicopter rescue costs three thousand dollars. "

"I'll be fine," I said with certainty as I gulped down the medication.

"What did the guide say?" asked Pepe.

"I have an electrolyte imbalance. Failure to drink the medication he gave me will result in my imminent death. I was not engaging in Jewish complaining. Insisting upon speaking up saved my life. No matter how ill I feel, it's time for me to mount up on Buttermilk."

"Why?"

"Mount-up failure will result in a three-thousand-dollar helicopter rescue."

"Start mounting, Sondra." The return trip to the rim was arduous and uncomfortable to the extent that I was on the verge of fainting. I hung on to the saddle horn for dear life. After a seemingly interminable time period, we reached the rim. I dismounted, said goodbye to Buttermilk and Meesekite, and burst into tears. Pepe was sympathetic and calming.

"I promise. No more mules. We have the satisfaction of experiencing a big adventure, though."

"True. One big adventure is enough. I look forward to relaxing and looking at scenery tomorrow."

"I've scheduled a helicopter ride."

"Absolutely not. There's no way that I'm going into that canyon via helicopter. Further, you will fly in over my dead body. I mean business. As you are aware, my body was almost dead a short time ago. "

"Maybe I did schedule too much. I suppose that we don't have to push ourselves to the limit and prove ourselves every day. You're right. The mules were enough. No helicopter." Three days later, we heard that a Jewish family from Brooklyn died when their helicopter, owned by the same excursion company Pepe contacted, crashed into the canyon. As we headed toward Monument Valley, I mourned their loss and counted my blessings.

John Wayne had nothing on Pepe and me as we rode our horses accompanied by an Indian guide toward the foot of Hollywood's most iconic western backdrop. The guide gave me permission to ride fast. *Marlboro Man*, eat your heart out, I thought, as I cantered across the flat terrain toward the clichéd precipices (I do not mean "cantored": the horse was not Jewish. And, unlike Ms. Ed, he can't sing). Pepe was impressed by the sight of me disappearing into the sunset. "It is not just any wife who can canter a horse," I emphasized. He nodded in agreement as he rubbed his lacerated *cul*.

The Yoknawpawtawpha Hilton

The honeymoon was over. This is certainly not to say that all good things between Pepe and I had come to an end. We managed to live harmoniously in our small one bedroom apartment. Every morning we had a discussion session where we aired any potentially tendentious issue. This morning's agenda: the kitchen garbage bag imbroglio. I was happy to use grocery store bags as garbage bags. Pepe viewed the store bags as an appalling nuisance. His reason: the bags were four point two inches shorter than the garbage can.

"I hate buying products which we don't need. Grocery bags are good garbage receptacles. The idea of purchasing garbage bags which precisely fit the garbage can is too obsessive."

"This is a quality of life issue. I can't stand fumbling with garbage bags. Having the correct bag size coincides with my idea of order."

Before I could say "I consider your utopian garbage can set up to be a pain in the ass," our kitchen cabinet contained a six month supply of custom size garbage bags.

"I hate these bags. They make me nervous. It is not fair that you purchased them without consulting me."

Pepe responded by putting up his flag. He developed a flag system to signal when I was not allowed to talk so as not to interrupt his train of thought. Red bandanas tied around the living room lamp served as "the flag." Rule number 23.4F read as follows: "When the flag is up, Sondra is not allowed to speak unless there is an emergency situation such as death or nuclear attack." I also had the option to put up the flag to silence Pepe. As someone who loves to talk and welcomes interruption, I never availed myself of this opportunity. My friend Carol says that Pepe's flag reminds her of a nautical distress code system. Tomorrow's morning meeting agenda: I will initiate a special flag to represent a Pepe over the top neatness SOS.

Pepe's flag and meeting systems were effective. During my years as an academic, I observed that scholarly conference attendees kiss the ground when they secure time away from their spouses. They welcome the chance to use conference venues as happy hunting grounds for extramarital sexual activity. I hear tell that the Modern Language Association Convention, routinely called MLA, is often referred to as ML-layed. ML-layed does not interest me. After years of hunting husbands at academic conferences, I never again wanted to try to find love and sex at one. After making sure that the flag was down, I asked Pepe if he wanted to attend MLA with me.

"Where is it?"

"At a new venue, the Yoknawpawtawpha Hilton in Mississippi. This particular Hilton has a sole proprietor. He gave the conference organizers a good financial deal."

"Sounds great. We can go to Florida *après* the conference."

"I have an idea for New Year's Eve. My friends Jeffrey Blumberger, his girlfriend Charlotte Frick, and Jonathan Goodman are attending. Should I invite them to join us for New Year's?"

"Sounds great, too."

Jeffrey and Charlotte agreed to the plan. Jonathan described his special requirements. "The Yoknawpawtawpha Hilton -- and even the giant Yoknawpawtawpha Marriott as well as all surrounding hotels -- are booked for New Year's. My plantation is a forty-five minute highway drive away from downtown Yoknawpawtawpha. I couldn't possibly undertake that drive after midnight on New Year's. Could I share a room with you and Pepe?"

"I'll ask him."

I approached Pepe gingerly.

"I have to ask you for something big. It's worse than when I brought home the two tons of thrift shop clothes. I will trade you something major if you agree. I am, for instance, ready to agree that the purchased garbage bags are worthwhile investments.

"What's your question?"

"All the hotels in Yoknawpawtawpha are full. Jonathan has nowhere to stay on New Year's Eve. He does not want to drive back to his plantation late at night. Can he stay in our room?"

"Yes."

"Yes? That's it? No rules, restrictions, or codicils?"

"Quit while you're ahead. Don't pursue."

Faster than one can say "Yoknawpawtawpha," Pepe and I checked into the Hilton.

"Shouldn't we ask about the extra cot for Jonathan?" he inquired.

"Not yet."

"They could run out."

"You're just being overly precise as usual. I'll take care of the bed in a day or so."

I became involved in the MLA Conference to the extent that I completely forgot about Jonathan's cot. On the morning preceding New Year's Eve, I learned that Pepe's prediction about lack of cot availability was right on target.

"You're going to kill me."

"I'm afraid to ask but why do you say that?"

"Yoknawpawtawpha, we've got a problem. You were right about the cot shortage possibility. There are no more available cots."

"How do you propose to solve this problem?"

"One person can sleep on the floor."

"This lack-of-a-cot situation is totally your fault. You're the designated floor-sleeping person. Jonathan can sleep in the queen bed with me."

"You're going to sleep with Jonathan?"

"There's nothing else to do. My honor depends upon it. I can't violate good host rule number 35.5H: guests do not sleep on the floor."

"I don't mind the floor. I'll make myself comfortable with the extra pillows and blankets." I neglected to tell Pepe that I was absolutely *plotzing* -- even though I was not sure if he knew from what "*plotzing*" means. Regardless, the great cot shortage definitely called for *plotzing* -- even meta-*plotzing*. Other women have affairs at MLA. I was carrying marital fidelity too far. I was bringing one of my former lovers into my husband's bed, creating a scenario in which my husband would be sleeping with a man who had slept with me. At least, *vis-à-vis* Pepe and Jonathan, "sleeping" would mean "snoozing," not "sexing."

I explained the situation to Jonathan. After enjoying a lovely dinner with Charlotte and Jeffrey -- capped off by watching fireworks' red glare burst in air over kudzu, Spanish moss, and swamp (kudzu, Spanish moos, and swamp are not a few of my favorite things) -- Pepe, Jonathan, and I settled into our Yoknawpawtawpha Hilton room. I looked up from the floor and saw Pepe and Jonathan recoiling on their respective sides of the bed. The space between them was the size of the Grand Canyon -- and you know that I know from the Grand Canyon. A mule would be required to most efficiently traverse the chasm which separated them (I was almost tempted to summon the extraterrestrial Sondra clones to request that they send in Ms. Ed to serve as a mule substitute. She was often stubborn). Jonathan's loud snores engulfed the room. Exasperated, Pepe looked down at me.

"You owe me big time. I mean you owe me to the extent that you're going to have to remove the totality of clothing mountain number four."

"No. Not that. Not all of clothing mountain four. Mountain four contains my favorite things: German jumpsuits and leather pants."

"And mountain five too. Mountain six is in grave danger."

I was relieved to hear the sound of two men snoring. Moonlight illuminated Pepe's and Jonathan's bodies -- along with the bed chasm which separated them. The scene was quite extraordinary. Anyone could shack up in a Hilton. But how many women can look up from a Hilton Hotel room floor and see the somnolent forms of their husband and former lover? Their snores were lolling me to sleep -- until I heard the sound of a definite snort. The snort was not human. I know a horse snort when I hear one. The horse snort and the now clear sound of a pawing hoof were emanating from directly outside the room. Ms. Ed would never behave in this fashion. She would call and tell me to expect her. I rose from my makeshift floor bed, tip toed across the room so as to avoid waking Pepe and Jonathan, and opened the door. A large black horse met my eyes. It was evident that the horse was a stallion. He walked inside the room and began to sniff Jonathan. Looking as if he discerned a familiar scent, he made himself comfortable while standing over my makeshift floor bed. Jonathan's trusty and beloved stallion Beauregard Jackson Pickett Burnside had become my third roommate.

Luckily, Hilton rooms contain refrigerators -- and pens and notepads. I made use of these accoutrements to contact the Sondras:

"Dear Sondras. Urgent. Please send Ms. Ed to room number 2204 in the Yoknawpawtawpha Hilton. Tell her to whisper when she arrives. Thank you, Sondra." Pepe heard the refrigerator door close.

"Why are you making noise? What's going on?"

"Nothing. Jonathan's stallion Beauregard Jackson Pickett Burnside is in here and I have to send for my talking horse, Ms. Ed -- I never did get around to telling you about her -- to find out why. Go back to sleep."

"Two horses? There's no room in this room for two horses." I soon again heard two separate human snoring sounds -- accompanied by two sets of horse snorts. Ms. Ed had materialized in front of the television cabinet. I threw my arms around her neck and kissed her muzzle.

"The Sondras told me to whisper. Why am I in Yoknawpaw-tawpha Hilton room 2204? Oh. I see. My fellow equine is also in room 2204."

"Ed, you arrived just in the nick of time. Meet Beauregard Jackson Pickett Burnside, my friend Jonathan's stallion. Ed, Beauregard; Beauregard, Ed. Jonathan is the man in that bed sleeping with my husband. But don't ask -- even though you can. You speak fluent horse and fluent English. I need you to ask Beauregard in horse why he is here. Tell me the answer."

"Beauregard is a stallion?" Ed exclaimed as she cocked her ears.

"How can you think of sex at a time like this?"

"Beauregard is such a stud," Ed panted. "Okay, I'll get down to business. I'll talk to Beauregard."

"Neigh?" said Ed to Beauregard.

"Neigh." He replied earnestly.

"Neigh. Neigh. Neigh," said Ed to clarify the details Beauregard expressed. The horses were beginning to sound like a bad Shakespeare play. I was worried that their conversation would, God forbid, wake Pepe and Jonathan.

"Well?" I asked to hasten the conversation.

"Beauregard says that, since he missed his master Jonathan, he came here to find him. He got the idea when he heard Jonathan's children reading *Lassie Come Home* aloud in the barn. Unlike me, Beauregard is a Jewish horse. He was really worried about Jonathan."

"Tell Beauregard not to worry. Jonathan is scheduled to return home tomorrow."

"I love Beauregard. He's gorgeous, sexy, single -- and Jewish."

"Ed, you have spent too much time around me. You just met Beauregard."

"I'm sure that this is love at first bite. Do you think Jonathan has room for me on his plantation?"

"I don't see why not. Jonathan owns a large plantation. It's not like you're asking Pepe if you can move into our apartment. In terms of his potential response, he would finally be correct in relation to his routine 'we have no room for that' edicts. Even if Pepe did own a plantation, he would surely say that there is no room for you to live on it. Such is not our present problem, though. I have to get you and Beauregard out of here. The Sondras already beamed you down. I disturbed them enough for one night. I've packed my red clogs. I'll get Ilya to zap you both to Jonathan's plantation. In the morning, I'll ask Jonathan if he's willing to keep you. It certainly couldn't be that hard for him to install you in a spare stall."

"I want to live in the same stall as Beauregard."

"Stop causing problems. Thinking about your preferred stall will cause me to stall in regard to the immediate need to summon Ilya."

Just as I was about quietly to click my red clogs together, I heard a knock at the door and motioned to Beauregard and Ed to hide behind the bed (I was, for once, grateful that Pepe always books expensive and, hence, large hotel rooms). They complied by kneeling on their haunches and lowering their heads. Once again, I tiptoed across the hotel room and opened the door. Two exceedingly large exposed breast tops met my eyes. The cleavage was as long as the Grand Canyon and, hence, as long as the chasm separating the sleeping Pepe and Jonathan. I saw none other than Sara Scottywitz. I was startled to the extent that I lapsed into horse language.

"Neigh? I mean what are you doing here at this time of night?"

"Sondra, I realized that I am madly in love with you. I want to sleep with you. We should get married. I think lesbians can now get married in Mississippi. If not, Canada is definitely on the verge of legalizing gay marriage. As a British citizen, maybe I can arrange for us to get married in Canada and live there."

Obviously, Sara had realized that I had as much professional clout as the hordes of middle-aged male science fiction critics she had seduced with career advancement in mind. Obviously, she wanted to marry me because I had recently been appointed to the Pilgrim Award nomination committee.

"I wouldn't marry you if you were the last person on Earth. You probably have not heard that I am already married. One spouse associated with Canada is enough. Just what I need: Canadian bigamy arrest. Flattery -- and your exposed breasts -- will get you nowhere with me. And I'm not voting to give you the Pilgrim Award. Never. No way."

"This marriage proposal is obviously backfiring. Please forgive me. Please understand that I am desperate to be you."

"Lower your voice. People -- that is to say my male friend and my human husband -- are sleeping."

She brushed by me and entered the room. She saw Pepe and Jonathan asleep in the queen bed.

"Two men. A *ménage-à-trois*. No wonder you don't want to sleep with me. You obviously have your hands full." I was praying that Ed and Beauregard would continue to keep their heads down. I did not want Sara to discern that the alleged *ménage-a-trois* was really a *ménagerie-à-cinq*. Further, if either Pepe or Jonathan woke up, I would be sunk.

"Oh my God. That's Jonathan Goodman. You're sleeping with Jonathan Goodman. Since you won't sleep with me and advance my career, I'll just hop into bed and seduce Jonathan. And who is this other person? I don't know him."

"My husband."

"Jonathan is sleeping with you and your husband? I have to hand it to you. I never cheated on my husband while he was in bed with a person I was cheating with. Is your husband a science fiction critic? If so, I will seduce him too."

"Don't you dare. Leave Jonathan and my husband alone. Just because I slept with your husband, you don't have to sleep with my husband. We should be above playing tit for tat."

"I won't listen to you. Getting into bed with Jonathan and your husband serves my best interests. Once I seduce Jonathan --

just like all the other male science fiction scholars I've seduced -- he will salivate over my big breasts and do my career enhancing bidding. And science fiction scholar or not, your husband is very cute. First, I'll do Jonathan. In the manner of your sexual involvement with my husband, one good turn deserves another: I'll roll over and turn to your husband. I've slept with two male science fiction scholars at once before. I can go for a *ménage a trois* right now. Sara prepared to jump on to the bed and land in the big chasm. Hoarse horse sex noises emanated from behind the bed. Jonathan began to toss and turn. Pepe opened his eyes and looked down toward the floor. He expected to see me. Instead, copulating horses met his eyes. Thank God my red clogs were on my feet. I clicked them together with all my might. Ilya appeared. The smoke detector went off. Ed and Beauregard neighed in alarm. Sara picked up her head from its vantage point between Jonathan's legs and saw Ilya. "Are you a science fiction scholar too? This is my lucky night."

Pepe, thinking that he was dreaming about copulating horses, tried as ever to create a semblance of order and adhere to logic. He dealt with the horse sex odors wafting past his nostrils. "Sondra, something in here smells funny. We should call housekeeping immediately." He sat up in bed, put his foot on the floor, and emitted a large scream. Pepe, fastidious to the extent of wearing white socks in the house to keep his feet clean, had just stepped bare-footed into a horse manure pile. Pepe fainted.

There was a knock at the hotel room door. Walking gingerly across the room to avoid Pepe's foot's fate, I opened the door and saw a man wearing a pale blue polyester leisure suit. "Egor, what are you doing here?"

"I was bored sitting alone in Florida waiting for your mother to arrive from Forest Hills. So I got in the car and drove to Mississippi in order to spend New Year's Eve with my daughter. I'm sorry that the drive took longer than expected and I missed the midnight celebration. Are you having a party in your room?"

My mind focused back to my freshman year at SUNY Albany (a.k.a. SUNY-A) when my visiting father accompanied me to my dorm room. He followed immediately behind as I opened the door and beheld the sight of my naked roommate in mid-copulation. I reacted instantaneously by jabbing my elbow into his stomach and pushing his doubled-over body outside of the room. A mere normally fornicating couple had caused me to go into emergency father's-attention-distraction mode. Egor was now decades older. I don't think he could survive the sight of amorous horses, a prostrate husband, and Sara fellating Jonathan and Ilya. I could hardly survive the scene. Good old reliable elbow jabbing came to the rescue again. I jabbed with all my might and locked the door.

My Yoknawpawtawpha Hilton room phone rang. "This is your mother, Herbert. What's ensuing in that room is ludicrous -- even for you. But, since you're married, I don't care. Now that you're finally married, you can do whatever you want. Put your father on. I'm coming to Florida tomorrow. I want to tell him to unpack the broiler, pressure cooker, broom, linens, and plastic carpet runners I shipped from Forest Hills to our completely furnished condominium. I want to make sure that he covers the couch with the plastic carpet runners." I hung up and took stock of the hotel room -- especially the livestock (which included the two horses and Sara the sex pig). It was clear that the first item on the agenda was to separate Jonathan's and Ilya's penises from Sara's orifices. "Break it up guys. Jonathan, would you mind keeping another horse on your plantation? Ilya, may I see you in the bathroom, please." He stepped over Pepe and the horse feces and sat down on the edge of the tub.

"Only for you Sondra would I extricate myself from the embrace of that Sara woman. She's something else."

"Ilya, do something. Help. This situation is out of control."

"What would you like me to do?"

"Zap my father to Florida. Return Jonathan and both horses to his plantation. Zap Sara to mid-embrace with the science fiction scholar she was seducing last night. In addition: conjure up some *Bewitched* Samantha-the-witch domesticity spell to get this room clean instantaneously, revive Pepe, and do the zapper-forget thing so that no one recalls anything. Then you can go home."

"Okay." Ilya twitched his nose. Everything returned back to the way it was when Pepe and I first checked into the hotel room.

Pepe awoke from his now peaceful repose in the large bed he did not share with anyone. "I think I had a bad dream. This room smells. I'm calling housekeeping." Even supernatural cleaning powers did not meet Pepe's sanitation standards.

"The room smells fine. We're scheduled to check out now anyway. Let's just go and get on with our trip. Next stop, the Everglades. I have never been to the Everglades. MLA always exhausts me. After all the politicking I witnessed, I am ready to go to a big swamp."

The long drive enabled me to unwind from all the Yoknaw-pawtawpha Hilton tumult. I felt relaxed while strolling with Pepe in the Everglades. Relaxation was short-lived. Pepe choose to stand very close to a crocodile.

"The Everglades is not a petting zoo. Nothing is separating you from becoming crocodile lunch. Crocodiles run very fast. I disa-gree with your insistence that purchased kitchen garbage bags are necessary because they exactly coincide with the garbage can size. Now I see that size does matter in relation to our garbage bags: the bags are not large enough to hold your potential croc-chewed corpse. Do you know about the crocodile in *Peter Pan*? If this croc attacks and you survive, you might have to spend the rest of your life being terrified of alarm clock ticking." The purchased kitchen garbage bags are a capitalistic crock. Not so for my warning about clear and pre-sent croc attack danger.

The crocodile blinked. Pepe decided to heed my warning. Like Captain Hook, Pepe survived his crocodile close encounter. I was grateful that he had been granted more time to be hooked on me.

En Famille à la Ville de l'Orignal (a.k.a. Mooseville)

Sunrise. Sunset. Swiftly flow the days. Spring semester passed uneventfully. It was time for summer vacation. Our plans were to attend the Le Pew family reunion held in Orignalville, a small town in Northern Quebec, before setting off on Canada Trek -- a trip to the wilds of Nova Scotia, that is.

On our way north, I insisted that we exit the New York State Thruway to stop at SUNY-A. Unlike the ivy covered walls of great universities, SUNY-A does not invoke nostalgia. There's no ivy. There's no football team. SUNY-A, though, is the most architecturally unique university in the world. Designed by Edward Durrell Stone, it resembles a Lincoln Center clone. Maybe I became a science fiction scholar because I graduated from a university which is a dead ringer for a rocket launch pad. Four phallic dorm towers, akin to mini World Trade Center towers, surround a podium replete with spurting fountains and a carillon tower. The carillon resembles a rocket awaiting liftoff. After all the years which had passed since my undergraduate days, the once-white SUNY-A concrete was graying. Regardless, the campus still uplifted me.

All of the SUNY-A campus's spurting phallic imagery was not lost on undergraduate Sondra. Armed with my *Norton Anthology of American Literature,* I would lie on library study area couches in wait for cute boys to pass by. In retrospect, it's clear that I was then just beginning to learn husband-hunting techniques. The campus I now visited seemed to be located in an alternative universe in relation to the one I had inhabited. It was at once the same and different. The saplings I remembered were now full-grown trees. Computers, unthought of then, were omnipresent. The current students were not yet born when undergraduate Sondra staked out a prime boywatching position on a library sofa.

Pepe tried to remain patient as I attempted to reconnect with my lost youth.

"I know that our time here is limited, but come with me to the library. I want to visit the place where I used to study so diligently."

In truth, I wanted to sit with my husband on one of my boywatching couches. Maybe by doing so, I could send a time travel message back to undergraduate Sondra to let her know that a nice husband would be a part of her future. I entered the lounge where the couches used to be located. It was now filled with hard chairs and computers. Where were the couches of yesteryear? Where were the girls with long straight parted-down-the-middle hair and the boys with hair down to their shoulders? They wore work shirts and torn jeans when they flirted while lying on those couches. They had become the parents of today's conservatively coiffed and dressed students. Maybe hard chairs and computers suited today's undergraduates better than languorous couches. At SUNY-A, both the couches and the hair blowin' and flowin' long as I can grow it hair were gone with the wind.

The wind, by the way, still howled through the SUNY-A podium's open structure which was more suited to Tahiti than to Albany. You can't go home again. As I sat on a hard desk chair and looked at Pepe, I decided that, if given the choice, I would much rather be middle-aged me than undergraduate Sondra lying on a couch boywatching. My few gray hairs blended with SUNY-A's now-gray concrete. I didn't belong there now. Regardless of this truth, the campus's resemblance to a futuristic NASA site still inspired me. I continue to love the on-the-verge-of-thrusting-forward towers and carillon which seem as if they can forever go onward and upward. Undergraduate Sondra could continue to inspire me too. If it were not for her, I would not have jabbed my father's rib cage to spare him from being done in after witnessing the Yoknawpawtawpha Hilton doings.

"Are you ready to leave?" Pepe asked.

"Yes. I was happy to show you my undergraduate school. I got a kick out of walking with you on the very spots where I used to hunt for boys. I was very attractive in those days, you know."

"You're still attractive. I love your *belle cuisses* and your *belle fesses. Je veux manger ton cul,*" said Pepe the husband, echoing Pepe the cartoon skunk's exaggeratedly French seductive tone.

"So much for the past. Onward to our motel. Where are we staying tonight?"

"The Burlington, Vermont Holiday Inn." A blast from the past hit me dead on. Even though this particular Holiday Inn caused me to spiral into meta-*plotz* mode, I tried not to reveal my agitated state. I didn't want to tell Pepe that I had lost my virginity with a SUNY-A history professor in the Burlington Holiday Inn. At the time, I thought that virginity lost in the Burlington Holiday Inn had a nice ring to it. I imagined mentioning it in the novel I would one day write.

"The Burlington, Vermont Holiday Inn?"

"Yes. Have you been there before?"

"I'm not really sure. Maybe I stayed there a few years ago when I gave a lecture at the University of Vermont."

Shielded from the truth, Pepe still suffered a panic attack when we entered our motel room—the very same one I had momentously occupied before. "This room lacks a suitable chair for you to stand on during our sex appointment. By the way, we have one scheduled for 6:33 PM -- sharp. How can you be my sex goddess if there's no chair to function as your pedestal? How will I be able best to caress and kiss your entire naked voluptuous body? There must be a way to solve this quandary. Would you stand on the luggage rack?"

"After traveling for eight hours, standing on a luggage rack is the very last thing I want to do." I did not add that if, I fell between the rack's plastic slats, I would lose more than my virginity at the Burlington, Vermont Holiday Inn.

"I guess I understand. Using one of the outside porch area rocking chairs won't work. The folding beach chair we have in the car trunk is too flimsy. I suppose that you would not want to stand on the bathtub."

Pepe eventually solved the chair lack problem (no Lacanian phallic lack) by dragging a very sturdy bench into the room from the hall. The bench, which was just right to stand on, solved the too-soft and too-hard chair problem. With me positioned up on my pedestal, Pepe became hard. The appointment began. When I lost my virginity in this Holiday Inn room, I never thought I would one day return as a gray-hair-streaked goldilocks acting as one of two bares.

Once again, Pepe and I were en route to Quebec, the land of his multitudinous thin sexy sisters. Taking my cue from the expression "it girl," I secretly called his sisters the "*ette* girls." I encouraged Pepe to describe his relationship with his family.

"It must have been hard for you to leave your big family."

"Yes. They didn't really understand what studying art history entails. For seven years, I said nothing about what I was doing. They thought that I was working for the CIA."

"You didn't give your family any information for seven years? My mother demanded fresh updates about my husband hunt every seven minutes. And this ensued throughout a twenty-seven yearlong hunt. I can relate to what you say about your family not understanding your work, though. Whenever I showed my mother one of my newly published books, she always said that sleeping with a book is less satisfying than sleeping with a husband. I guess she had a point. She never thought that I would write a memoir about having sex with a husband. It is, by the way, good of you not to object to my mining of our relationship for material. I just described the motel room chair trauma scenario.

My father is not interested in literary criticism in general and feminist science fiction in particular. He does try to be enthusiastic about my publications, though. When he took one of my feminist critical theory books to the beach club, his card game friends looked at page one and read four sentences. 'We don't understand this,' they all said in unison. I guess they have a point. I'm not sure that the literary criticism I wrote years ago currently makes sense to me. Maybe it never made sense. Maybe no one really understands literary theory. Maybe you were right about withholding information from your family. Working for the CIA is more comprehensible than creating scholarly analyses. Your family is so different from mine. It is giant and it has been in North America for centuries. Do you know about your ancestors?"

"There are family legends about how the family founder, Honoré Amoreuse Le Pew, accompanied Samuel de Champlain when the first French colony in Canada was established in 1604. I'm particularly enamored of Honoré Amoreuse Le Pew the third. When the British removed the Acadians from Nova Scotia in 1755, Honoré Amoreuse the third led a mutiny, commandeered the British ship, and sailed to Quebec. Upon arrival, he married an Acadian named Evangeline and had twenty-one children. I've seen a portrait of him brandishing his sword. He cut a striking figure attired in his body armor and helmet. His thick wavy shoulder-length hair resembles yours."

I was involved in Pepe's family stories to the extent that I failed to notice that we had arrived in Orignalville. Our plans called for us to spend the night in Hadassah Le Pew's house before going to the reunion Nanette, six years Hadassah's senior, was hosting on her farm.

Hadassah greeted us with open arms. As I dragged my luggage into her living room, I noticed Pepe eying the chairs. When Hadassah disappeared into the kitchen, Pepe mounted an upholstered chair and bounced on it tentatively.

"Get down. Down Pepe. Down. Don't even think about asking me to stand naked on your sister's chair."

"I was just testing its stability. This chair is much too soft. It is unsuitable. I wouldn't subject you to standing on it." Not one to give up, Pepe stood on the bed at 8 A.M. hovering over my just waking body."

"'No' means no. And that goes for every piece of furniture in your sister's house," I stipulated." Hadassah was already preparing breakfast.

"Good morning, Sondra. I've just put the cover on my wooden table. I want to protect it from potential scratch marks." Although I found it hard to believe that anyone could surpass Pepe's neatness obsession, Hadassah did. Her home resembles a *House Beautiful* ad. Everything was orderly to the extent that the house didn't look lived in.

"I understand your attention to protective covering. My mother is also very into covering things to protect them."

"Really? What does your mother cover?" I could not bring myself to tell Hadassah that my mother covers all her furniture in plastic and puts plastic runners over the carpet. The news might over tax her aesthetic sense to the extent that she might expire due to domestic horrific vision overload. I ducked for verbal cover.

"Oh, I really can't exactly recall how my mother's penchant for covering things manifests itself. My memories of this aspect of my childhood home are very hazy." I bit my tongue. During my last visit to Forest Hills, tripping on a curled plastic runner nearly killed me.

Plastic runner descriptions or no, Hadassah's breakfast-cooking techniques flawed me. In the manner of how I imagined Honoré Amoreuse Le Pew would wield his sword, she brandished two wire implements that were dead ringers for racquet ball racquets over sizzling bacon and ham.

"Hadassah, I'm very curious. May I ask you why you cook with two racquet ball racquets? I've never seen anyone do this."

"They keep the grease from splattering. I would die if a grease molecule landed on my kitchen floor. Just yesterday I examined the kitchen floor with a microscope. It is grease molecule-free. I want to keep it that way." I decided never to tell her about the wildebeest appearing in the Forest Hills apartment kitchen.

"You could learn a lot from Hadassah," Pepe interjected as he navigated his breakfast consisting of ham, bacon, fried eggs, fried potatoes, beans, toast, tomatoes, orange juice served in long stemmed crystal glasses, and whipped cream-covered strawberries presented in crystal bowls. Linen napkins and sterling silver cutlery adorned the table.

"Is this breakfast normal? Do you eat like this all the time?"

"This is a typical *Quebeçois* breakfast. What would you be served for breakfast in your family? Hadassah asked.

"Shredded wheat and skimmed milk which are respectively located on the shelf and in the refrigerator." This information caused Hadassah to have a heart palpitation. Pepe tried to distract her attention from the shock she derived from envisioning a milk container, rather than a cute ceramic milk-filled pitcher, appearing on a breakfast table. "Can Sondra use your iron? I've informed her that she must iron the outfit she's wearing to the family reunion."

"Pepe, I think the outfit you picked to wear is a little much. It's over-the-top for a family reunion held on a farm."

"I've considered your opinion. Since I see my family so infrequently, I must look my best. My outfit decision stands. There is no procedural irregularity. You have no recourse."

"Does this go for my outfit too? Do I have to iron the sleeves?" I inquired.

"You know the answer."

Nanette greeted us in a manner which repeated Hadassah's open-armed warmth. She deserved an Academy Award for the best guarded response by a *belle soeur* witnessing inappropriate attire for a family reunion held in a garage converted from a barn. A New York Jew attending the Le Pew reunion was the biggest thing that happened in the family since the following two circumstances ensued: (1) Honoré Amoreuse the first sighted land when he sailed up the Saint Lawrence with Champlain and (2) Honoré Amoreuse the third commandeered a British ship. Our outfits made the family forget that they were welcoming *moi*, the world's first Jew Le Pew.

When Pepe's brother Michel the Moose Hunter muttered "Oh, Christ," he was not responding to a Jew sitting at the Le Pew reunion table. He was instead reacting to a tuxedo-clad Pepe and his red-gown-wearing *épouse* entering the barn/garage. Knowing that he had committed a huge sartorial faux pas, Pepe stared at his formal black leather shoes sticking out like a sore thumb from amidst his family's sandals and sneakers. At least, since he granted me a dispensation from high heels, I took advantage of the opportunity to use my white clogs to accent my gown (My red clogs clashed with the red gown).

Pepe had orchestrated attire for the wrong French event. His top hat and tails and my gown and elbow-length gloves were appropriate for Jack and Jacqueline Kennedy meeting de Gaulle in France, not for Pepe and me meeting the Le Pews in an Orignalville barn/garage. With succulent hot corn cob in hand, I waited for Pepe to resolve the situation. No, I was not going to reenact the corn cob scene from Faulkner's *Sanctuary*. I had merely scouted the terrain and noticed that everyone was eating corn. Despite my gown and gloves, not to mention my Jewishness and inability to speak fluent French, I just wanted to fit in. To do so, I held my corn like a true Le Pew: I mimicked Honoré Amoreuses the first and Third brandishing their swords -- and Hadassah wielding her racquet-ball splatter-control kitchen utensil. Pepe finally took control of the situation.

"This corn could splatter all over my tuxedo and Sondra's gown. I think it would be best for us to go into the house and change," Pepe announced in French Canadian to the assembled Le

Pews. The throng applauded in relief. Pepe and I disappeared into Nanette's bedroom. Her home was a *House Beautiful* clone of Hadassah's impossibly clean abode. Now that the attire fiasco had been resolved, I tried to derail further trouble.

"What goes for Hadassah's chairs also goes for Nanette's chairs," I informed Pepe. Knowing that he had erred so egregiously in relation to the improper clothes, Pepe, rather than mounting a chair to test its stability, opted to keep his now sneaker-clad feet firmly on the floor. Finally appropriately dressed in shorts and tee shirts, we rejoined the party.

Not being a clinging wife, I ventured out alone to engage with the family. I started a conversation with Michel the second, the son of Michel the Moose Hunter, a gorgeous, strapping forty-five year old.

"When I heard that Uncle Pepe married a native New Yorker, I was very anxious to meet you. Welcome to the family."

"Anxious" was a polite way to say "I and all of my relatives were curious as hell and we were chomping at the bit -- not to mention *plotzing* -- to set eyes on you. I could have cleared a large profit if I made every Le Pew buy tickets to step right up to see the strange new alien Jewish Le Pew."

"I'm thoroughly enjoying meeting you all, which is not to be confused with 'y'all.' That's from another story about teaching at Blackhole State University which I described in my novel *Oy Pioneer!* Pepe tells me that you're his godson. Now that I'm married to him, does that mean that you're my godson too?"

"It doesn't really work that way. But, hey, you can still be my godmother."

"Jews don't usually have godchildren. But, for you, I'll make an exception." I embraced Michel the second. "Son. My long-lost godson. I've found you at last. Who would have known that I have a long-lost son. And a tall, middle-aged old one at that." Michel the second laughed with me.

"I'd like you to meet my wife Nicolette and my two year-old son," said my godson.

"He's so cute. He looks just like a mini Pepe. His resemblance to Pepe is amazing. Is he Michel the third?"

"His name is Jolan. I named him after a superhero from another planet called Jolan, a character in the French comic *Thorgal*. I hope you don't think it is strange for me to name my child after an alien superhero," explained Nicolette.

"I don't think that your choice is strange at all," I said casually, omitting to mention that some of my best friends are extraterrestrials -- e.g. that, in addition to being a feminist science fiction scholar, I am well acquainted with spaceship travel. It was better that Nicolette did not know from exactly who she was talking to. I brushed a mosquito off my leg and noticed that his colleague was buzzing around contemplating how to turn Jolan into lunch. Much to my surprise, the mosquito expired immediately after contacting Jolan's skin. True, Pepe did explain to me that *Quebeçois* mosquitoes are much more hardy and vicious than their American counterparts. I named the *Quebeçois* mosquitoes Superbugs. Superbugs, figments of my imagination, were not really faster than speeding bullets and more powerful than locomotives. Not so for Jolan. A "Superbug" expired immediately after nose diving into Jolan's skin. I began to suspect that Jolan was a superhero not just in name only. Encountering a real superhero would be par for the course for me.

"Jolan is adorable. I especially love him because he looks just like Pepe. Would you allow me to take care of him for a while?" I asked Nicolette.

"Sure. Maybe you can help him to learn New York-accented English."

I took Jolan by the hand and led him to Nanette's back porch. I wanted him to be out of sight during his superhero flying test. "*Vole* Jolan," I instructed him. Because he was too young to understand a verbal command to fly, I jumped down from the porch step to act out what I had asked him to do. Giggling while anticipating a fun game, he descended from the step in a decidedly non-supernatural fashion. Not one to give up, I flapped my arms. "Can you fly Jolan? Can you fly?" He obviously thought that I was a big *meshuganeh*. Still refusing to give up, I tried to be more explicit. I took him into the house and perched him in front of Mozart, Nanette's pet bird (Even though Mozart lacked a tail and didn't sing, Nanette still loved him). My agenda: use the bird to indicate to Jolan that he might be a high-flying superhero.

I pointed to the bird. I flapped. I pointed to Jolan. I grasped his arms and moved them up and down. I pointed to the bird again. Jolan's cute little face registered a look of recognition. He began to squeal and to flap. "By George, he's got it. I think he's got it," I said aloud. Onward to the Jolan Superhero Flying Test trials. I took Jolan back to the porch stairs and positioned him at the edge of the step located closest to the ground. I thought of Pale Male the hawk who famously built a nest on a Manhattan Fifth Avenue apartment building. Super powers or no, Jolan certainly had it easier than Pale Male's children. The little baby hawks had to fly while looking down at traffic choked Fifth Avenue.

"Jump, Jolan. Fly." I tried to be as encouraging as Mrs. Pale Male. Jolan jumped -- and soared upward. My hunch was right. Thank god that he couldn't inform his parents about his superhero status. I had the luxury to wait until he figured out how to talk before I had to figure out what to do. First things first. It was time to return Jolan to his parents.

"Here's your son back. We had fun exploring the house and the backyard. Jolan particularly likes Mozart. I used the bird as a means to teach him about flight." I believe in truth.

"Thanks for taking him off my hands for a while," said Nicolette.

"I have to ask you two something which I guess is a big deal. I hope I'm not being presumptuous. Michel, the idea of my being your godmother is, of course, a joke. I have a special interest in Jolan, though. Could I be his god mother for true?"

"We're sorry. Jolan already has a designated godmother," said Michel.

"Maybe Jewish culture can save the day. Jews have something called a T. G. May I be Jolan's T. G.?"

"T. G.?" questioned Jolan's bewildered parents.

"Yes. T. G. The T.G. was invented when the Jews were roaming the dessert and manna fell from heaven. Although the falling manna was a *mitzvah*, they worried that if it could appear so too could something big and heavy. They did not want to get hit in the head, that is to say *kabonged* on the *kup*. It was the job of the T. G., or *Tsuris* Guard, incessantly to gaze up and issue a warning in case something big and bad began to fall from the sky. One T. G. took her job too seriously; she became known as Kosher Chicken Little."

"I'm a little confused. I don't understand the word '*tsuris*'," said Nicolette.

"'*Tsuris*' is something that ya shouldn't know from."

"Of course, it is all perfectly clear now," said Michel, not wanting to admit to his confusion with regard to alien cultural rituals.

"It seems to me that a *Tsuris* Guard is a good thing. No child should be left behind in regard to having one. Yes, you can be Jolan's T. G." said Nicolette. Let's have a T. G. induction ceremony. Sondra, do you have a bathing suit?"

I nodded affirmatively. I packed it because I suspected that, if swimming was on the agenda, I would be changing out of my gown.

"Good. Put it on and report to Nanette's hot tub for the induction ceremony appointment in exactly ten minutes sharp."

"Does Nanette keep a beach chair by her hot tub?"

"Why?"

"Oh nothing important. It's just that if Pepe wanders over, it would be nice for him to have a chair for the ceremony appointment." Wearing my bathing suit, I reported to the tub exactly at the designated time. Nicolette, Michel, and Jolan surrounded it and looked very somber. Michel told me to submerge myself.

"I, Nicolette Le Pew, mother of Jolan Le Pew, do hereby baptize Sondra Lear, the first Jewish Le Pew, as henceforth the official *Tsuris* Guard of Jolan. From this moment on, Sondra Lear will be charged with scanning the skies to make sure that Jolan is not *kabonged* on the *kup* by *tsuris* which ya shouldn't know from." She splashed water over my head and applauded. I hugged Jolan, went into the house to change into dry clothes (i.e. shorts and a tee shirt, not the ball gown), and rejoined Pepe.

"Why is your hair wet? You're right that my tuxedo and your gown are not appropriate for this party. But surely dripping hair is carrying informality too far. I like your hair when it is fluffed out. You look like a drowned rat."

"I have a perfectly logical explanation. Nicolette and Michel baptized me. Strange things happen when you marry outside of your culture. My baptismal ceremony is not original. The WASP husband was baptized in *My Big Fat Greek Wedding*."

"That's fiction. I like reality. I know that I shouldn't ask. But why did they baptize you?"

"To signify that I had become Jolan's *Tsuris* Guard. He already has a godmother."

"Teaching my family Yiddish is the limit. Some of them do not even speak English -- and now you have them speaking Yiddish. I turn my back for a few minutes and you turn Nicolette into a *Yiddishe momme*."

"She has a long way to go before she becomes Totie Fields. But, under my tutelage, she's making progress. I can't believe that I've been baptized."

"Serves you right. This is my revenge for when you made me wear a *yarmulke* and *talis* when we attended Carol's daughter's *bar mitzvah* at the Forest Hills Jewish Center. If I can wear those Jewish contraptions and dance the *horror*, you can get baptized."

"That's the *hora*."

"Same difference. I'll be right back. I have to *pish*. Go and mingle some more with my family. And remember the Prime Directive: don't interfere." Pepe, who has a great facility for learning foreign languages, was now using Yiddish and science fiction terminology.

"I won't," I said innocently. I neglected to add that I teaching Jolan how to be a superhero constitutes big-time Prime Directive breaking. Overwhelmed by the events I had just experienced, instead of mingling further, I decided to hide behind Nanette's house. Just as I was about to savor some peace and quiet, I saw a rather obtrusive and definitely magical smoke puff. This could not be good. Since I had not used my red clogs to call Ilya, I was not expecting a magical smoke puff. I braced myself. The smoke cleared. A man who was the image of Pepe appeared wearing armor. His sword was sheathed. Maybe he was peaceful.

"Greetings, Sondra, my future Jewish kinswoman. I am Honoré Amoreuse Le Pew."

"Are you Honoré Amoreuse the first or Honoré Amoreuse the third?"

"I am Honoré Amoreuse Le Pew the third."

"Nice to meet you. I've heard a lot about you. I've engaged with many Le Pews for the first time today. Even though I am only a Le Pew by marriage, and a Jewish one at that, I guess that I can welcome you to the family reunion."

"I am not here for the party. I materialized in the future simply to meet you, my dear."

"To what can I attribute the pleasure of your company -- or this blast from the past?"

"I want personally to welcome you to the Le Pew family precisely because you *are* Jewish. I know how it feels to be a persecuted minority group member. I was forcefully removed from my home in Nova Scotia and imprisoned on a British ship. I led a rebellion and commandeered the ship. Sondra, I have *chutzpah*. I just had to come and meet the world's first and only -- and probably the last -- Jewish member of the Le Pew family. I had to talk with the only Le Pew who knows what '*chutzpah*' means."

I immediately warmed to Honoré Amoreuse. Sensing that I would welcome his embrace, Honoré took me in his arms. He felt just like Pepe -- and he acted just like Pepe. One of his hands clutched my buttocks and the other caressed my breasts.

"Do they have stable chairs in the twenty-first century?" he asked in an amorous tone that only a Frenchman could accomplish. I grabbed his sword.

I pointed the sword directly at Honoré's crotch. "I have had enough *tsuris* with stable denizens and stable chairs. Being seduced by a Le Pew ghost is the limit. Enough is enough. I will not cheat on Pepe -- even though it would be fun to get it on with an eighteenth century version of him. And, Pepe aside, I will not hurt your wife Evangeline. How dare you try to seduce me when at this very moment she is probably giving birth to your eighteenth child. You know, the one who is the direct ancestor of Pepe. *Non*. '*Non*' means '*non*.' If you can't take *non* for an answer, maybe this will make my point," I said as I thrust his sword even closer to his crotch. Go back to where you came from. It's immediate return smoke cloud mode for you Honoré, or should I say Dishonoré."

"I am right about the ethnic affinity between us. Jewish you is as feisty as Acadian *moi*. I will do as you wish. The sword is too close for comfort. Return my sword and I will go. *Adieu*, Sondra." He pushed the sword point into a stone and disappeared in the predictable smoke puff (This text is starting to need a nonsmoking section). Thinking that a Le Pew might like to own an ancestor memento, I tried to remove the sword from the stone. It wouldn't budge. Just as well. I had no desire to become the King of Quebec. I emerged from behind the house to reconnoiter with Pepe.

"Do you have a relative named Arthur Le Pew?"

"Not that I know of. Why?"

"Oh, nothing. I was just thinking that if the separatists win the day and Quebec secedes from Canada, maybe Arthur could pull Honoré Amoreuse's sword from a stone."

"Your attention to fiction is just too much for me."

"Arthur Le Pew, if he exists, could very well become King of Quebec. You told me that Jean Chrétien went to college with you here in Orignalville. Chrétien is Prime Minister of Canada. Anything is possible."

"Enough of this conjecture. At least your hair is dry. Why do you look so startled?"

"No reason. Just chalk it up to seeing Casper the Friendly Ghost. Casper is an American Baby Boomer cultural icon. I don't think you know from him." I noticed that various Le Pews were frolicking in the hot tub -- naked. To change the subject, I called Pepe's attention to them.

"Look Pepe. Yonder. There are naked people in the hot tub. Wow, they don't have any clothes on. Let's join them."

"*Non. Pas pour moi.* I like you standing naked on a chair, not dunking naked in a hot tub surrounded by my family. You join them. You go. I'm going to sleep." I removed my clothes and plunged in.

"We're glad you joined us. We're discussing next year's family reunion. We would like to do something different for a change. Any suggestions?" asked Hadassah.

"Yes. If you would like a different venue, I suggest the Forest Hills Jewish Center. My friend Carol just had her daughter's *bar mitzvah* there. She told me all about the Center's wonderful caterer. The caterer's name is also Hadassah. Hadassah, you should talk to Hadassah. You two Hadassahs can decide if the Le Pews would rather eat *tsimes* or *kreplach*. For good measure, you can consult with the entire membership of the Forest Hills Jewish Center Hadassah chapter. All of the Forest Hills Jewish Center's catering is kosher. I'm not sure if they cook with tennis racquets, however."

"What a wonderful idea, Sondra" enthused Hadassah. The entire family would love to come to New York. We can stay with you and Pepe. What is a *bar mitzvah*?

I gulped hot tub water as I recoiled in horror at the thought of what Pepe would do to me when Annette, Claudette, Georgette, Lynette, Nanette, Pierrette, Suzette, Hadassah, Marcel the Mountie,

and Michel the Moose Hunter and all their kinfolk (a.k.a. multitudinous children and grandchildren) showed up at the door step of our
one-bedroom apartment. Scratch that vision. Our one-bedroom
apartment does not have a door step. Even if Jolan were old enough
to be in full control of all his superpowers, he would not be able to
save me from the wrath of Pepe.

"Next year in the Forest Hills Jewish Center," said the hot
water-sodden, naked Le Pews in unison.

Northern Exposure

Although I love to proclaim that I'm a science fiction scholar who is married to an alien, my proclamation is false advertising. Despite my mistake involving Pepe's electric shaver masquerading as an interplanetary communicator, he is from French Canada -- not outer space. When contemplating this discrepancy in relation to Pepe's idiosyncrasies, I sometimes think that Quebec is in truth a different planet. I am not acquainted with any New York Jews who are married to outer space aliens -- or to *Quebeçois*. I did not conduct an official poll to arrive at this conclusion. I am just drawing on my knowledge of all the New York Jews I have ever heard of and my participation in receptions organized by Manhattan's Canadian Cultural Consulate. To make my poll more accurate, I attended a Consulate reception and addressed the white-haired, rotund Canadian cultural ambassador.

"Excuse me, Mr. Ambassador. May I ask you a question?"

"Yes."

"Do you know any *Quebeçois* who are married to New York Jews?"

"No."

The Lear/Le Pew unique ethnic union again became a conversation topic when Pepe and I stood on Madison Avenue viewing the Immigration Day Parade. We watched as floats filled with costumed dancers from countries as diverse as Bangladesh, China, Korea, and Peru rolled by.

"Do you think that Canada has a float?" I asked Pepe.

"No."

"We should have our own float to represent *Quebeçois* who are married to New York Jews. I could throw bagels and you could wave a blue fleur-de-lis independence flag. I could dance the *hora*. I am stumped as to what dance you could do to represent your culture. Ditto for distinctive *Quebeçois* costumes." I felt culturally shallow as I watched the Chinese contingent represent themselves as legs positioned beneath a long colorful streaming dragon.

"Canadians -- even French ones -- should have a float to represent them in the Immigration Day Parade. You are from Mars and I am from Venus; I'm only speaking metaphorically. Yet, we don't stand out as being glaringly different ethnically from each other. Yes, I am fatter than all of your sisters put together. Stop agreeing. I'm exaggerating. My nose is normal size. Our skin is the same color. We don't look like a mixed marriage. No one raises an eyebrow when, for simplicity's sake, we use the same last name to make a reservation. I fit in fine as Sondra Le Pew. People accept you as Pepe Lear. 'Lear-Le Pew' has a certain ring to it. Does Chrétien, the surname of the Canadian Prime Minister you went to college with, mean Christian?"

"Yes."

"Then it is a good thing that you are not named Chrétien and I am not named something exceedingly Jewish like, I don't know, like Lipshitz. Could you imagine if we were the Lipshitz-Chrétien family?"

"We don't have that problem. All of this talk about immigrants and ethnicity and America is making me think of my book project. I want to get going on my book that explains American culture from the viewpoint of an alien outsider. I'm starting with a chapter on race relations. To encourage me to write, I want us to go to the annual Civil War reenactment in Gettysburg. Can you imagine seeing Pickett's charge recast on the very place where it happened? Don't you find the mere thought of Pickett's charge thrilling?"

"No." I was still kissing the ground that I was not charged for Beauregard Pickett Jackson Burnside's presence in the Yoknaw-pawtawpha Hilton

Pepe began to pack for a trip to Gettysburg. I circumnavigated the apartment while carrying a sign picturing a circled cannon with a slash through its middle. Furthermore, I vociferously chanted "Hell no, I won't go. Hell no, I won't go." Picketing against Pickett's charge got me nowhere. Faster than I could say "*oy vey*" ("*oy vey*" is not very Civil War-ish; but having "fiddle-dee-dee" emanate from my lips defies credulity), I found myself smack in the middle of a July heat-sodden Pennsylvania field. I was surrounded by blue coats, and gray coats, and cooking fires, and cavalry, and horse manure -- oh my. As I checked out the horses, I was relieved: Ms. Ed had elected to stay with Beauregard Jackson Pickett Burnside on Jonathan Goodman's Mississippi plantation. Realizing that the next two days of incessant battling would cause me enough problems, I dismissed the thought that Ed and Beauregard would fit in well here. Ed could potentially blow her normal nonverbal horse cover and neigh "Charge!"

No. On second thought, her imagined battle cry would never take place. After spending so much time in Forest Hills, Ed thought "Charge!" meant Visa card. In reality, the Northerners and the Southerners were in fact charging -- both across the battle field and in the motels and restaurants.

"The Civil War is not really my thing. I fought my own version of the Civil War as a New York Jew who was trying to survive in Virginia at Blackhole State University. The Blackholians were certainly not civil to me. Some would say that I lost that war. But I consider myself to be a big winner: rather than remaining in southwest Virginian *Goyimville*-from-Hell surrounded by cows, I now live in Manhattan surrounded by subways and ethnic diversity. But don't think that I don't know from the Civil War. I remember my first day of the Blackhole State semester experiences. I would go into classrooms and say, "Good morning. This is American Literature 101." Upon hearing my New York accent, the students would glare and think "damn Yankee." They didn't come out and say it, but they definitely thought it. I remember the time my Southern gentleman colleague -- that is to say a racist geezer who really lived on a plantation -- took the Hanukkah decoration I had hung in the English department lounge and ripped it to shreds in front of my face. He said that the decoration is ugly. But he's dead now. He hung himself with a belt from his dining room chandelier. That's no stretcher; that's the truth.

And then there's the time that I stood up in a department meeting and explained to the entire racist geezer-from-hell platoon (a.k.a. the Blackhole English department) that the slaves were free and women could now vote. Well, maybe I did provoke them: I routinely wore my father's genuine World War Two army jacket -- replete with its China/Burma/India patch -- to department meetings. I wanted to stress that the departmental civil war involved the feminists pitched against the ultra-conservative WASP males. You think that Pickett's charge was bad? Well, you should have seen what happened to the English department's feminists at Blackhole. But don't get me started. Even though I've fought a Civil War (and I did it sans time travel accoutrements -- but that's another story, don't ask) -- and even though the historical Civil War is not my thing -- I'm here at Gettysburg and I might as well make the best of things."

"That's the spirit, Sondra. Besides, I'm in dire need of your help."

"Why?"

"I must start my book. I want to interview Northerners and Southerners to discern if they have different conceptions of race relations. Because I'm not a native speaker of English, I can't tell the difference between Northern and Southern accents. I want to send you out on advance missions in which you speak to people, figure out if they are Southern or Northern, clue me in, and let me take it from there to conduct interviews."

"You don't need my help. Telling the difference between Northerners and Southerners is as easy as pie -- Boston cream and pecan -- but I'm not counting calories. The Southerners wear gray uniforms and the Northerners wear blue uniforms."

"No, it doesn't work that way. Regardless of where they're really from, the Civil War reenactors can play any part they want."

"Let me get this straight. Despite my terrible life experience as a Jew living in the South, you want me surreptitiously to identify which people are Southern? That's weird. I suppose it could be worse. Finding Southerners is not as bad as being a Nazi hunter. And there's all my husband-hunting experience. Okay. I'll do it. I'll help you. I have to add something, though. In addition to your nonexistent ability to discern the difference between American accents, as an alien in relation to American culture, your cultural code radar is way off. You just can't directly ask American strangers what they think about race. Americans aren't comfortable talking about race."

"I'll capitalize on being an alien. I'll just exaggerate my French accent to the level of, say, Maurice Chevalier, and tell interviewees the truth: I'm a foreigner researching American culture. If this research method was good enough for Alexis de Tocqueville, then it certainly should be effective for Pepe Le Pew. There's no time like the present to begin. Go behind the Southern lines into that wooded camp area over there. The people are cooking over fires and chatting. Behind the Southern lines yonder looks like a good place to start."

"'I'm not comfortable in woods. Nor am I comfortable going behind the Southern lines -- even if all of this Civil War *mishegas* is fake. You can take the New York Jewish Yankee out of New York and put her in the woods. But, you can't take the Yankee out of the Jewish New Yorker. The real Southern Southerners, as opposed to the Northerners dressed up as Southerners, will immediately discern that I am a New York Northerner. What if they don't like me for real? What if I take off one of my white clogs, attach it to a stick, and wave it around -- and they don't understand that I come in white clog waving peace. The Civil War is not really over. As I learned from my time in Virginia, a New York Jew surrounded by Southerners can end up as dead meat -- and those cooking fires are real enough. I will be much more comfortable starting out with Northerners. In fact, here comes the guy playing General Grant now. General Grant just can't be Southern -- even here."

"Don't be so sure."

"I'll start a conversation, return, and report back to you about which American region he hails from. This very easy task is unworthy of Professor Henry Higgins' linguistic expertise. Any American can immediately tell whether or not his fellow American is Northern or Southern. Enough said. Off to Mission Possible I go. Hi ho" (No, this is not a Kurt Vonnegut novel. Kurt Vonnegut once flirted with me -- but that's another story). "I'm your wife. I choose to undertake said mission."

"Hello, General Grant. May I call you Ulysses? What a nice sword you have. Please keep it sheathed," I insisted, with Honoré Amoreuse in mind. "You look resplendent in your blue uniform. Allow me to break out of reenactment mode. I'm Sondra Lear."

"Pleased to meet y'all, ma'am. When I'm not General Ulysses S. Grant, I'm known as Mr. Clayton Cockburn Snopes the third."

"Nice to meet you, Mr. Snopes. Command well."

I returned to Pepe and reported my findings. "General Grant is a Southerner. I would say that he hails from around Yoknawpawtawpha, Mississippi. Maybe he knows Jonathan Goodman."

Actually, I'm clueless as to whether or not the real General Grant fought at Gettysburg. My Forest Hills Elementary School curriculum was not at all that big on the Civil War. New York Jewish teachers taught New York Jewish students the following abbreviated version of the Civil War: Southerners owned slaves. The Civil War was fought to free the slaves. Lincoln was a great president. The North won the war. Lincoln freed the slaves. End of story.

"Go find another Southerner," commanded Pepe. Go over there into the woods beyond the Southern lines to the Southern encampment. The Southern encampment is a promising place to find Southerners who play Southerners."

"Don't send me behind the Southern lines. Going there could be a fate worse than death for me. I'm afraid to go behind the Southern lines. I won't like it there. I don't want to talk to Robert E. Lee -- even if I find out that he comes from Brooklyn."

"Stop acting like a baby. All the people here are very nice. Go talk to that woman near that big tree who is cooking with a large black pot over the camp fire."

"I don't like the looks of that pot. What if she is a cannibal Southerner? I was a child in the days before political correctness; I watched all those racist Warner Bros. cartoons featuring African cannibals dancing around big black pots." I decided to try to get out of my impending Southern line close encounter by inventing new American racism on the spot. Perhaps Pepe would be unable to discern this narrative white lie about Southern white subterfuge: "Since you're Canadian, you're not aware that Southern swamps are filled with big fat white male cannibal Southerners. Do you know the Civil War story called *Swamp Fox*? I hear tell that white Southern males ate both foxes and people in the swamp. What if there is a great fox and human population shortage and the cannibal Southerners are hungry? They could eat me. If I don't return from my mission behind the Southern lines, you could find me being boiled to death in that big black pot. You would feel very guilty if you condemned me to a watery grave in which I drowned surrounded by boiled cabbage -- sans corned beef, yet. I know, corned beef cholesterol would kill me first. You will find yourself in the soup when you have to tell my parents that you caused their daughter to become Southern soup. True, my mother wouldn't be that concerned, because at least she would know that I died married. She wouldn't be happy, though."

"Sondra, enough. Just go." I approached the woman that Pepe had chosen to be my designated quarry. She was at once tending the fire and stirring the large black pot's contents.

"Hello. What's cooking?"

"*Kreplach*. Crappy *kreplach*. Campfire-cooked *kreplach* cannot fail to be crappy." I wasn't conversing with a cannibal Southerner after all.

"What brings you to the reenactment?"

"My Izzy. My Izzy wants that he should be a Confederate soldier. In all the annals of the Civil War, I bet you that there was not one Confederate soldier named Isidore Insdorf the first. For this nonsense, I have to *schlep* from Borough Park to Gettysburg. At least for this I didn't have to buy new clothes. Long dresses. Long dresses I "hafta" wear in Borough Park -- and I can also wear them here in the Southern camp. Why can't my Izzy be happy eating *matzo* at home like everyone else? No. For my Izzy *matzos* aren't good enough. He drags me here because he wants that he should be a cracker."

"Nice to talk to you. Maybe your *kreplach* will come out less crappy than you think." I crossed the border of the Southern line and gave Pepe *the report*.

"Northern or Southern?" he asked.

"Northern. Definitely Northern."

"Are you absolutely certain? You know that I am a perfectionist."

"Absolutely. The woman is a self-described crappy *keplach* cook. All *kreplach* cooks, crappy or not, are Northern."

"Introduce me to her. I want to ask what she thinks about race relations."

"I know what she'll say. She'll tell you about 'the *schwartzes*.' Talk to General Grant instead." We set off to penetrate the Northern lines.

"General Grant, I mean Clayton Cockburn Snopes the third, I would like you to meet my husband, Pepe Le Pew. He's writing a book on American culture. He's up to the race relations chapter. Would you mind if he interviews you about current race relations?"

"Why ma'am, I would be plum tickled to participate in the study y'all is undertakin'. Fire away, Mr. Le Pew. I don't mean that as a General Grant-articulated military command. This weekend, when

I say 'Fire away!' all hell breaks loose. Seems to be that I know some folks named Le Pew from Louisiana."

Pepe and General Grant/Mr.Snopes the third made themselves comfortable sitting on a fat log located outside the main Northern military command center tent. I hoped that Honoré Amoreuse Le Pew the third, sensing that I was fraternizing with someone acquainted with his Cajun kin, would not see fit to materialize. I was having enough trouble facing Civil War cannons. It would be too much to have to deal with a sword, too.

"So, Clayton. I hope it's proper for me to call you Clayton instead of 'General?' How would you describe race relations in your neck of the woods? Sondra tells me that she thinks you're from Mississippi."

"Clayton is certainly fittin'. Yes, I'm from Mississippi. It's easy for me to talk about race relations. Everything's fine. No problems at all."

"Are you sure?"

"Yes, I reckon so."

"Do you think the Southern Civil War battle flag should still be depicted on Southern state flags?"

"Of course. That flag symbolizes the proud heritage of white Southerners. My great grandpappy fought and died in the Civil War. That flag symbolizes his sacrifice in the great war against the damn Yankees. We white Southerners don't want any damn Yankees or uppity black folks sticking their noses in our white Southern business. I want my little son, Clayton Cockburn Snopes the fourth, to be proud of his Southern heritage. I want his heart to pound when he sees that flag unfurled and fluttering against our proud Southern magnolia trees."

"I see. What's your opinion of Trent Lott being chastised for saying that race relations were fine during 1945?"

"He's right on. The uppity black folks knew their place back then. My parents didn't have to contend with no uppity black folks. You know how uppity those uppity black folks can get. I voted for Trent. I would be right happy to vote for him ag'in, too."

"How, then, do you summarize your view of contemporary American race relations"

"Everything's hunky-dory. Right as rain. Right? After all, ain't no black folk callin' no white folk hunky now. Excuse me. I hear a bugle call I can't refuse. I have to go mount my horse and lead a charge up that there knoll yonder. I love my horse. His name is Beauregard Jackson Pickett Burnside the second. His pappy, Beauregard Jackson Pickett Burnside the first, lives on the plantation located up the road just a holler from my plantation. Beauregard the First sure loves his owner, my neighbor, who goes by the name of Jonathan Goodman. He's a Jewish fella -- but he's nice anyway. You know how those Jews can be. Some of my best friends are Jewish. You must excuse me. We Southerners are prone to storytellin'. The Faulkner thing. None of this must mean a hill of beans to y'all. First, the damn Yankees take away all the darkies, oops, I mean African Americans -- we all need to be politically correct nowadays -- from our plantations. Then the Jews start livin' on plantations. What's next? Rest assured, though, that everything is now fine in the South regardin' race relations. The battle call calls. 'Bye, y'all." Ulysses/Clayton rode off into the sunset astride Beauregard Jackson Pickett Burnside the second. I made sure not to tell Pepe that Beauregard Jackson Pickett Burnside the second, who was obviously Ms. Ed's son, was kin to me.

"Before we call it a day, Sondra, I would like to talk to the pot-stirrer from the North." I embarked upon Northern line penetration and introduction round two.

"Mrs. Insdorf, please tell me your view of contemporary American race relations," Pepe asked earnestly.

"Everything's absolutely fine. It's so fine, ya shouldn't know from it."

"What about the early nineties Borough Park tragedy when rioting broke out after a Jewish driver accidentally ran over a black child?"

"That whole horrible mess riled me and my Izzy. If the *schwartzes* stayed in their own neighborhood where they belong, the whole thing never would have happened. There's a clear dividing line between the *schwartze* section and our section of Borough Park. When the *schwartzes* stay on their side where they belong, we have peace and everything's all right. I don't have to tell you. You know about the element."

"I'm glad that you think all is well. Thank you for your time," said Pepe, while sticking his nose in the big pot. "This certainly smells good. Those big white floating things look like crepes."

"Crappy *kreplach*. Crappy crepes. Same difference. I just *hafta* have it all ready in time for when my Izzy comes home from the battlefield. Nice meetin' ya. Be well. Get home safely." Pepe and I made our way back to the motel.

Black Like Me?

Pepe was uncharacteristically animated. "I have a brainstorm: you're a person, Sondra."

"Thanks a lot. I should hope so."

"Take the desk chair, and sit down."

"What's goin' on? First, you decide to include me in the Declaration of the Rights of Man. Then, even stranger still, you ask me to sit down on a motel room chair like a normal person. I can't believe you're telling me to sit on the chair rather than stand on it. Why aren't you checking out the chair for stability to prevent me from crash-landing after you turn it into a sex goddess pedestal?"

"I'm making perfect sense. You're a person. I can interview *you* about race in America." Pepe placed his tape recorder in front of my mouth. Because of my long-term Pavlovian conditioning about what Pepe considers chairs and motel rooms to connote, I half expected him to ask me fellate the tape recorder.

"Speak, Sondra. I want to know what you think about race."

"I think that, in relation to job candidates, merit should receive first priority. I mean, regardless of race, the best qualified person should always land the job. I can only speak from my experience in Academia. The quality of a person's mind, not the color of a person's skin, should be the deciding factor. This is not how things work, though. Academic jobs are very often awarded on the basis of race. This practice, which assumes that all blacks are underprivileged, is unfair. What if, for example, a black millionaire's daughter or son wants to be an English professor? Why should this person receive preferential treatment? Yet, this hypothetical privileged black academic wannabe would be the most sought-after job candidate.

More than one person has told me directly that Jewish feminists are a dime a dozen on the job market. Jews should count as a
minority with regard to academic hiring. Jews *are* a minority. Jews
face discrimination when they move to universities located in God-
knows-where American hinterlands. I know. It happened to me at
Blackhole State. I faced more discrimination there as a Jew than any
black did. I was a highly qualified person who suffered through a
tenure battle. My highly qualified black female colleague was venerat-
ed. She became a dean. The Southern academics -- and for once I am
not exaggerating -- almost killed me dead; the German and Austrian
academics killed me with kindness.

I even faced discrimination as a Jew among feminist Jews.
Did I ever tell you about my experience as a Fellow at the Balabusta
Brand-ex University Jewish Feminist Research Institute? During the
initial interview, Institute head Leona Rhinestone told me that being
a Forest Hills Jew was not exotic enough to meet the Institute's
needs. A Forest Hills Jew couldn't cut it at Brand-ex in employment
competition with foreign Jews. She asked me to accept half the salary
the Institute originally stipulated. Why? Rhinestone wanted to fake
the usual one-person-to-one-job ratio expectation; she wanted to
hire both me and an exotic foreign Jew. I swear that she was salivating over her opportunity to hire an Ethiopian Jew."

"What should be done about the situations you describe?"

"All hiring should be race-blind. Numbers should replace
candidates' names on vitae. Candidates should be interviewed by
phone. All MLA interviewees should wear clothes that cover their
skin. I would go so far as to say that they could put paper bags over
their heads to mask their race. Back in the early 1980's when I was
first interviewed at the MLA Convention, drunken male English department members routinely spoke with female candidates while
sprawled out on hotel room beds. What's a mere paper bag in relation to this lack of decorum?

Another thing: why do hiring committees assume that race --
and gender too -- are integral to subject matter? A man can teach
feminist literature. A Gentile can teach Jewish literature. A Caucasian
can teach black literature. An Earthling can teach science fiction. I
know. If professors are relegated to teaching texts that match their
backgrounds, I would have to specialize in Forest Hills Jews. I
would have to spend my whole professional life teaching Forest Hills

denizens such as Burt Bacharach, Art Buchwald, and Simon and Garfunkel. If I became really desperate, I would have to research whether or not Bob Keeshan (a.k.a. Captain Kangaroo), another Forest Hills native son, wrote anything. Maybe, just maybe, I could sneak Art Spiegelman into my syllabus. He's from Rego Park. The border between Forest Hills and Rego Park is quite porous.

If a space probe find life on Mars, will only Martian professors be hired to teach Ray Bradbury's *The Martian Chronicles*? I can teach Bradbury just fine, thank you -- and that was before I ever flew in a warp drive-powered starship. Oops. Sorry. Only kidding. I'm just getting carried away. This whole race emphasis thing in academic hiring is unfair. Take Condelezza Rice, for example. She got to be Provost at Stanford even though she only published two edited books. Two edited books would not result in tenure at Blackhole State -- or at any Dreck Tech in this country. If you include what I have to say in your book, people will get angry. Nevertheless, I have told you the truth as I see it."

"I appreciate your candor. I can identify with you. When I left Canada, the race preference you describe worked in my favor. As I told you when we first met, I supported myself in graduate school by becoming a *maitre d'* in very expensive Manhattan restaurants. Being a handsome French-accented person got me many American restaurant jobs. The Tavern on the Green customers loved it when I smiled and said '*Bonjour, suivez moi madame et monsieur.*' When I was young in Canada, the French were considered to be inferior; the best jobs went to the English Canadians. I don't harbor resentment toward the English, though. I don't agree with dwelling on the past. '*Je me souviens*' is the official motto of Quebec. Instead of remembering past wrongs, I say: move on."

"I understand. You mean 'enough already' with '*Je me souviens.*' I want to apply that motto to the enmity between many American Jews and Germans. All Germans born after World War II -- and we're talkin' the preponderance of the population -- are, without question, innocent of committing Nazi-era atrocities. I had great experiences in Germany and Austria. I'm glad that I lived there. By the way, I'm also glad too that I was open to marrying an alien *goy*. Your Frenchness served you well with me as well as restaurant owners. I was initially drawn to your accent. '*Suivez moi*' sounds more sexy to me than 'Hey, move ya self.' This conversation gives me an idea.

Why don't we take advantage of your background and travel some-where where they speak French?"

"I like it. Bring it up when we get home. I will file it on an index card under 'T' for 'trip'." I broached the subject as soon as we returned and finished unpacking.

"What about the French travel destination I suggested in Gettysburg?"

"Where should we go? France is too far away. How about the Caribbean?"

"I've never been to Martinique. How about Martinique? I can check it out with my SUNY-GV friend Pamela Boriskovitch. She's the head of the Latin American Studies department, and she speaks French and knows a lot about the Caribbean."

"Boriskovitch is a Latina?"

"Her mother is Cuban and her father is Russian. I'll ask her about Martinique when I see her on campus tomorrow." I gave Pepe the *Boriskovitchian Caribbean Report*: "Pamela says that Martinique is beautiful and we should certainly go. She specifically suggests a hotel which has a great pool with an across-the-harbor view of Fort-de-France. She emphatically stated one proviso, however. She warned that you should not speak French to the black people there. The blacks in Martinique abhor the French. They will be hostile to you."

Pepe did not follow Pamela's advice. As soon as we checked into the sumptuous hotel she suggested, Pepe began to speak Parisi-an French. The black desk clerk, who was perfectly cordial to Ameri-can English-speaking me, glared at him. The Francophone Pepe fias-co intensified at dinner. Pepe, in French, asked the black waitress demanding questions about the menu. I then ordered in my New York English. She served me politely -- before she slammed Pepe's plate on the table.

"Maybe you should have listened to Pamela. The waitress obviously hates you; she thinks that you're from France. All of Mar-tinique's heavenly atmosphere will be ruined for me if I have to watch seething people express hostility towards you because of what your ancestors did." I wondered what our waitress would do if Honoré Amoreuse Le Pew the third took it upon himself to materi-alize and become our dinner guest.

"Pamela can't be right. I'm innocent. I never hurt these peo-ple. They can't hate me."

"But they do. Maybe Honoré Amoreuse Le Pew the third sailed to Martinique and mistreated black slaves. Obviously, our waitress thinks that this is the case. I hate the historical facts underlying her hostility. I also hate the fact that an innocent person is accused of the horrors that members of his tribe committed in the past. But, thus it is." When the waitress slammed Pepe's dessert plate on the table, I took matters into my own hands.

"*Il n'est pas Français. Il est né au Canada*," I informed her. I hoped that my fifth grade French would save the evening. My efforts failed. Pepe continued to speak Parisian French -- and the waitress continued to be rude to him. I was glad to return to New York.

Because I wanted to increase my SUNY-GV salary, I decided to go on the academic job market. My twenty page vitae includes four scholarly books, six anthologies, one novel (not including this one), numerous articles, and a plethora of lectures delivered throughout the world. But who is counting? No one. When it comes to academic job market success, vitae size does not matter. The most prized job candidates are young, gifted, and black. To say the least, being middle-aged, female, and white is not a plus. The academic job market has nothing to do with merit and everything to do with being monetarily cheap and expendable. Young scholars are routinely disposed of in the manner of so many used fast food containers. Adjunct professors, separate and unequal in relation to their full-time counterparts, are treated as migrant workers. I do not respect this exploitative system. When I went on the job market, my rebellious nature kicked in big-time. I resented the fact that all of my publications would get me nowhere. I responded by having a brainstorm involving juxtaposing my disdain for the system with my trip to Martinique. If the academic job market favored blacks, I would appear to be black. *Sans* magic.

And *sans* prevarication: as a married woman living under a patriarchal system, I was absolutely entitled to use my husband's last name. *Voila*. Faster than a speeding bullet, Sondra Lear could become Sondra Le Pew. Sondra Lear was automatically assumed to be Jewish; Sondra Le Pew could be a Francophone black, someone who hailed from, say, Martinique. Sondra Le Pew, to explain her New York accent, could claim that, as an infant, her parents left Martinique and brought her to Queens (Remembering Balabusta Brand-ex University Jewish Feminist Research Institute head Leona Rhinestone financially penalized me for not being an Ethiopian Jew, I contemplated claiming Sondra Le Pew hails from a marriage between a Martinique denizen and an Ethiopian. On second thought, I decided to go the completely Martinique route. Why complicate things?). People would immediately assume Jamaica, Queens, not Forest Hills. Name change accomplished. Accent accounted for. Onward to my vitae.

While trying to prepare a vitae appropriate for Sondra Le Pew, I experienced how Alice felt in Wonderland. Twelve pages was too long. One page was too short. How to settle upon a page length that would be just right? Honesty required black Sondra to share my educational history. Since it is perfectly kosher to omit information on one's vita, I started black Sondra's career with my post-Blackhole employment experience. Like me, black Sondra was a visiting professor in South Africa and Austria. Like me, black Sondra is employed at SUNY-GV.

Next category: publications. Transforming my vitae into black Sondra's vitae required a hatchet job. Although I could not fake her age and the dates when she received her degrees, I could shorten her publication record with impunity. Fewer publications would make Sondra cheaper to employ and, hence, easier to hire. I mercilessly cut nine pages from my vitae. Deleting four scholarly books was no sweat. My books were, in truth, nothing more than impediments which made me expensive -- that is, unemployable. Chop, chop. Fizz, fizz. Oh what a relief erasing one's books is? I'm not sure. When creating black Sondra, necessity was the mother of invention.

Some of my existing publications could believably emanate from black Sondra's pen. Not so for *Oy Pioneer!* The delete key chomped my vitae's reference to my Jewish feminist novel. *Au revoir, Oy Pioneer!* Black Sondra, like myself, could be writing an as-yet-untitled ethnic feminist novel. She, of course, shares my academic interests. I have written about Samuel Delany and Octavia Butler. I am contracted to produce the first critical anthology about black women and science fiction. *Voila*: Sondra Le Pew is an expert on black science fiction. On second thought, make that speculative fiction; science fiction is discriminated against. My job application letter would contain the truth, the whole truth, and nothing but the truth. I was not obligated to disclose that my experience in Martinique boiled down to a long weekend. The letter:

> Dear Department Head:
>
> I am a SUNY Buffalo Ph.D. who wishes to apply for your advertised position in Black Literature.
>
> My experience in Martinique has impacted my writing and research interests. Please know that I am presently writing an ethnic feminist novel. My research involves black speculative fiction. I have written articles about Samuel Delany and Octavia Butler. My critical anthology, the first study of black women speculative fiction writers, is in press.
>
> I thoroughly enjoyed my teaching experiences as a visiting professor in South Africa and Austria. I particularly appreciate my chances to engage with urban minority students as a faculty member at SUNY-GV.
>
> Thank you for your attention to my application.
>
> Sincerely,
> Sondra Le Pew

The letter is short, sweet and true and much more direct than my usual two-page description of my four books. Sondra Lear did not receive one interview in ten years; Sondra Le Pew immediately received five hundred interviews.

"Pepe, I'm having success on the job market."

"Really? How come?'

"I made a few changes. By the way, would you still love me if I had darker hair?"

"Suit yourself."

"What about darker skin?"

"What?"

"Darker skin. Would you love me with darker hair and darker skin?"

"Do I *vhat*? Do I love you? For five years my bed (and my chairs) were yours. For five years, I solved all of your computer problems. For five years, I put up with your mother. For five years, I navigated your ever-burgeoning clothing mountains. For two hours, I wore a *yarmulke* and a *talis* in the Forest Hills Jewish Center. Do I love you? If that's not love, *vhat* is?"

"It doesn't mean a thing. But even so, after five years, it's nice to know."

Extreme metamorphosis was in the air. Black Sondra seemed suddenly to be married to Jewish Pepe who sounded like a male *Quebeçois* version of Tevye's wife Goldie. This made perfect sense. *Oy Pioneer!* is about how I spent twenty years demanding "Matchmaker, matchmaker, make me a match, find me a find, catch me a catch." And I live in a world where matchmakers are an endangered species, yet. I was on my own as far as finding a husband was concerned. So, too, for finding my way as black Sondra. Husband-hunting is a well-worn path; passing as black Sondra was *terra incognito*. Never fear. I am an expert on the feminist lesbian separatist planet -- *terra incognito* incarnate. Passing as black Sondra would be no sweat.

Sweating is precisely what could cause me problems. My interview attire would consist of pants, boots, and a long-sleeved turtleneck shirt, and sunglasses (Black Sondra could not have big blue eyes). The MLA Convention was being held in San Diego. Dressing too warmly would enhance my sweating possibility and cause dire consequences. I could not risk the possibility that the brown theater makeup which covered my hands and face would begin to melt in mid-interview. The thaw could cause my black wig to slip off of my head. Yes, I was presenting myself as a speculative fiction expert. Still, it would be inappropriate for me to melt in the manner of the Wicked Witch of the West. "Don't sweat it" and "Don't let them see you sweat" are clichéd job interview advice. This advice now literally applied to me.

Following it was futile: I couldn't avoid sweating. I was, after all, wearing a too-heavy sweater, too much packed-on theater makeup, and a wig which functioned as a too-warm hat. What to do? Successfully landing a job as black Sondra was clearly a job for the Sondra clones. I had to call them in. At least Pepe was not home. He would not be able to deal with black Sondra *and* the Sondra clones. I took my job letter and placed it in the refrigerator -- with a postscript attached: "Dear Sondras, HELP!!!!"

Two white Sondras immediately materialized in the living room. They looked puzzled.

"We no longer resemble you. Your skin and hair color have changed. They are darker. Your genes and DNA have remained the same and, hence, so have we. Oh, by the way, we -- and you -- have not lost any weight," said a Sondra clone.

"My color change is fake, not biological. I'm wearing brown face makeup and a black wig."

"No wonder we don't look like the 'new' you. Why are you doing this?"

"Don't ask."

"Sondra, when you have to tell your extraterrestrial clones to 'Don't ask,' don't you think you have gone a little too far?"

"No. I'm merely fighting institutional discrimination. To do so most effectively, I need you to make a biological alteration that is beyond the means of current Earth scientific capabilities. Can you please turn off all my sweat glands in a manner which enables me to survive?"

"Why? Are you tired of your low salary as a scholar and novelist? Are you giving it all up to become a deodorant entrepreneur? That could work. You could call your deodorant formula manufactured by aliens *Secret*."

"*Secret* could fly. My great relationship with all of you clones aside -- in regard to extraterrestrials -- humans should keep themselves secret, mask their presence. Science writer Michael Lemonick says that no one on Earth should send out signals to let aliens know that we are here. His thinking: it would have been a big mistake for the Native Americans to send up a signal flare to direct Columbus. Sounds good. Since humans, with the exception of me, don't know from whom is out there in outer space, we should leave well enough alone. News about the existence of a feminist science fiction theorist's feminist clones would not be welcomed on this patriarchal planet. But enough of this. Please turn off my sweat glands."

"Sure. No sweat," said another Sondra clone reassuringly. "Let me use your computer." An image of my body appeared on screen. The Sondra clone typed "ban sweat glands," pressed the well-worn delete key, and pointed at me. A beam of light emerged from her outstretched finger. My sweat glands were nullified for three days.

"Anything else we can do for you?"

"No. Thank you. On second thought, maybe there is. Can you zap me over to the San Diego Hilton? I have to survive the five hundred interviews which will all take place during the next three days. I need to save my strength."

"Sure. And remember: you are always welcome to return to our starship."

My clones zapped me over to the Hilton and beamed back up. Disguised as black Sondra, with no sweat, I went to my first interview.

In early January, I reported the results of my job hunt to Pepe. "I've been offered positions as President of Berkeley, Brown, Harvard, Stanford, Yale -- and Blackhole State."

"Turn down all the offers. I like you as you are: a Manhattan resident who takes the subway to SUNY-GV. I don't want to leave New York. If you become a college president, you will be consumed with appointments while sitting on plush office furniture chairs -- and you will have no time to have sex appointments with me. I will not move to another city. Hell no, I won't go. And I don't want you to go either."

"Okay."

"Okay? I thought that you're a feminist. I thought that you'd never give up career advancement because of a husband. How do you explain your complacency?"

"I don't like to wear makeup. If I were a college president, I would have to wear makeup every day. I would also have to get dressed up. I don't like getting dressed up." I neglected to tell Pepe exactly how much makeup and body-covering clothing being college president black Sondra would require. In addition, the Sondra clones, in order to prevent me from expiring from never perspiring, would very soon have to turn my sweat glands back on. Being the president of a major university was definitely not something to die for. The black Sondra subterfuge was not sustainable. All of the college president offers were offers I had to refuse.

"Didn't you interview at Columbus University? Why didn't they offer to make you President of Columbus? At least, if you were president of Columbus, I wouldn't have to leave Manhattan. We could move to the Upper West Side. Maybe you could sometimes come home during the afternoon to have a sex appointment. Or, we could have an appointment in your presidential office. Wow, new-fangled chairs."

"I did interview at Columbus. Nothing happened. The Columbus English department, it turns out, wanted to hire a very high-powered white feminist theorist. In order to interest her, they offered her partner the presidency. You know how the spousal hiring thing works: all the usual procedures in relation to merit and fairness are suddenly dropped. The new Columbus president is a white female feminist theorist's transsexual husband." I didn't add that, in relation to Columbus University, my black Sondra masquerade got me nowhere. According to academic hiring rules, superstar whites take precedence over entry level blacks.

Resigning myself to remaining white Sondra of SUNY-GV, I politely declined all the positions I was offered. My letter read as follows.

> Dear Search Committee:
>
> Thank you for offering me a position as president of your college. I regret to inform you that your offer did not meet my particular needs. I am abdicating as president to remain in Manhattan with the man I love.
>
> Sincerely,
> Sondra Le Pew

Sondra Le Pew was never heard from again. No loss. Someone routinely called Mrs. Sondra Le Pew never existed. Dr. Sondra Lear would plod on in her true middle-aged, gifted, and Jewish form -- which was, from time to time, subject to alteration by her feminist clones and a horny vampire.

Let Me Entertain You, Or Performance Anxiety

My decision to remain white did not completely preclude professional metamorphosis. The publication of *Oy Pioneer!* signaled a career emphasis shift from literary scholar to novelist, a change which required me to master a completely new public performance mode. Reading a novel in public is a very different skill from presenting an academic paper. I was accustomed to delivering papers via monotone drone tone. Now, I had to interest audiences in characters such as Fred Bob, the Blackhole State redneck English department head from Hell. Pepe advised me to act out my protagonists' different voices.

I was able to successfully project a fake Southern accent into a microphone. This is not a stretcher. The problem: "Southern" was the only accent I could do. All of my accented characters sounded alike -- regardless of where they hailed from. Hence, Ilya, an Eastern European vampire, had the same speaking voice as Fred Bob the hillbilly. My verbal ineptitude was reasonable. I had, after all, spent years in Blackhole, Virginia, and zilch time in Transylvania. Who knew that Ilya would be miffed because I gave him the same accent as Fred Bob?

I stood behind a lectern podium during a reading at a Pennsylvania State university branch campus. I thought nothing of impersonating "Southern" Ilya as usual. The usual ended. Ilya was sitting in the audience with furrowed brow. He snapped his fingers. The whole room -- including Pepe -- went into suspended animation.

"You are depicting me incorrectly. It is bad enough that you are now married and you won't have sex with me anymore. I understand that you want to be loyal to your husband and there is now no room in your life to have antigravity flying sex. But making me

Southern is the limit. You are misrepresenting my national identity. I won't stand for the rape of my subjectivity lying down. Perfect your Eastern European accent. And do it immediately, if not sooner."

"Calm yourself, Ilya. This is not about you. The audience believes that you're a figment of my imagination. Who would think that I really had sex with a vampire? Certainly not Pepe. Audiences can't even fathom that your non-fantastic characteristics are real. Remember the part in *Oy Pioneer!* where you state that you must have sex with me immediately if not sooner because your sexuality is analogous to washing machine cycles? You argue that lack of sex causes your spin cycle to go awry. Who would believe that we had this conversation? Who would believe that a supernatural being recast himself as a washing machine? I told one audience that the washing machine/sex conversation really happened. They gasped. Pepe believes that I made up the part about having flying sex with a vampire. Please don't blow my cover. To contend with the supernatural competition, he might suspend a chair from the ceiling to simulate flying sex." Ilya kissed my hand and disappeared in a smoke cloud. The audience was immediately reanimated. As soon as I finished reading the flying vampire sex passage, two people stormed out of the auditorium. Unlike my similar response to Kurt Waldheim, they did not express their displeasure by clunking their clogs.

During the reception which followed my reading, I introduced Pepe to Dina Matza, the faculty member who had organized the event. Dina advised me not to worry about the couple who had left so abruptly. "They always leave whenever they feel that their conservative sensibilities have been insulted. They define 'insult' as all references to sex. Your fiction is sometimes hard to take. You're not at fault now, though."

"Her fiction is even hard for me to take," Pepe told Matza.

We analyzed the event during the drive home.

"Is Dina Matza Jewish?" Pepe asked.

"Of course. With a name like Matza, she has to be Jewish. In two weeks I'm doing a reading organized by Leah Bagelman. While surrounded by Dr. Matza and Dr. Bagelman, it's good that I'm not on Dr. Atkins' diet."

"Your fiction reading ability has improved greatly. But you should read more intensely. Sing out, Sondra. Let it all hang out. 'Let it all hang out' is correct colloquial English, *n'est-ce pas*? Neither Pepe nor I could foresee exactly how loose my readings would become -- or exactly what would hangout.

I was asked to perform *Oy Pioneer!* in a Greenwich Village night club. I got the gig because my SUNY-GV officemate knew someone who organized comic performances. After hearing about *Oy Pioneer!* he put me in touch with his contact. Hired on the spot, I was booked into a Greenwich Village venue which was a Japanese restaurant by day and a performance space by night. The compensation deal: I would be paid in free sushi. This payment method, albeit peculiar, made sense to me. The Indians gave Manhattan to the Dutch in exchange for twenty-four dollars' worth of trinkets. *Moi*, a fledgling Jewish feminist comic voice, would give a ten-minute performance in exchange for twenty-four free sushi pieces. This was a good deal. I like sushi -- especially free sushi. If my performance bombed, I could always chomp on my sushi and bid stand-up comedy *sayonara*.

To distract myself from the performance anxiety derived from being a scholar attempting to devise a comedic performance, I decided to attend a discussion between Eve Ensler and Grace Paley held at The New School. When Paley asked Ensler about being optimistic about women's place in the world, she answered in terms of washing machine imagery. "The situation is like a washing machine in the drying cycle. It goes haywire, is uncontrollable while it shakes up everything and you can't stop it. The washing machine drying cycle symbolizes the new era we women are on the verge of." I couldn't believe my ears. Ilya, as I have said, told me that I had to have sex with him because his body was like a washing machine. And now Ensler was providing a feminist version of Ilya's washing machine complaint. He had to hear Ensler. Luckily, I wore my red clogs to The New School (My brown clogs were at the shoemaker). I clicked them together. Ilya appeared and placed Ensler, Paley, and the entire audience in suspended animation. He likes suspended animation.

"Glad to see you, Ilya. I called you because you must hear Eve Ensler's version of your sex-and-washing-machine analogy. Her discourse is feminist, not phallocratic like yours."

"She has already articulated her washing machine verbiage."

"Can't you go into un-freeze and re-freeze mode and play back Ensler's lecture, like a tape?"

"I suppose so."

"Ilya caused Ensler to speak in a high-pitched too-fast manner discernible only to him. He then pressed his stop button and looked at me thoughtfully.

"I met the original Eve in the Garden of Eden. This Eve Ensler is interesting too. I have a passion for this new Eve."

"I know you will try to seduce her. She, however, might not be as open to a supernatural vampire as I am. Remember, my field is feminist science fiction; her field is talking vaginas."

Talking vaginas were obviously too much, even for Ilya. He immediately placed the auditorium on play and disappeared. The discussion between Ensler and Paley proceeded without a hitch.

"Excuse me. I'll be right back. I'm going to the rest room," I heard Paley say to Ensler at the end of their public conversation.

I followed Paley into the bathroom and parked myself directly in front of her chosen toilet stall. I stared into a mirror in order to unobtrusively watch Paley's closed stall door located directly behind me. The door opened. Paley emerged. Before I went in for the predetermined seemingly chance encounter, I gave her time to wash her hands. I pounced when she put hand to paper towel.

"Hello, Ms. Paley. What a wonderful surprise to meet you by accident in the bathroom! I don't mean to be intrusive. Can I tell you about my new novel, *Oy Pioneer!*?" I reached into my backpack for an *Oy Pioneer!* flyer (I never leave home without them). I placed one in Paley's now-dry hand.

"This looks very interesting. I'm glad to know about your work."

"I'm getting up all my courage to ask if you would review it."

"I have to decline. I don't have time to read all the new stuff that's published."

"But I'm trying to write in your tradition. Ms. Paley, I have to tell you the truth. Because I want your review so much, I purposefully followed you into this bathroom. I feigned surprise when your toilet stall door opened. How many new Jewish feminist novelists have the balls to stalk you in a woman's bathroom? I bet that I'm the first and only one. I have extreme *chutzpah*. I want a review from you more than anything. Please say yes."

"Yes. Write to me in Vermont." Victory. *Chutzpah* gets me everywhere -- even outside Grace Paley's toilet stall. There should be no limit to feminist *chutzpah*. The washing machines in spin cycle should fly. If Ensler can speak out in the voice of talking vaginas, I can ratchet up my *chutzpah* quotient. I can be even more daring than usual. My stand-up comedy routine became clear to me as I watched Paley pocket my flyer and exit the bathroom. Mama Rose told Gypsy to "sing out." I could become the first feminist theorist stripper.

I informed Pepe that he was required to attend my performance. "I've been asked to do a comedy routine at a Village sushi restaurant. You're coming. I'm on at midnight."

"Midnight is past my bedtime. You know that every night I go to sleep at ten precisely."

"Please come with me. I'm going to do a striptease. You can't miss it."

"Are you sure that stripping is decorous?"

"We're talkin' the Village, not a Parisian finishing school."

"I've survived the fact that my wife has published a novel which depicts her as the slut of the planet. I suppose that I can also survive her new incarnation as a feminist theorist stripper. Okay, I'll go. But only this once. I don't want to make a habit of deviating from my sleeping routine."

The sushi restaurant was dark and packed. "Heeeere's Sondra," the emcee announced. I appeared on stage carrying a brown leather briefcase and wearing a tweed jacket, black wool pants, black pumps -- and my black Sondra wig. The audience did not yet know that my outward attire -- which once served as my MLA Convention job candidate Halloween costume -- covered a sartorial *pièce-de-résistance*: a skin-tight gold *lamé* bodysuit. For two full minutes, without moving and without speaking, I stood in front of the audience and stared dead on. They wondered how the schoolmarm nerd who faced them, a woman who made Ruth Buzzy look like a hot babe, could make them laugh. Since it is impossible for me to remain silent for more than two minutes, I launched my monologue.

"Good evening. My name is Dr. Sondra Lear. I'm an English professor. The audience cringed. "More specifically, I specialize in feminist theory. The audience gasped in horror. "I know that you don't expect a literary theorist -- especially a feminist one -- to be funny. But you're wrong. First impressions can be deceiving. You can't tell a book by its cover," I said as I yanked the black wig off my head. My very-much-in-need-of-a-haircut much-too-thick shoulder-length hair made its appearance. Ruth-Buzzy-clone me now looked like a poster girl for *Hair*. "See. Fooled ya. Growin'. Flowin'. Long as I can grow it -- my hair. When I keep my twice-yearly haircut appointments, the beautician revs up the lawn mower she keeps just for me. My husband helped me to prepare for this evening. 'Sing out, Sondra,' he insisted. Sing out, Sondra? Sing out, Louise is more compelling. So, hello boys -- and girls too. Even though my name is Sondra, not Louise, 'Let me entertain you. Let me make you smile.' I decorously stood in front of college classrooms for years. Enough already. It's time for me to let lose my inner stripper."

I took off my tweed jacket, slung it over my shoulder, and traversed across the stage to allow the audience best to see my big breasts outlined beneath the skin-tight gold *lamé* bodysuit. "You thought that feminist literary theorists are frigid, unfunny ice maidens. Ha. Were you wrong. 'I can do a few tricks. Some old and then some new tricks. I'm very versatile.'"

Gesturing toward my briefcase I said, "Bet you think that I have a scholarly paper or an academic journal in here. Ha. Wrong again." I reached into the briefcase and flamboyantly removed two white feather dusters. I took one in each hand, held them over my head, and then exaggeratedly swung them back and forth in front of my breasts. "It's logical for me to carry pasties in my briefcase *à la* Gypsy Rose Lee; I was a gypsy scholar. Gypsy's colleague said 'Well, I do it with a horn.' Well I do it with feathers." I swung the feather dusters even more fervently. The audience applauded. "You ain't -- have you ever heard a literary theorist, feminist or otherwise, say 'ain't' -- seen nothin' yet. You're gonna see more. Before your very eyes, Dr. Sondra Lear, Ph.D. is gonna take it off, take it off -- but not take it all off."

I dropped the feather dusters and reached for my pants zipper. I started to unzip. "Do ya know what word Erica Jong famously paired with 'zipless?' No? Well, I do. See. Being a feminist literary theorist does have practical uses. No ziplessness for me. Boys -- and girls -- I'm ready to zip. I'm zipping. I'm zipping right now. Let 'er rip. Thank god these pants won't rip from being too tight. I've been on a diet. Weight loss is a consummation devoutly to be wished (I know from *Hamlet* too) for a middle-aged woman -- especially for one appearing in front of a packed house attired in a skin-tight jumpsuit." I stepped out of my pants and stood in my jumpsuit. "Yes, I am *zaftig*. But all the *zaft* (since Yiddish Is not my field, I feel free to take liberties) is still in all the right places."

The audience applauded enthusiastically. I bowed deeply as I closed my monologue. "Don't think it's easy to be a feminist theorist, especially a middle-aged one, who looks as toned as this? Feminist theorists don't get much exercise. I mean what is it that I do every day? I stand and teach and I sit and read and write. My time's up. This is my cue to skidoo. That's not feminist theory jargon. Goodnight, folks." I gathered my clothes, briefcase, and feather dusters and exited stage right -- neither bare nor pursued by a bear. That goes for a feminist talking horse, clones, and a displaced wildebeest. My present reality was more onerous than these business-as-usual scenarios: I had to face Pepe.

"What did you think?"

"You were very interesting. It appears that you have taken learning to 'sing out, Louise' to heart. How long did they want you to perform?"

"Eight minutes."

"You short-changed them. I timed you. You spoke for precisely six minutes and twenty-two seconds. In the future, you need to work on your timing and speak for exactly the required time. Precision is all-important. It's late. Let's retrieve your sushi payment and go home."

"Good idea. I want you to be rested for tomorrow night's activity."

"Don't tell me about it now. I deal with one day at a time. Tell me about tomorrow tomorrow. Not now."

Tomorrow, as was to be expected, dawned. I met Pepe on the sofa to begin our daily organizational consultation meeting.

"I'm afraid to ask. But what's on the agenda for this evening?"

"I am scheduled to give a reading from *Oy Pioneer!* at the City University of New York Graduate Center with Wendy Wasserstein. My friend Charlotte Frick is an event coordinator there. She arranged for me and Wasserstein to do a benefit reading for the Grad Center Child Care Center. You can't miss my reading with Wasserstein. Will you come?"

"Okay. I never wanted to marry an artist. You didn't tell me when I married you that you would drag me to your fiction readings. You also didn't tell me that you would stop cooking *kasha varnishkes*. You deployed *kasha varnishkes* as a trap to lure me into the marriage. This is my fate. No *kasha*. Multitudinous performances. I'll come with you."

"Thanks. I'll need you for moral support. It will be difficult for a first-time novelist like me to hold the stage with Wasserstein. The Grad Center president and provost will be there too. I can handle it. I have the novel-reading thing down pat by now. I'm not nervous. At the very least, I won't have to strip at a Grad Center event. I don't think that the president and provost, not to mention etiquette loving Charlotte, would suffer stripping at a Child Care Center benefit gladly. After last night, I will be relieved to return to the normal public performance realm." The near future would reveal that I had spoken too soon.

I entered the Grad Center's Skylight Room and greeted Wasserstein.

"Good to meet you, Ms. Wasserstein. I admire your work and I'm honored to appear with you. I will be reading from my first novel."

"Congratulations on your publication. I look forward to hearing you."

"You, of course, know that first novelists need all the help they can get."

"Yes, of course."

"I hope that I am not being presumptuous. Would you be willing to consider writing a review for me?"

"No. I can't. I don't have time." I knew that, unlike my recent experience with Grace Paley, following Wendy Wasserstein into the bathroom would get me nowhere.

"That's fine. I absolutely understand." I lied. Wasserstein's definitive "no" was not fine. I did not understand. Once upon a time, Wendy Wasserstein, and all present celebrity writers, were fledgling authors just like me. Some famous writer must have given Wasserstein a helping hand. She should act in kind. She should be open to helping a fellow Jewish female writer of her generation. I was so angry, I wished that I could turn Wasserstein into a frog. Faster than a speeding bullet, the truth hit me. I did have the means to turn Wendy Wasserstein into a frog -- or anything else I saw fit to ask to be conjured.

As this thought entered my mind, I smiled at Wasserstein and watched Grad Center president Laurette Leibowitz take microphone in hand to begin the evening (Laurette Leibowitz and Hadassah Le Pew could benefit from swapping first names. This swap would enable my most feisty *belle soeur* better to fit in with all of her "ette" named sisters). One can smile and smile and be a devil. Or, more personally, I can click my red clogs and click my red clogs and cause my guardian angel vampire to appear (Okay, guardian angels aren't Jewish. But ya gotta do what ya gotta do). I just happened to have the clogs in my briefcase. One can never be too careful, after all. I wouldn't dream of performing in front of a celebrity author, a provost, and a university president sans red clogs.

The audience applauded after Wasserstein finished reading from *Shiksa Goddess*. President Leibowitz gave me a gracious introduction. I stepped in front of the lectern -- with red clogs and without feathers. No one noticed when I clicked my lectern-hidden red clogs together. Ilya appeared. As ever, he froze the audience.

"Sondra I'm always glad to come when called. But what now?"

"I'll tell you in a minute. I just have to make sure Pepe is frozen solid. As I have let you know, he would be a little perturbed if he knew his wife fraternized with a vampire. He can hardly deal with my new role as a novelist. Are you sure Pepe is frozen?"

"Of course. Do you think I would do a half-assed audience-freezing job?"

"I trust you. But one can never be too careful. You know all the trouble I went to find a husband. I don't want to rock the boat. Bear with me while I double-check." I walked to the back of the room where Pepe was seated. I poked him with my pen tip. I yelled at the top of my lungs: "I'm inviting all your siblings and all their kin to live in our apartment. I'm mounting a new thrift-shop-clothing-pile mountain to greet them upon arrival. I'm getting a Great Dane." Pepe did not respond. "Yup. You're right, Ilya. Pepe is frozen -- solid."

"I told you so. Now what is it that you need?"

"Fairy dust."

"Fairy dust? There are limits. I'm a perpetually horny vampire, not a fairy. I'm almost afraid to ask. But why in Hell do you need fairy dust?"

"I'm giving a reading with Wendy Wasserstein. I want to make Wendy fly. Don't you dare try to have flying sex with her."

"She's not my type. Making Wendy fly makes perfect sense. I should never have asked." Ilya snapped his fingers. He placed a bag of fairy dust in my hands. He snapped his fingers again. He disappeared.

"Wait. Ilya. Come back!" I screamed while frantically clicking my clogs.

"Sondra, even though you won't have sex with me anymore, I put up with you because you're a good person and I treasure my memories of you as a great fuck. But you're becoming a pest. What's the matter now?"

"What am I supposed to do with a room full of frozen people? I don't know how to un-suspend suspended animation. Fairy dust makes people fly. It doesn't function like antifreeze. This is a procedural irregularity, as the frozen provost in the front row can tell you. I might also need the forget-zapper thing."

"Sorry. You're right. I should not have dashed off without first giving you all the necessary magical accoutrements. Here, take this water-filled vial. Bye."

"Wait. You still can't go. I have no idea how to work this water vial. Despite my forays into the fantastic, I'm still a normal, mortal human being. I can't use a magic water vial to nullify fairy dust and bring people out of suspended animation. This was not part of the SUNY Buffalo English Ph.D. program -- even though Buffalo has the most far-out liberal English department in the country. Leslie Fiedler and Norman N. Holland did not teach me anything about fairy dust. You can't assume that I have the magic contraption expertise you take for granted."

"I must be more patient. First, deploy the fairy dust. Then, *spritz* the flying people as well as the audience with the water. After you *spritz*, everyone will forget everything and return to normal."

"*Spritz*? Since when do *goyish* vampires mention *spritzing*? The label on the vial says 'holy water.' *Spritzing* with holy water is not kosher."

"Details. Details. I'll unfreeze the audience. You have your directions. Deploy the fairy dust. *Spritz.* 'Bye." The Skylight Room's no smoking sign did not hold water *vis-à-vis* Ilya's usual smoky departure mode.

I sprinkled the fairy dust on Wendy, President Leibowitz, and myself. The Empire State Building's spire, visible outside the Skyline Room's glass ceiling, backgrounded our activity. Neither Wendy Wasserstein, President Leibowitz, nor I are thin -- to say the least. Picture three hefty Jewish women hovering overhead within view of the Empire State Building. The scenario violated Pepe's sense of propriety.

"Sondra, what are you, Wasserstein, and President Leibowitz doing? Come down from there," he screamed while craning his neck upward.

"We're flying. Oh, what lovely fun. Watch us everyone. Take a look and see how easily it's done. We're flying."

"Come down immediately, if not sooner. I told you that you can do whatever you want when I'm not with you. This is not now the case. You're my wife. I don't want to be associated with someone who causes a celebrity author and a college president to fly. Furthermore, to say the least, none of you are thin. What if one of you falls on someone's head and squashes them? You're being reckless. Why are you behaving improperly?"

I wondered what Pepe would think if Jonathan Goodman's colleague Penelope the Fat were hovering with us.

"There's a glass ceiling in the Skylight Room. Women hit glass ceilings all the time. Wasserstein and President Leibowitz have shattered the glass ceiling. If a woman Pulitzer Prize winner and a woman college president are seen flying beneath a glass ceiling, it becomes perfectly clear exactly how untenable the very real glass ceiling is. As for myself, I'm no fiction writer comparable to Wasserstein; I'm no college president. But -- as a woman, a feminist, and a science fiction specialist -- my head is sore from continued glass ceiling-hitting. My head hurts. The success I enjoyed while wearing a black wig did not cushion the blows to my head. Meanwhile, in terms of the implication of this flying thing for our relationship, there is no big dog named Nana to make everything right. You won't let me get a dog -- especially a large sheepdog."

"What did I do to deserve witnessing your complicity with this appalling public spectacle? Again, why are you doing this?"

"Would you believe that I lost my shadow? Would you believe that I'm sick of being judged in terms of the image my body presents. Or my color. Or my age. Or my sex. My body and the social shadow which must always appear in its wake are not the sole means of defining me. I should be scrutinized in terms of the merit of my work. My work, though, functions as a mere shadow in relation to my body. Okay, I now know that I staged this entire scene to get this matter off of my chest. I feel better now. I have to put everyone back to normal. Even though no one will remember what has taken place, I suppose I should apologize. I am a mere shadow. I did not mean to offend."

I *spritzed* Wasserstein and the President with the magic water contained in the vial Ilya provided. They landed smoothly in their respective chairs. The audience, believing that they had thoroughly enjoyed a normal evening listening to Wasserstein and Lear, applauded. My friend Gary Shapiro favorably reviewed the event in his *New York Sun* column. No one was worse for the evening -- with the exception of Pepe. I joined him after saying Goodbye to Wasserstein and President Leibowitz.

"You look crestfallen. What's wrong?"

Pepe pointed to his shirt. Do you see this little blue pen mark on my sleeve? It wasn't there before. I can't imagine how it got there. My shirt is now unwearable. Perfectionist rule number 806.9 : throw out all shirts that have imperceptible stains. I clearly see 5.5 specks on your jacket. What's their source?"

"Fairy dust flotsam."

"Bravehearts: Men In Skirts" Or Jews 'Я' Us?

No one throws fairy dust at a gay marriage. What follows is the tale of how, during this time of gay marriage controversy, I was not hired for an academic job because my metrosexual husband refused to pass as my lesbian partner.

Why the need to ask Pepe to participate in a masquerade? Very simple: as I have emphasized, exotic minorities (you know -- Eskimos, Native Americans, and I suppose Swazis) are the darlings of the academic job market. The more exotic the minority, the better to please a search committee -- i.e. a transgendered Eskimo would be a more highly prized job candidate than a straight Eskimo. Jews, especially dime-a-dozen middle-aged white heterosexual feminist Jews like me, need not apply. Unable to present myself as an Eskimo, a Native American, or -- in light of the black Sondra disguise disaster -- as a Swazi of any gender or sexual orientation, my best chance for salary-enhancing job-acquiring success rests upon being perceived as a Jewish lesbian. Confronted with a job market which places ethnicity and sexual proclivity before merit, who could blame me for capitalizing on the fact that search committees immediately conclude that a feminist lesbian planet expert is a lesbian, not a newlywed husband hunter? Hence, during the following phone call (when the caller automatically assumed that I am a lesbian), I decided to play the lesbian card.

"Hello. Professor Lear? This is Tricia Cox of the San Clemente State University Women's Studies department. We want to interview you. Would you and your partner like to undertake a campus visit?"

The word "partner" resounded. I made a snap decision to comply with what was obviously this job's most important requirement.

"Why certainly, Tricia. My partner and I look forward to meeting you."

"Wonderful. Do you and she have any particular dietary requirements?"

"She and I would be happy with a generic California sprout salad." I began to wonder if Pepe liked sprouts.

"Let me be frank. My colleagues and I are quite excited about your candidacy. We want to do everything we can to welcome you and your partner. What, by the way, is her professional expertise?"

"What? What? We seem to have a bad connection. The doorbell is ringing. My partner called the exterminator because roaches believe they own our kitchen. You know how it is in Manhattan apartments. New Yorkers are always in a hurry. Just think of all the roach killing the exterminator who is at this very moment standing outside my door has on his calendar for today alone. I can't keep him waiting in the hall. Gotta go. Just find some nice kosher sprouts for me and my partner -- and please don't house us in a roach motel. Bye."

Saved by the ringing doorbell even though no bells are ringing. So much for naming my nonexistent lesbian partner Judy Holliday -- despite the fact that Holliday was a Jewish actress who hailed from Manhattan. Both she and Lauren Bacall went to high school with my mother -- but who's counting. For whom does the bell toll? It tolls for me. How could I ever convince Pepe to wear a skirt to play my lesbian lover during the campus interview? I was doomed. But maybe not. Hope emerged as Pepe headed for our sometimes-truly-roach-inhabited kitchen to prepare lunch.

"There's a great new show at the Metropolitan Museum Costume Institute. How would you like to see "Bravehearts: Men In Skirts?"

"Men in skirts are not my thing. Remember, I'm an art historian, a visual person. When I go to the Met, I want to peruse Picassos and van Goghs -- and only superior Picassos and van Goghs. I absolutely do not want to see men in skirts. I always advocate dressing appropriately."

"I most certainly do know your feelings about always wearing unobtrusive attire. I didn't forget what happened when we were in the Philadelphia Marriott attending that science fiction fan conference. The fire alarms blared at five A.M. while details about fire investigation emanated from the loudspeaker. Throughout the entire commotion, you calmly asked what constitutes proper hotel evacuation attire. I'm sorry that I lost my patience and sarcastically advised you to throw on a silk designer parachute. But I kept my cool when you took me literally and asked where one could buy a silk designer parachute in Philadelphia. I logically suggested *Parachutes 'Я' Us*."

"Just because I took your parachute suggestion seriously, don't think I'm amenable to attending a men-in-skirts exhibition. *Non*. I'm not interested."

My response to what seemed to be a *fait accompli*: I hung my head to try to look as sorrowful as possible.

"Please."

"Okay. Maybe men in skirts can be artistically compelling. I'll accompany you. Don't bring it up again."

Pepe, after spending an hour contemplating what appropriately to wear to a men-in-skirts exhibition, was ready to venture to the Met. Upon arrival, as we stood in front of a male skirted mannequin whose knees were particularly knobby, I could no longer skirt my pressing issue.

"So, what do you think of men in skirts? Could you see yourself wearing one?"

"*Non. Jamais.* Don't bring it up again."

"Open your mind Pepe. Skirts are very practical   especially in hot weather. Wouldn't you rather wear a skirt in the summer? A skirt would allow air to flow between your legs. Marilyn Monroe wasn't *schvitzing* when she stood over the grating."

"Some like it hot."

"Men in skirts can assuage male *schvitzing*. Just for argument's sake, if you traveled to, say, Death Valley, wouldn't you rather fight male sartorial convention than *schvitz*?"

"*Non*. When I taught in California, I dressed to fit in. I was resplendent in my chartreuse paisley shoulder-padded suit. I threw out that outlandish suit immediately upon arriving in black attire-obsessed Manhattan. Men in skirts are even beyond California taste."

"If you wore a skirt in California, you could start a trend. You could be famous. You could help humanity. Pepe, you could be the father of male *schvitzing* cessation."

"*Non. Jamais. Pas pour moi.*"

"Does your response mean that you won't help me to land a Women's Studies job? I need to appear to be a lesbian lesbian planet expert. I need you to wear a skirt to impersonate my lesbian partner during my campus visit."

"*Jamais* up the wazoo."

"Maybe the Californians will hold the interview in a hot tub. How about wrapping a towel around your waist, wearing a bikini top, and putting a mop on your head to represent a woman's worst bad-hair-day nightmare?"

Knowing that it was time to throw in the towel, I phoned Tricia Cox.

"I must decline the campus visit."

"Why? You're such a perfect match for our department. You and your partner would love it here."

"My partner does not want to move to California. She would not fit in with your community."

"How can you be so sure? We would welcome her potential diversity. Is she by any chance an Eskimo, a Native American, or a Swazi? Has she always been a woman? We could not be more open to difference. Some of our best friends are Jews. Why do you think we would object to her?"

"She doesn't dress right. Please excuse me. The exterminator is here for a return *spritz.* Our roaches recognize his footsteps. They're *schvitzing* and *kvetching* in their nests as we speak. No Manhattan denizen takes *schvitzing* and *kvetching* roaches lightly. My partner and I are off to shop for skirts. If you ever come to Manhattan, I suggest that you patronize *Skirts 'R' Us.* Great store. 'Bye."

My decision was for the best. I couldn't expect Pepe to spend his life being one of the "men in skirts" to enable me to meet the academic job market's exotic diversity requirement. I would just have to resign myself to succeeding as my true self: a Jewish feminist separatist lesbian science fiction planet expert and debut novelist who recently married a perfectionist *goyish* male alien. *Oy* feminist planets. I mean, if Katharine Hepburn never wore a skirt, why should Pepe? I would have to resign myself to treating the job market as a come-as-you-are party. Instead of trying to transform my husband into a lesbian, I could simply present myself as a Jewish fiction writer. Creative writing is a much hotter field than lesbian planets.

Noticing that the Knitting Factory, one of the coolest performance venues in Manhattan, was holding a marathon fiction reading, I tried to interest program planner Yalan Papillons in *Oy Pioneer!* I didn't care that, when Papillons initially contacted me via email, I could discern neither this person's sex nor ethnic background. Regardless of whether or not this female or male was from France, Israel, or Haiti, Papillons proved to be an excellent planner: I was unexpectedly offered the chance to curate an event devoted completely to Jewish fiction.

"If you bring in an audience of four hundred people, you can have the main stage," Papillons declared.

Papillons might as well have asked me to bring the Wicked Witch of the West's broom to sweep the stage. As a debut novelist, I kiss the ground when even a handful of people attend one of my readings. I couldn't in good conscience tell the planner that my reading night at the Knitting Factory would be different from all other nights in relation to audience dearth.

"I can't promise four hundred people. But I can provide superb Jewish writers."

"Are you sure you can deliver Jewish writers?"

"Certainly. All I have to do is call *Jews 'Я' Us* and order takeout from the Jewish writer's menu. I am well acquainted with Jewish writers listed under Group A and Group B."

"Fine. We have a done deal. I'll just give you a smaller room."

While presenting Pepe as being out of central casting for "Braveheart: Men In Skirts" was a mission too impossible, portraying myself as a Jewish writer was just right. I generated a title for the Knitting Factory event: "Mazel Tomes: The Jewish Write Stuff." With title established and event under construction, I was off to attend a reading for *The Believer,* the cool new hot literary journal devoted to smart writing about fiction, music, and art which Heidi Julavits edits.

I closely encountered literary "it girl" Julavits holding ultra-cool court (hot Julavits was definitely not *schvitzing*) in front of a filled auditorium.

"Would you like to participate in a Knitting Factory reading?" I asked the tall, thin, blonde, blue-eyed Julavits.

"Yes." Her affirmative answer certainly improved upon Pepe's "*non.*"

"'Yes?' Please don't say you will participate unless you really mean it."

"I do." It took twenty-five years of husband-hunting before I heard Pepe say those very words. But, as I have explained, my interminable husband search is another story. Dismissing husband-hunting memories, I immediately discerned that Julavits was someone to be trusted. I, however, wasn't sure what to believe in regard to whether or not she's Jewish. Did I think that this Eastern European-surnamed woman, someone who resembled a poster child for a stereotypical *shiksa* incarnate, could appropriately participate in "Mazel Texts?" I could see it now: I would be ostracized from the *Jews 'Я' Us* writing community for passing a *shiksa* writer off as a Jewish writer. Then it hit me. A Jewish woman who suffers in the job market because she isn't a transgendered Ethiopian Eskimo should be open to including a potential *shiksa* in a Jewish literary reading.

I simply changed the event's title: "Mazel Tomes: The Jewish Write Stuff (With A Potential *Shiksa* Thrown In)" was born. Despite Julavits's undisclosed religious background, The Knitting Factory's Jewish fiction night was resoundingly successful. The audience applauded the now-close-knit group of accomplished writers I had assembled using talent, not ethnicity, as a first priority. Pepe, wearing a black suit and black turtle neck, applauded with the most enthusiasm. I would like to think that Judy Holliday and Katharine Hepburn gazed down at my Jewish reading (which might or might not include a *shiksa)* approvingly from some nondenominational place in the sky where talent and merit are the most important criteria. Bravehearts, after all, are nonsectarian: Scotty could appropriately beam up his Jewish starship Captain while wearing a skirt. (Since I just discussed Julavits, this is no time even to think about Scottywitz. Sara, as far as I am concerned, is not an 'it' girl. And Julavits is definitely not to be counted among the Austrian Heidis.)

Last but not least: I had a new brainstorm relating to enhancing my job prospects. The real world, unlike a feminist separatist lesbian science fiction planet, is a discriminatory patriarchy which perpetuates a reward system based upon racial, religious, and gender categories. Marriage to Pepe provides a new means for me to counter the fact that the job market does not favor middle-aged Jewish feminists. Although membership in the groups comprising Eskimos, Native Americans, and Swazis will forever elude me, as Mrs. Pepe Le Pew, I'm eligible to become a Canadian citizen. All the wonderful universities in all the desirable Canadian metropolitan areas (locations devoid of cows) give first employment preference to Canadians. While these universities would never consider American Dr. Lear, they would welcome Canadian Mrs. Le Pew.

Potentially saved by the wedding bells -- i.e. the combination of a Ph.D. and a Mrs. Degree authenticating my marriage to an alien, a Canadian citizen. Such is the way of the real world. No wonder I choose to immerse myself in science fiction's feminist separatist utopian planets. There's no place like home? Is Dorothy a Jewish name?

Angels in Barnes & Noble

The name Dorothy is nonsectarian. A Dorothy could appropriately be off to see that specific wizard of ours: the Wizard of *Oy*. Leona Rhinestone, in contrast, is a shining example of a Jewish appellation. Leona is no Patricia Cox. She phoned to make me an offer I couldn't refuse.

"Leona Rhinestone here. I would like to interview you in regard to your application to be a scholar in residence at the Balabusta Brand-ex University Jewish Feminist Research Institute. I am the head of the Institute -- and I am married to the president of the university. That is to say, I am the Queen of Brand-ex. What Leona wants at Brand-ex, Leona gets. I wanted a feminist research institute. So hubby gave me a building to house it. I want to interview you. If I like you, you're in. I will be in New York tomorrow. Where can we meet?"

Finally, after all my years teaching in Germany and the Austria -- after all my masquerade attempts to get a job via appearing as something that I'm not -- I had the chance to be welcomed as a Jew at a Jewish university. Goodbye face makeup to appear as a black. Goodbye dressing Pepe in a skirt to appear as a lesbian. *Au revoir* to convincing Pepe to return to Canada. Shalom authentic Jewish me.

"The chance to participate in a Jewish feminist research institute strikes me as a heaven. I'm very interested. Can we meet at the Upper West Side Barnes & Noble?"

"Sure. See you at noon."

I threw my black body makeup into the kitchen garbage can, exited the apartment, and made my way to Barnes & Noble. Leona was twenty minutes late. I tried to relax over a cup of coffee in the bookstore's café. Suddenly, I heard a loud cracking noise emanating from the ceiling. As I moved my eyes upward from my coffee cup, I noticed that all the Barnes & Noble patrons were placed in suspended animation. I was so mad at Ilya and the Sondras. How could they mess around with my temporal reality when I was about to have a job interview? I panicked when I realized that Ilya and the Sondras could not be at fault. I had neither clicked my red clogs nor put a note in the café's refrigerator. The ceiling cracked open and the crack became increasingly wider. The large ceiling gap enabled moon light to shine directly into the café. I could see it now: I was on the verge of adding a werewolf to my supernatural animal menagerie. What did I need with a werewolf? Ms. Ed would not suffer a werewolf gladly; a werewolf could eat Norris. Pepe, who had forbidden me to get a dog, would not welcome a werewolf. He would say that we have no room for one. These trepidations became immediately irrelevant: I saw a white-robed, winged female figure suspended between the moon and the café floor.

"Hello Sondra. I, Queen Leona Rhinestone of Brand-ex University, have come to bring you to academic heaven." She snapped her fingers. A ladder appeared held in place by another white-robed, winged female figure.

"This is my Balabusta Brand-ex University Jewish Feminist Research Institute co-director, Rhoda Morgenstern. I fundraise, and Rhoda generates scholarship. She's writing a book on intermarriage."

"Intermarriage. Great. I'm intermarried -- to an alien."

"Is he Jewish?"

"No. He's French Canadian. For the record, Jewish French Canadians are rarer than feminist lesbian planet experts. But that's another story."

"Silence. I am in the middle of *my* story." Leona flapped her wings in consternation. Rhoda grasped the ladder harder.

"Climb this ladder. Enter the Jewish feminist research institute I have created with the help of my sidekick Rhoda."

When I was a Visiting Professor at an Austrian university, my feminist colleagues never required me to climb ev'ry mountain or ford ev'ry stream. Two Jewish feminist angels were now asking me to climb a ladder to ascend to Jewish feminist academic heaven.

"Sure thing," I said as I placed my foot on the first rung.

I've spent my professional life trying to climb the academic success ladder -- an academic misfit's mission impossible, rather analogous to a female Jew striving to become a priest. I say this because the success ladder's rungs were always made increasingly steeper for me. How could I believe that two academics -- even Jewish feminist academics -- were suddenly offering me the chance to enter academic heaven? There's no such thing as academic heaven. And then it clicked: there is also no such thing as Jewish angels -- and ditto for a Jewish heaven replete with pearly gates. The Jewish angels I was encountering in Barnes & Noble smacked of being decidedly unkosher. They could be golems. But whoever heard of golems in America? What if Leona and Rhoda were evil spirits? Or, the dark side of the Force? Or, winged, white-clad angels in sheep's clothing? Possibilities for supernatural *tsuris* from hell (especially the academic kind) were endless. This was a matter beyond the purview of a mere mortal; this was a job for the Sondra clones. How to summon them without ruffling the feathers on Leona and Rhoda's wings?

"This ladder is very high and steep. I'm going to stick my head in the café's refrigerator to find a refreshing cold energy drink. Be right back." I surreptitiously removed a discarded reading event flyer from the garbage and used it to scrawl a note: "Dear Sondras, Help! Love, Sondra." I placed the note in the café fridge -- and hoped for the best. Six Sondras clad in skin-tight gold *lamé* bodysuits and brandishing phasers set on kill appeared. They at once looked *zaftig* and formidable.

"Here we come to save the day. That means that more mighty Sondras could be on the way. What can we do for you?" said the Sondra in charge.

"Jewish feminist angels in Barnes & Noble are trying to force me to climb to academic heaven. I don't trust them. That's why I called you in."

"Rightly so."

The Sondras gazed up at Leona and Rhoda, suspended in midair, and pointed the phasers at their heads. The exceedingly perturbed Jewish angels furiously flapped their wings to express their displeasure.

"Let my people, that is to say Sondra, not climb to academic heaven. Let her not go," ordered a phaser set on stun toting Sondra.

"Never. I will get the specific Jewish feminist science fiction scholar I came for. Jewish feminist science fiction scholars are in short supply. I want Sondra, not that Scottish slut Sara Scottywitz.

Hell hath no fury like a Jewish feminist academic Balabuster scorned," snarled Leona.

"You are powerless against the force of Sondra's extraterrestrial clones. Surrender, Leona," responded all the Sondra clones in unison.

"Never."

The phasers fired. Leona and Rhoda evaporated. The rupture in the Barnes & Noble ceiling closed.

"Did you kill them?" I asked my clones.

"No. They will return in their normal non-supernatural form. Your interview will proceed in a usual fashion. Bye."

I anticipated experiencing interview rewind as I stood against the Barnes & Noble mezzanine-level café railing scanning the selling floor below. The patrons stepped aside to make way for the woman who had just entered the store. She was impressive looking in that she was tall with short cut salt and pepper hair. In fact, she looked like a normal handsome woman -- with one exception. Her skin-tight sleeveless jersey black dress was covered with an ermine-trimmed floor-length cape. I also noticed her diamond tiara. A rather nondescript woman carried her cape train. I had taught in Cape Town; I could deal with a cape train.

"Excuse me. Are you Leona Rhinestone?"

"Yes. I am Leona Rhinestone, the great and powerful. That is to say, I am the founder of the Balabusta Brand-ex University Jewish Feminist Research Institute. I hold an endowed chair -- and my husband is the President of the University. The short version: suffice it to say that I am the great and powerful Queen of Brand-ex. This is my Institute co-director, Rhoda Morgenstern. And who are you?"

"I am Sondra. I am not small and meek. As you can see, I can stand to lose ten and three-quarter pounds. And, as you are aware, there is no such thing as a meek Jewish feminist."

"I have no time for you, Sondra. But I suppose that we have to progress with the interview. Rhoda, take my cape to the cleaners. 'Bye. Sondra, let's sit in the café and talk so we can get this interview over with as quickly as possible. I have to generate funds for the Institute. Sorry that I am an hour late. I'm very busy. I "hafta" call Barbra -- and other people."

"Whatever you say."

"Do you have any questions?"

"What exactly are you looking for?"

"I want someone who will not bother me."

"I can fit that bill. I've taught and lectured all over the world; hence, I'm exceedingly independent. I promise that I will never bother you. Are there any other characteristics that you are seeking?"

"Excuse me. My cell is ringing. Hello, Barbra. You can donate five million? Fine. Thanks. 'Bye."

"That's a lot of money."

"Barbra is not hard up for cash. Now where we? It's the cell again. Be right with you. Hello, Barbara. You can donate three million? Fine. Thanks. 'Bye."

"These multimillion dollar phone calls are slightly beyond me. Why did Barbra call you twice."

"That was Walters, not Sreisand. The B list is big. I am racking my brains about how to add Barbara Bush. There must be some way to interest her in a feminist Jewish research institute. Where were we? Oh, other characteristics. We would like to hire an exotic Jew."

This was the limit. Here I was interviewing for a Jewish feminist position and my ethnicity was still not right. I momentarily contemplated what color body paint I would need in order to appear to be exotic before again deciding that disguise would not work. I was sitting directly in front of Leona; my true racial characteristics were plain to see. Painting myself as a Jew of a different color would get me nowhere. No lesbian husbands or black-like-me this time. I had to tell the truth.

"I, of course, know that during job interviews the candidate should try to conform to the interviewer's stated requirements. But there's no way I can claim to be an exotic Jew. I'm a Jew from Queens. Jews from Queens are a dime a dozen. There's absolutely nothing exotic about me in relation to Judaism."

"True." Leona removed her tiara, put its end between her teeth in the manner of someone thinking while chewing on eyeglass frames, and furrowed her brow. "It occurs to me that if you will accept half of the advertised salary, I could get two Jews for the price of one Jew: mundane Jewish you and an exotic Jew. Would you come to Brand-x for half the money?"

All the black body paint and male lesbian husbands in the world would not help me now. It was unfair of Leona to pose this question before offering me the job. Since I wanted to share my Jewish feminist novel *Oy Pioneer!* with a Jewish feminist academic community, I agreed to this decidedly unheavenly -- and unkosher -- proposition.

"I accept your terms."

"Glad you agree. Since you do, I'm willing to overlook the fact that you're a mundane garden variety Queens Jew. Anyway, for this job, any adult Jewish female who exudes a scholarly aura suffices. You can impress the Institute's financial backers simply by existing. You'll do. You're hired."

"Great. What does the job entail?" And so began my semester-long commute between New England and New York.

"The position is unstructured. Come to our board meetings, staff meetings, and Intermarriage Conference."

"Sounds good. I'm intermarried, by the way. Maybe I could contribute to your Conference. I'm happy to accept the position."

My happiness was short-lived. After a few sojourns at the Institute, I realized that there was absolutely nothing for me to do there. Leona should have named me the Seinfeld scholar; my job was about nothing. My primary purpose was to show up to impress the Institute's board and its financial backers; I merely had to be present to prove that they were paying for a living, breathing scholar in residence. I was a Stepford Scholar. Only my body mattered. I was in no way expected to say anything or to contribute my considerable professional expertise. How could I have known that a Jewish feminist research institute would treat me like a cheap whore? Leona and Rhoda had bought my body for a very small monetary amount. Now they had the power to tell me to place my silent and silenced body in Institute meetings and conferences. Academic heaven? Definitely *non*.

The Intermarriage Conference was particularly excruciating. I had to endure hours of sociology paper presentations during which slides and charts were used to discern that if 6.22 Jews married 8.23 *goyim*, their progeny would consist of 2.34 Jews and 3.46 *goyim*. Although Pepe might appreciate such precision, listening to endless intermarriage procreation statistics were decidedly *pas pour moi*. I took advantage of the silence expected of me. Under the guise of appearing to take copious conference notes, I wrote this *Oy Feminist Planets* chapter.

I, however, could accomplish no such writerly deception during the Institute staff meetings. Writing subterfuge does not work while sitting at a small round table with six people. I was expected to weigh in on questions of great pith and moment. Examples: How do we sell Rhoda's intermarriage book? How many staples do the staplers need? During these deliberations, my mouth and brain might as well have been stapled shut. What could I possibly say while Leona and Rhoda deliberated how best to hit up Palm Beach Jewish feminists for donations to their Institute?

"We're having a reading series in the largest home in Palm Beach. The owner doesn't work. Not working is a sure sign that a person is exceedingly rich. But Palm Beach, we have a problem. We need popular books about Jewish women. Our Brand-ex University Press series does not publish popular books. Where can we get a popular and entertaining book about Jewish women?" Leona inquired.

Not being able to contain myself, I broke my enforced silence. "Me. Me. Take me. I'd love to present my work to Palm Beach Jewish feminists. *Oy Pioneer!* is exactly what you need." Leona, someone who relentlessly hounds people until they submit to her will, ignored me.

"Izzy Izzwitz has been one of our biggest benefactors. Should we invite Izzy to our next board meeting?"

"I think Izzy Izzwitz is dead," interjected Rhoda.

Is Izzy dead, or isn't he?"

"Only his funeral director knows for sure."

"Invite him anyway -- just in case he's still with us." Leona's hey ya never know end of life attitude was at least more benign than a rumor about how death was handled at a Blackhole State English department meeting. I had heard that, some years before my arrival, the conservative geezers from Hell held a committee meeting in which a female colleague who routinely challenged their authority was present. As the story goes, she had a heart attack and keeled over dead mid-meeting. The geezers, applauding her demise, did not call an ambulance. Did this happen? Hey, ya never know. I believe that it did.

Recalling this story made me feel grateful that, when I keeled over, my efficient husband did not leave me to die.

Meeting over, Pepe and I drove back to New York. When we exited I-95, I complained to him about being treated like a Stepford Scholar cheap whore. To cheer me up, he suggested that we have dinner at my favorite neighborhood restaurant. It is no garden-variety restaurant. I'm enamored of a combined Mongolian barbecue, Japanese, and Chinese all-you-can-eat buffet place. It's no exaggeration to say that this restaurant contains an entire city block of sushi and a plethora of unidentifiable raw fish species. Unlike academic heaven, culinary heaven most certainly exists. Pepe, who exercised restraint in regard to buffets, had a cow when I returned to our table with my second plate-load of sushi.

"Haven't you had enough?"

"What? Enough? What's with enough? This is only my second helping. I have not yet begun to eat."

"Enough already." Pepe was sounding like me? I was really in trouble. I felt decidedly dizzy as I eyed sushi piece number twenty, but who is counting leaning against a succulent spare rib.

"Pepe, I'm going to faint." And I did. Pepe acted immediately. "Help. Help. My wife is unconscious. Call an ambulance." While two cell phone-brandishing hostesses appeared and directed their attention to my prostrate body, Pepe calmly paid the check and calculated the tip to the penny. He accompanied me as paramedics lifted me on to a stretcher, placed me in an ambulance, and drove me to a hospital. This is not a stretcher.

I opened my eyes and saw a doctor placing electrodes all over my body.

"Where am I?"

"SUNY-GV Medical Center.."

"Good."

"I'm Dr. Honoré Amoreuse Chevalier."

"Honoré Amoreuse? I know that name. You must be French Canadian."

"Most definitely. I am named for Honoré Amoreuse Le Pew the first, the founder of our family."

"Oh yes, I know him well. Sorry, I am a little delirious. You must be related to my husband Pepe Le Pew."

"Probably so. Nice to meet you, long-lost cousin Pepe," he said, extending his hand. I noticed that, as my hospital gown began to fall off my shoulder, both Pepe and the doctor were staring at my electrode-laden breasts. I had no doubt that these men were indeed related.

The nurse appeared to put in a needle in my arm and engaged in conversation to distract me.

"Where do you work?"

"Brand-ex University."

"How interesting. What do you do there?"

"I do nothing." She frowned. "They pay me to bring my body to their activities to impress donors." Knowing that this conversation was not fulfilling the purpose of a simple distraction, she turned me into a blood donor.

"Let me check out these electrodes," said the amorous doctor as he fondled my breast and eyed the chair in my emergency room alcove. "For this medical appointment, it would be best for you to stand on the chair. I'm stepping out to get your blood test report. Hop up on the chair to be ready when I return. And, oh yes, I have to do a rectal exam."

"Pepe, help. Did you hear your long-lost cousin say that he wants to have an appointment with me on a chair? You've never met this distant relation of yours. What is it with you Le Pews and being turned on by appointments on chairs? Is there a gene for this sexual peccadillo?"

"Relax. He's an attractive young doctor who is probably mired in middle-aged female patients. So what if he is turned on by your breasts? He will get a thrill if he exams you while you stand on a chair. His behavior is harmless. I would be thrilled to watch him being thrilled. Being in an emergency room at two AM is not the most wonderful experience. Why shouldn't we liven things up with a little sexual titillation? I can't wait for the rectal exam."

The Le Pews had their sexual thrills and discharged me from the electrodes, the hospital, and being sexually electrifying. Pepe and I drove back to New England. Wearing my hospital bracelet to communicate that my prostituted body was a little disconcerted, I proceeded to show up for the morning Brand-ex Institute faculty meeting. For once, Rhoda noticed that I was present.

"Why are you wearing a hospital identification bracelet?" she asked in an agitated voice.

"Because I was hospitalized."

"What happened?"

"I was eating dinner in a restaurant, and I passed out."

"Did you eat anything unkosher?"

"Did I eat anything unkosher? I pigged out on a mile-long all-you-can-eat Japanese sushi and raw fish bar. Unkosher? I think that I ate crustaceans and bivalves which are as yet uncharted in zoological nomenclature." Rhoda looked pale to the extent that I feared she was the next candidate for Pepe's relative's chair. On second thought, I reasoned that Orthodox Jewish women do not keep sex appointments which involve standing on chairs. Leona brought the meeting back to a professional focus.

"Let's see. Action item six: acquire a million-dollar donation for the Institute. Sondra, do you know anyone who can give me a million dollars?"

"No. Not off hand."

"Give this matter more thought. Meanwhile, tonight, we are having a signing and reading for Rhoda's intermarriage book. I know that we have already had two conferences on intermarriage. But one can never generate too much publicity. We are charging the highest admission fee that we can possibly get away with. Six rabbis will elaborate on Rhoda's work. I want you and Pepe to be there."

"We wouldn't miss it for the world. Pepe will absolutely love listening to intermarriage procreation statistics to the tune of six rabbis." I omitted mentioning that I was not sure whether or not Pepe, in his entire life, had ever set eyes on six rabbis. Blaring fire alarms suddenly interrupted the meeting.

"Evacuate," ordered Leona. The building's human contents, twenty-five Jewish feminists, cooled their flat shoe heels on the porch as they tried to engage each other *sans* meeting discourse or study-carrel isolation. The Brinks truck approaching the Brand-ex University building, which housed the Fiscal Unit Office as well as the Jewish Feminist Research Institute, attracted everyone's attention. Seeming to run amok in the face of so much unexpectedly approaching money, Leona bounded down the porch stairs while wildly waving her arms at the Brinks driver. She stuck her head inside the truck window.

"Would you take our picture?" she asked the burly driver sweetly. Twenty-five Jewish feminists complacently arranged themselves in stereotypical group-picture-on-stairs mode as the driver exited the money-filled truck and grasped Leona's camera. He raised his arms and, hence, left his gun vulnerable. Leona diverted his attention by issuing picture-taking orders. "Everyone smile and say 'Cheese, milk and, no meat," she said as the driver snapped. Leona, luckily, did not snap as well. Her hand inched toward the driver's gun while he held the camera and focused. Obviously, as someone who does not mix milk and meat, she concluded -- at the very last moment -- that it was not kosher for her to fund her Institute via holding a gun to the head of someone entrusted to deliver a university money truckload. "Thank you so much for your help, sir. You made our day by recording our firedrill moment," Leona said as she bounded back up the stairs.

"The sight of you running after a Brinks truck was nothing short of hysterical," I interjected.

"Yeah. I really want a million dollars for the Institute. I planned the whole thing. I arranged for the fire alarms to coincide with the truck's scheduled arrival time. But when push came to shove, I couldn't go through with the idea. Maybe I just wanted to see if I could orchestrate the heist without carrying it out. I mean, as the university president's wife, I couldn't actually hold up a Brinks truck. My husband would say that Leona and Mordecai Rhinestone are not Bonnie and Clyde." Leona turned to the assembled women. "Everyone back inside. Back to work."

I told Pepe about Rhoda's book event and omitted to mention Leona's at-once-premeditated-and-aborted heist. If I told Pepe about the funding-obsessed Leona/gun/Brinks truck scenario, he would never stop mentioning his negative opinions about Jews and money.

"We have to go and hear six rabbis talk about Rhoda's intermarriage book," I simply said.

"Will there be a reception?"

"Yes."

"Okay. I'll go. Do you think there will be any shrimp?"

"Any event which includes six rabbis entails zilch shrimp."

"You're no longer hospitalized. If you're well enough to go to a reception, shrimpless or otherwise, you're well enough to have an appointment. Drape the pillowcase over your shoulders to mimic that sexy hospital gown. Get on the chair," said Pepe in an effort to parody his sexuality.

"I will trade you a sex appointment for turning on your French charm to Leona and Rhoda. I have to work with them. They certainly are not charmed by me."

"I don't know what kind of mood I will be in later. I may not want to talk to anyone. I can't just turn my charm on and off like a water faucet."

"Please."

"You win. I'll be charming. Let's go."

Rabbi Number One introduced Rhoda by proclaiming that she was one of the most profound intellectual lights in the Jewish scholarly world. I somehow endured Rabbi Number Four's Intermarriage Conference follow-up lecture about what progeny results when a particular percentage of Jews marry a particular percentage of *goyim*. Pepe never made it to Rabbi Six. He fell asleep during Rabbi 2.5.

"Wake up. The rabbis' lectures and responses are over."

"Thank god."

"Time for you to turn on your French charm for Leona and Rhoda. Go to the reception and do your stuff." Pepe approached Rhoda as she sat at her book signing table.

"I must tell you what a joy it was to hear your articulate and enlightening lecture. The flow of your body movements was so impressive. You have a particular gesturing style which at once calls attention to your ideas as well as the attractive way your beautiful red form-fitting sleeveless dress accentuates your lovely figure." I could clearly see that Rhoda's politely beaming face reflected the fact that she was inwardly swooning with ecstasy. Pepe flashed a Charm-Rhoda-mission-accomplished look in my direction.

"Great. There's Leona. Do your stuff with her."

"Ah, *bonsoir* Leona. It is so nice to *voir*, not to mention to *regarder*, your scintillating presence this evening," he said in fake French while grasping her arm.

"Oh Pepe, your French accent is such a delight. I am going to Montreal next month to raise money. I could raise much more money if I could speak French. Unfortunately, such is not the case." She pronounced the city as "*mount-tree-aal.*"

"That's "*mon-ray-al*," he said as he touched her lips to position them optimally to elicit the desired corrected French pronunciation.

"Oh Pepe, "*mount-tree-aal*" sounds so sexy when it emanates from your mouth." Help me to try to pronounce it again."

Despite Pepe's repeated efforts to place Leona's lips in exactly the right position, her "*mount-tree-aal*" failed to sound anything like his "*mon-ray-al*."

"*Non.* By George, you definitely have not got it."

"When I try to speak French properly, the rain in Spain unsuccessfully falls on the plain. I have a wonderful idea. Why don't you accompany me during my weekend stay in *Mount-tree-aal?* You would be such a help if you would speak French to the potential funders I'm targeting. The University is springing for a sumptuous suite in the Fairmont Queen Elizabeth Hotel. I couldn't possibly get along without you."

Pepe looked directly into Leona's eyes and again grasped her arm. "I would love to come. And so would Sondra."

"My invitation is not such a good idea after all. The extra expenses two people would generate would strain the budget allocation. Excuse me. My cell is ringing. It must be Barbra."

"How did it go with Leona?" I asked.

"Great. She invited me to spend the weekend with her in Montreal."

"What? Have I created a monster? I told you to be charming, but not that charming. You turned on entirely too much charm. How did you handle the situation?"

"With finesse and aplomb, of course. I merely told her that you'd like to come to Montreal too. In the end, the whole trip idea was relegated to much ado about nothing. Leona wasn't insulted. She didn't try to kill me. You don't have to worry about which emergency room you'll be visiting tonight."

"Good. I appreciate your efforts. They will help me to survive next week's boring faculty meeting."

Due to Pepe, the next meeting did not turn out to be boring after all. I sat down resigned to tune out during the usual staple count, fund raising hysteria, and book promotion rendition. I looked forward to the meeting highlight: the definitive answer to is Izzy

Izzwitz alive or dead. I never expected Leona to deviate from the agenda.

"Sondra, your husband exudes *savoir faire*. It was such a pleasure to talk with him. When he grasps you, you're really aware that you're being grasped. Oh, but I do suppose that you must know how it feels to be grasped by Pepe? No?" Leona had gone from one meeting voice extreme to another. Her usual focused upon money and stapling had been redirected to Pepe and grasping. What was I supposed to say? I knew that, in mid-academic meeting, I could not describe how I felt when Pepe grasped my breasts -- not to mention all my other body parts -- in mid-chair appointment mode. I thought it best to opt for the most conservative approach.

"Yes." Although I left it at that, the meeting agenda still centered on Pepe. Rhoda chimed in.

"Your husband is so nice. Speaking with him was the highlight of my evening." She went on for ten minutes. I never thought that I would miss hearing about generating money, monitoring the staple supply adequacy, and discerning Izzy's mortality status. Pepe was impressed with himself when I described how the subject of his charm had dominated the meeting. He suddenly asked an unexpected question.

"When I took your blazer to the dry cleaner, it was covered with white powder. Why is there white powder on your blazer?" The white powder was, of course, the plaster which descended when the Barnes & Noble ceiling opened. My choices: (1) tell Pepe the truth about how two angels crashed through the Barnes & Noble ceiling or (2) lie and say that I was a coke addicted anthrax terrorist. Neither alternative was acceptable. I had to resort to distraction. I had to direct Pepe's attention from the angels to the Martians. The Martians, at least, were real.

"I'm sure the cleaners can easily take care of the white powder. I need you to help me with the Martians. Jonathan Goodman and I are co-editing the first science fiction issue of *PMLA*. This is momentous. *PMLA*, *Publications of the Modern Language Association*, is the most prestigious, conservative stick-up-the-ass literary journal in the country. They accepted my idea for the cover: I suggested juxtaposing a pulp science fiction Martian with an image from the NASA Mars rover. Co-editing the *PMLA* science fiction issue is one of the most important events in my career. Salk cured polio; Gates gave us software; Lear is putting a Martian on the cover of *PMLA*.

I have finally fulfilled my destiny. In the whole history of literary criticism, no one has ever placed a Martian on the cover of *PMLA* -- and no one has ever written an introduction for that journal which is replete with Jewish jokes and a giant feminist talking squid from Mars. I named the squid Leona. I'm having trouble with the Martians. I can't decide which image of a Martian should appear on the cover. The *PMLA* managing editor sent me a whole slew of e-mails with the subject line "Martians." This, too, is a first. I have to pick between Martians one through ten. Come look. Three Martians have horns and big noses. They look too anti-Semitic. I tend to go with Martian Number Four, a picture of a woman and a man pointing zap guns at this Martian mechanical eye thing. I need the full force of your art history talent. What do you think?"

After meticulously analyzing the representational pros and cons of multitudinous Martians, Pepe forgot about the white powder. What a life. I instigated the Martian invasion of *PMLA*. I survived the Hell the angels in Barnes & Noble created.

September Mo(u)rning

"Having your dinner interrupted when paramedics placed me on a stretcher was unpleasant. I'm going to make it up to you. I'm going to take you to a great surprise place for your birthday," I informed Pepe.

"It had better be good. You know my high standards."

"I'm going to meet your high standards in an exceeding high place. I will wear something special, too. I'll be right back."

Recalling that the skin-tight jumpsuit clad Sondras were really me -- and that they looked sexy -- I decided to follow suit. I put on my gold *lamé* bodysuit, held in my stomach as tightly as I could, and stood in front of Pepe.

"What do you think?"

"You look a little on the naked side. Your outfit is not to my taste. I hate to attract attention. If this gaudy attire makes you happy, it's okay with me. You can carry it off. You've lost a little weight lately. Have you been using the scale I gave you for your birthday?"

"Giving a woman a scale for her birthday does not constitute a Hallmark moment. Actually, you gave me two scales."

"Two scales?"

"Yes."

"That's right. I gave you one for Hanukkah, too."

"Did you give me a scale for Hanukkah because you were hoping for a miracle? If so, you were turning Hanukkah into a fractured fairytale. You never do get the right spin on Jewish holidays. Remember how at last year's Passover Seder you called the *Haggadah* a brochure? You also confused the search for Elijah the prophet with a nonprofit organization job agenda"

"Hope always springs eternal. You lost one scale under a clothing mountain -- and I replaced it. Even though you never used either scale, you look fine now. Let's get this birthday show on the road."

We hailed a cab and headed downtown. Pepe was impressed when we reached our World Trade Center destination.

"'Windows on the World' is a great choice."

He stared at the sensational view. I took great satisfaction in the fact that men were staring at me. But even the sight of a middle-aged woman, someone who was certainly no Twiggy, attired in a gold *lamé* bodysuit could not rival the glittering lights of Manhattan. Pepe, happy to spend his birthday at "Windows on the World," ignored the fifty-dollar price tag for four scallops. I was relieved that the small portions would not further expand bodysuit-wearing me. We ate, viewed, and toasted the future, oblivious to why this night would become different from all other nights. All the scales in the world could not adequately weigh the import of one of the last World Trade Center suppers.   Pepe's birthday is in September.

I coped with the morning of September 11 by reaching out to the science fiction community. Because Pamela Sargent told me that my experience was important and should be recorded, I published the following account on the *Locus Magazine* website:

> It is certainly strange at this time to be a professional science fiction critic *and* a native New Yorker. I saw the burning tower from the street. I live in a twenty-second-floor Manhattan apartment with a straight-shot view of what was formerly the World Trade Center. Out of all the millions of people who saw the events and are commenting about them, I think that as far as I know Samuel Delany and I are the only academic science fiction critics who live in Manhattan. This is a small minority perspective *vis-à-vis* the fact that every cognizant adult on the planet in the civilized world knows what has ensued. Professionals, of course, have been called upon to use their skills in the recovery effort. I, of course -- again -- can't remove the twisted steel or repair wounded bodies. But what I can do is to

comment in terms of science fiction in general and personal experience in particular. Since communicating traumatic events fosters healing, this exercise will be useful to me, and I hope that those who share my interest in science fiction will also find it useful.

***

I left the apartment on Tuesday morning at 8:45 to walk across Manhattan to the Port Authority Bus Terminal to catch the bus that would take me to a guest-lecturing appointment in New Jersey. Although the attack started while I was in the elevator, street life was perfectly normal. About ten minutes into my walk, I heard someone say "Smoke is coming from the top of the building, and you can see it." I turned and looked up at the buildings directly behind me. I saw no smoke. Since the sight of smoke emanating from a building would not deter a New Yorker trying to catch a specific bus, I continued on. When I was directly across the street from Madison Square Garden and Penn Station, I heard a solicitor for funds for the homeless who had a bull horn use the horn to say "The World Trade Center has been hit by a plane. We are all praying." I immediately thought that terrorists were responsible for this hit. Shocked, but unable to imagine that this situation could impact my bus, I thought that I should fulfill my professional responsibility. Once inside the bus terminal, I witnessed people's nervous reactions and thought better of entering the Lincoln Tunnel. I walked out of the terminal and found myself on streets filled with stunned and panicking people. This was calm panic; no one was crying or screaming. Everyone resembled dazed automatons. I was petrified. I thought that more planes were coming to attack more buildings. I thought that planes carrying nuclear weapons were coming. I walked to 34th St. and saw the Empire State Building directly in front of me. I told myself that I could not be there; I could not be in front of the Empire State Building when planes could come to attack this prime target. I turned to change my direction and passed a building which had its occupants standing in front of it. "Why are you standing out here?" I asked one of the people. His answer: "This is a tall building and we've been told evacuate." Not understanding how standing in front of a building which might be attacked at any second could manifest safety, I walked toward Madison Square Garden. I defined this building as another target. I realized that it was impossible to find safety anywhere. People who ran from Ground Zero said that they had become the war refugee that they have seen in pictures. I thought that I had become a character in a post-apocalyptic urban landscape science fiction novel. I have devoted my professional life to studying science fiction; now science fiction was real; now the science fiction critic had become a science fiction character. I walked and talked to myself. I really articulated these words: "I can't believe it. I can't believe it. This is a science fiction novel. I'm in a science fiction novel."

Because I knew that there was no such thing as finding a safe place, I began to walk home, looking as stunned as everyone around me. I paused to listen to a radio report emanating from a parked construction truck. I do not remember what I heard. Then, from a location I also can't remember (which must have been Seventh Avenue), I looked south. I saw it. I saw black smoke billowing from the top of a tower. I say "a tower" because I saw only one tower. It was ten o'clock. One tower had just fallen before I noticed the sole smoking tower. But my mind did not register that it was abnormal to see only one tower. My mind could not fathom the possibility that only one tower could exist. And this occurred even though I always saw two towers. I imparted normalcy to the situation by reasoning that one tower was somehow not visible from my particular angle. I really and calmly believed this to be the case even though it never was the case before. The burning tower struck me as just a more significant, horrible, and scary version of a normal building fire -- i.e. the supposed typical fire that did not deserve my attention that I saw at the start of my walk. Since the smoke was coming from a limited area at the top of the building, I thought that it could be contained and that the people inside would calmly leave via elevators. Death did not enter my mind. Even though groups of people were lined along the avenue staring transfixed at the tower, I reasoned that I had already seen the smoke and the burning tower and nothing would be gained by standing in the street continuing to look at it. Construing a visual version of the cliché "I have been there and done that," I turned to continue walking home. Again, knowing that finding safety was impossible, I resumed my attitude of juxtaposed trauma and calm. I have been married for a short time. Although having a husband is a very alien concept to me, it stands to reason that -- if one does have a husband -- one should call him when flames are emanating from the top of a World Trade Center tower. I went to a phone booth and dialed. "Do you know what happened?"

"Yes."

"I'm coming home."

"Okay. Good. Come home." He spoke calmly and succinctly even though he saw the burning towers directly from our apartment's window and he knew the magnitude of the explosions. Soon after we hung up, he had a direct view of the falling towers. In retrospect, I am glad that I did not see the towers fall. Since New York Jews resort to humor when they are distraught, let me tell you the difference between his subsequent telephone renditions of the event and my own. When his numerous sisters called from Quebec, what he had to say was always the same: "*Bonjour. Oui. Oui. Non. Je vais bien. Au revoir.*" And that was it. When people phoned me, I spent no less than an hour per call articulating various versions of the following: "Aaaaaaaargh!!! *Oy*!!! And the sirens and the smell coming into the apartment and what will happen next and all those poor, poor people... etc, etc."

When I arrived home, my husband and I watched television. I could not decide between looking at the screen and the framed space of my windows. I alternated between both views. I cannot articulate how it felt to have the scene on television enacted outside my window. Smell attached to a television screen is still science fiction; I smelled the smoke the television reporters were describing. At 5:20 PM, a reporter said that another building had collapsed. I looked out of the window and corroborated the report in that I saw more smoke.

And then it was the science fiction cliché of the day after. It was a day of more television. On Wednesday night, the smoke smell permeating the apartment became intense to the extent that I was coughing and my eyes were tearing. I closed the windows and got back into bed to watch more television. A reporter said that there was a bomb scare in the Empire State Building and it was being evacuated. Since I never had a chance to say Goodbye to my beloved World Trade Center view from my window, I got out of bed and went to the bathroom window to look at the Empire State Building and say Goodbye to it (It is seven blocks away). I never bothered to awaken my husband; if the Empire State Building fell in ruins, there would be nothing that he could do. If the bombed building threatened our lives, he might as well sleep through the trauma.

Another "the day after." I spent it at the Bellevue Hospital Missing Person Center trying to help a friend locate her missing cousin. The task was hopeless. He was not on any of the lists of the missing. Because of the number of people, I could not hope to file a missing person report. It is strange to stand on line with grieving people when you are not directly grieving. A chaplain asked me if I needed help. I said no and directed her toward a person who looked especially bereft. I returned home and watched more television.

Another "the day after." Traumatized to the point that I could not function normally or work, I resolved to try to have a normal day. I made an appointment to meet my lifelong friend Carol for lunch. She works on Park Avenue in a large office building. On my way to my usual sitting spot to wait to have lunch with Carol, located across the street from the Waldorf, I forced myself to walk through Grand Central Station. I told two businessmen on the escalator behind me that it was an effort for me to walk into the building. They provided thumbs-up encouragement. While I usually read while waiting for my friend in "my usual sitting spot," today I just wanted to "veg out" and stare into space at a normal urban landscape. Suddenly, I saw people running from the office building. The stunned faces appeared again. The traumatized cell phone conversations took place again. I walked up to a woman standing in front of me. "I am really afraid to ask this, but why are you all out here?"

"Bomb scare. The building has been evacuated."

I knew that the building could collapse at any moment. But I did not run. I stood on the street corner. I knew that Carol, the person who I had known since the time she was born eight months after my birthday, the person who had been in every grade with me from kindergarten to senior year of college, was prompt. Carol was due to meet me in four minutes. Carol would come. Even if the building crumbled, I had to wait for Carol. I saw her cross the street. She obviously did not know something was wrong. I grabbed her hand. "There is a bomb scare. We have to get out of here. We have to run. We can go to Central Park. In Central Park, the buildings can't fall on our heads." Holding hands, we proceeded to head north. Then she stopped in her tracks.

"Sondra, this is probably just a scare. I want to go back and ask the security guard the reality of the situation. Let's just go in the building and have lunch as usual in the cafeteria."

"No. The authorities told the people in the Trade Center to remain where they were. I don't care what the guards say. I am not going in that building." We talked to the guards. We compromised. We had lunch in the deli located at street level in another building.

Another "the day after." I had to teach my classes. I was afraid that some new horror would happen. Although I never intended to desert my students, I voiced my apprehension to my husband. He ordered me to go to school. I stood in front of the students who looked at me nervously because they know I live in Manhattan. I told them what I had been through. I then described the events in terms of the subject of my class. It took me som time before I could ask the class something normal such as "Does anyone need a syllabus?" Looking at those young scared people and reaching out to them as a fellow scared human being rather than as a professor constituted the most amazing teaching experience of my career. I thanked my students for their help -- and they thanked me.

***

I am now sitting in front of the computer with my hands cold and damp and some tears in my eyes. I am still scared. I do not really believe that things are back to normal. I still hear some sirens. If I look out the window, I will still see the smoke. I

can turn off the television; I cannot turn off the window view. I am trying to tell myself that the worst is over, that New York City will not really be destroyed in short order. But the truth is that a plane can come out of the sky before I put a period to the next sentence. I know that I cannot know the future -- even if I am a professional science fiction scholar. I reach the end of another sentence and type the period and the plane did not come. I do not want to reread my narrative or alter what I have said. Again, I just want to be a science fiction schol-ar who has communicated my experience to
the science fiction community. No matter what happens, even if New York ceases to exist, my books will be there as long as human civilization ex-ists. And someone will read this narrative. Is my sending this message a science fictional act? Well, without scrolling up and looking back at what I have written, I know my next future action. I am going to write "love, Sondra" and push the send button. Love, Sondra: *Oy*!!!!!!!!!!!!!!!!!!!

I printed my text and put it in the refrigerator. A Sondra clone appeared.

"I have one question."

"Yes."

"Will New York City in general and the United States in par-ticular survive?"

"Yes."

"Although I am stretching things, what does the future hold for me?"

"You know that it is not good for you if I answer a question of this sort. But since you are coping with an extraordinary circum-stance, I will be flexible. Pamela Sargent told you to write your ac-count. Well, you will be the Chair of the Pilgrim Award Committee, and she will win the Pilgrim Award."

"It is so reassuring to hear about the Award. It is simply one of my favorite things -- and the perfect positive thought for a terrible time like this. I know that it will be asking too much for you to name all the future Pilgrims. I will be satisfied if you just tell me who else win when I serve on the Committee."

"Eric S. Rabkin and Donna Haraway. And you will be able to speak from the so-called Committee grave. After your sojourn on the Committee is over, the new Committee will listen to your advice and give the Pilgrim to N. Katherine Hayles."

Donna and Eric and Kate? I love these extraordinary people. Being on the Committee which grants them the Award will be just as wonderful as winning it myself. And I bet that their award ceremonies, unlike mine, will be normal."

"Well, I wouldn't exactly say that. You will call in the Committee's presentation speech for Pamela Sargent. And, when you phone to tell Haraway and Rabkin the good news, you will act like you are placing a call emanating from Stockholm. But enough already with what will happen. Just get through this horrible occurrence and look forward to the future."

"Thanks for your good advice. I listened to Pamela's suggestion. I will do as you say, too."

Enormous Changes at the Last Minute Or Stop the Starship, I Want To Get On

I sat on my sofa and gazed at the empty space which the World Trade Center once occupied. Like many of my fellow New Yorkers, I was contemplating the meaning of life. If I again called upon the Sondras -- or even Ilya --they could concoct some supernatural way to set things right. Authors, after all, routinely write right. Martin Amis' Times Arrow, for example, is about how people survive the Holocaust after emerging from life camps. I can't follow suit in terms of 9/11. My supernatural coterie will not engage further with the disaster I witnessed. I will follow the Star Trek prime directive. I will not change history. I will simply imbue my own life with enormous changes at the last minute. Grace Paley is more my style than Amis. On second thought, make that Sholem Aleichem. I echoed Tevye when I told Pepe "let's start packing."

"I can't stand smelling these fumes coming from Ground Zero. I can't continue to face the fact that so many people died. Let's leave Manhattan for a while."

"What do you suggest?"

"A change of scene. How about spending a little time visiting my alma mater, SUNY-A. You liked the campus when we stopped there. I told you that it is a very special place designed by the Lincoln Center architect Edward Durrell Stone. Remember the campus' four towers? They're shorter versions of the World Trade Center towers which surround a podium replete with fountains and a phallic carillon. People say that the place looks like a science fiction spaceship launching pad."

I conveyed this description while feigning an innocent tone. If I wanted to take Pepe to a science fiction spaceship launching pad,

I, of course, could not directly tell him so. I wanted to escape post 9/11 Earth. I needed a vacation from the Bush administration. I wanted to make the metaphorical SUNY-A spaceship launching pad real. Pepe was still clueless about my sojourn in the Sondra clones' starship. What was I supposed to do if the clones turned my cat Norris into a gorgeous man and I married him? Could I help it if Norris, returned to his original cat form, was in the starship awaiting my return? At least I felt much more loyal to my human husband than to my cat transformed into a human husband. French Canadians, even if they are alien in relation to Jewish New York Americans, are real after all. Getting back to the starship was one problem. Convincing Pepe to join me was another. Surprisingly, he acquiesced.

I stood on the SUNY-A podium wondering what to do. "The fountains are wonderful. What a uniquely symmetrical campus. How do you feel being back here yet again?" Pepe asked.

"Trees really get taller after a generation of growth. It is nostalgic being here recalling how I spritzed in the fountain during my youth. I want to go back to my old dorm room. Next stop: Cayuga Hall on Indian Quad." I contemplated how to turn the SUNY-A campus into a functioning spaceship launch pad site. I was a little encouraged as I remembered that Kurt Vonnegut's brother Bernard Vonnegut was a SUNY-A science faculty member. Maybe a science fiction writer's brother's scientific connection to SUNY-A would somehow enable me to accomplish my unusual objective.

Reality quickly intervened. What was I thinking? Science fiction writers and their brothers are reality-bound. Turning SUNY-A into a real spaceship launch pad was not a job for the Vonnegut brothers. This was a job for science fiction -- not for a science fiction writer or a scientist. I was, in short, contemplating a job for the Sondra clones. I needed to contact them immediately.

"A dorm room really isn't that interesting to me. I'll accompany you to the quad and find a men's room while you commune with your past," said Pepe.

I stood outside my old Cayuga Hall room, knocked on the door, and addressed two identical-appearing approximately nineteen-year-olds. The two skin-tight tank top and low-rise navel-baring bellbottom pants clad nose-ringed female denizens of my former room stared at me quizzically. I returned their stare. I, at first, thought I was seeing clones, not twins. I regained my composure as I did an instantaneous reality check. I remembered that human clones were not real -- yet.

"Hello. Nice to meet you. I'm Sondra Lear, an Albany alumna. I lived in this Indian Quad dorm room many, many moons ago, before you were born. For nostalgia's sake, would you allow me to come in and look around? " I said extending my hand.

"I'm Jennifer-Tiffany Olsen. And this is my sister, Tiffany-Jennifer. Sure, come in. Make yourself at home."

"May I use your bathroom?"

"Sure."

"I remember exactly where it is located." I entered the bathroom, removed a pen from my backpack and scrawled a note on a toilet paper square. "Dear Sondras, Help. I want to return to the starship. I want to do so by turning the SUNY-A campus into a functioning launch pad. Pepe is using the bathroom. He will return at any moment. Please answer immediately, if not sooner. Thank you. All best, Sondra."

Now to the task of enacting my usual method of communicating with the Sondra clones. I had to manage to put the note into a refrigerator.

"Jennifer-Tiffany, I would like to wallow in my memories of living in this room while sipping a cool drink. The Diet Coke in my backpack needs some freshening up. May I pop it in your fridge?"

"No problem." I put the Diet Coke and note inside the refrigerator and closed the door. Three Sondras appeared. One flashed a forget-thingy beam at Jennifer-Tiffany and Tiffany-Jennifer. I suppose that Ilya let them borrow his forgetting contraption.

"You rang?"

"Yes.

I desperately want to return to your starship. I need a vacation. I can't stand looking out my window at the empty space where the twin towers once so majestically stood. This newly-made empty space resulting from their absence makes science fiction outer space look really good to me now. Enough already with terrorists. Enough already with Bush. Bush wants Americans to go to Mars. I want to go to science fiction outer space now. Sondras, please tell me how to return to the starship. While you're at it, throw in some advice about how to break the news of the truth of my science-fiction life to Pepe. He likes reality. One Sondra answered quickly.

"You have always been able to return to our starship."

"Really? How?"

"Just drink from the waters of the SUNY-A fountain, hug the carillon, and initiate a countdown from ten to zero. Upon reaching zero, merely state 'ignition lift off' and up to the starship you will go."

"Will this work for Pepe, too? I would never think of returning to the starship without Pepe."

"Certainly. To include Pepe, follow the procedure I have outlined -- with one alteration. Pepe must kiss you before you both drink SUNY-A fountain water. As soon as your lips separate, blast-off ability will kick in for you both."

"Great. Now explain how I can tell Pepe the truth about my life in a way which does not cause him to have cow."

"Humans have cows? Maybe a cow would be good company for Ms. Ed."

"Pepe is an alien French Canadian. He would probably have a moose. What am I saying? Potential cow emanation from a human is a figure of speech. Humans don't really have cows."

"How was I to know? Humans don't have alien clones either. And here I am telling you how to return to my starship. Be that as it may, science fiction turned real cannot help you control Pepe's reaction to your life's real science fiction. You must discern how to deal with Pepe yourself. 'Bye now, Sondra." This Sondra aimed her forget apparatus at Jennifer-Tiffany and Tiffany-Jennifer. She and her colleagues disappeared.

"Thank you so much for welcoming me to your dorm room, girls. You made my day. It's time for me to head out and find my husband. Good luck to you. 'Bye now."

I saw Pepe leaving the Indian Quad tower.

"Did you have a blast going back to your past?"

"Yes. But the blast is not my immediate concern. We gotta get out of this America place if it's the last thing we ever do."

"Although I'm not American, I understand how you feel about having your country attacked and being powerless to alter the designs of reprehensible President Bush. We can spend some time with my family in Canada. Terrorists are certainly not going to attack the Le Pew ancestral home in Orignalville."

"Canada is not far away enough. I'm talking about going to another galaxy."

"You're not making sense."

"Pepe, I have something big time to tell you. This isn't going to be easy. Let's take a walk as I try to explain." We arrived back at the central podium and sat down on the edge of the fountain. I recalled all the times my undergraduate self had perched on this very same spot while glancing over the top of my Norton Anthology of American Literature to check out the cute boys splashing in the SUNY-A fountain social watering hole.

"I love you, Sondra. I can deal with whatever you have to say."

"I don't know what to do other than to blurt out the truth, the whole truth, and nothing but the truth."

"Are you having an affair?"

"Absolutely not. The only affairs I go to involve 'affair' being synonymous with 'event.' I particularly enjoyed the pâté and brie orgy the Alliance Française organized."

"I know. You're about to announce that you have slept with Leona Rhinestone. You once mentioned that there's a bed in her Institute."

"Leona wants to sleep with you, remember? Enough. Enough guessing. Here's the fact: You're my second husband." Pepe almost fell into the fountain. "There's more. I fraternize with supernatural creatures. I've traveled in a starship my clones inhabit. It's in orbit overhead. The cat who they turned into a human is on board. I married him. Don't worry. He's presently a cat again. Before she decided to live on Jonathan Goodman's plantation with her favorite stallion Beauregard Jackson Pickett Burnside, my talking horse Ms. Ed often visited the starship with her lover, Pegasus.

"Enough. I've heard enough. This isn't news to me. I know that you know supernatural creatures. Your mother is out of this world -- and I don't mean that in a good sense. If I can deal with your mother, I can deal with your talking horse, starship, and first-husband cat. I can't believe that I'm saying this. I thought that the lengthy dream sequence on The Sopranos where Tony encounters a horse in his house was too much. If Tony can cope with a horse in his house, I can cope with a horse in your starship."

"The starship isn't mine. It belongs to the Sondra clones, in-habitants of another planet."

"Are you telling me that there's a whole planet of you? Wow. Can I sleep with other Sondras? Do they use chairs on their planet?"

"Absolutely not. Although all the Sondras are my biological copies, they're most certainly not me. I'm sure that no other Sondra on the whole planet of the Sondras would agree to stand on a chair during a sex appointment."

"What if I get confused when confronted with a whole pop-ulation of Sondras? How will I know which Sondra is you?"

"I'm the only Sondra who speaks with a New York accent."

"You're still the only Sondra for me." Pepe pledged his alle-giance to marital fidelity, put his arms around me, and kissed me. Good. The kiss requirement had been met. Now I had to convince him to drink SUNY-A fountain water and agree to blast off with me.

"I'm proud of you. You're really taking this all very well."

"I just want you to be happy. If you want to fraternize with clones, human cats, and talking horses, fine with me."

"I left out the horny vampire."

"Don't push it, Sondra. What will happen to me when you sojourn in another galaxy? Another galaxy is too far, far away. When we got married, we agreed that you would stay in Manhattan."

"You can come with me."

"To a starship and another galaxy?"

"Why not? Look at all the fun we have had traveling. You like to travel. You don't always make sense in regard to travel: you define the Upper West Side as another city and then you decide to drive to Las Vegas. So what's another galaxy? Pepe, this whole sci-ence fiction trip thing makes perfect sense. My Sondra clones told me how to include you. The lines between science fiction and the real world are becoming increasingly blurred. The World Trade Cen-ter disaster exemplifies science fiction busting out of its fictitious literary pages. By me, the two towers evoke Tolkien. And New York City blasted by alien terrorizers smacks of Independence Day. As long as I inhabit a science fiction world, I may as well seize the day and enjoy my chance to experience a science fiction world which is still fictitious."

"Count me in. I will be happy as long as I'm with you. What is the procedure for initiating a close encounter with Sondra clones on a starship?"

"The procedure is very simple. You just have to drink SUNY-A fountain water."

"What? Jamais. I would rather have a colonoscopy. This water is filthy. It could contain dog urine. I'm not drinking this water."

"The dirty water can't hurt you. Remember that the Sondras are from an advanced alien culture. They have health care methods beyond our wildest dreams. And universal health insurance too." Pepe cupped his hands, scooped up some fountain water, and swallowed it. I followed suit.

"Now what?" asked Pepe.

"We need to wade into the fountain, cross our arms around the carillon, count down, and say 'ignition, blast off.'"

"Drinking filthy water isn't bad enough. Now I have to wade into the fountain and ruin my perfectly pressed chinos and newly polished leather shoes. This is a metrosexual's worst nightmare. Crossing my arms around a carillon? Sondra, you're crucifying me."

"Let's not go there. I had enough crucification to deal with while trying not to throw up after hearing descriptions of Mel Gibson's The Passion of the Christ."

"I just want to get this science fiction shit I'm going through for my passion of the Sondra over with. I'm the only man in the history of the human race who is giving up his planet for the woman he loves. The Duke of Windsor has nothing on me."

"No. You don't understand. You're not giving up anything. During times like this, I wish you were a science fiction scholar. A science fiction scholar would immediately understand that the Sondras' temporal zone differs from humans' temporal zone. We can spend as much time in the starship as we want before returning to Earth a mere nanosecond after we left. No harm done."

"Let's just get this over with." We crossed our arms around the carillon, counted down, and said "ignition, blast off." The carillon ascended as a smoke trail appeared in its wake. No one realized that it had been missing for a nanosecond.

The carillon docked with the starship. The Sondras provided spacesuits for me and Pepe. We spacewalked to the starship hatch, opened it, floated through, appeared on the Bridge, and greeted the

Sondras on crew duty. A gray male cat emerged from under the Captain's Chair.

"Hi Norris. Pepe, this is my first husband, Norris. He's the cat the Sondras transformed into a human. You do recall that I said that we were married."

"Jamais. I'm your one and only husband. Transformed cat or no transformed cat, I will not tolerate this situation. You have me living in a science fiction novel. I'm going to change genres. I'm willing to sacrifice using that omnipresent Captain's Chair during our next sex appointment. It's time for my French heritage -- the world of swashbuckling swordsmen -- to kick in. It's time to evoke Scaramouche and The Three Musketeers. Norris, encore une fois, change into a human and I'll challenge you to a duel for Sondra's hand. En garde." Norris dove back under the Captain's Chair. The Sondra in command intervened.

"Professor Le Pew, you must understand that you are now living among separatist feminist science fiction planet residents. We will not stand for male violence. You, Professor Le Pew, are a stock feminist science fiction character: the lone male who encounters a feminist separatist science fiction utopia. And we all know what happens to him."

"I don't read science fiction. What happens?"

"Stop," yelled Sondra. You cannot under any circumstance kill Pepe. I won't have it. Do you know how long it took me to find a husband? You live on a feminist women's planet; you have no idea what husband-hunting is like. If you zap Pepe with a phaser set on kill, I will have to go back to husband-hunting square one."

"En garde," Pepe repeated. Norris emerged from beneath the Captain's Chair with a white flag attached to his upright tail.

The Sondra in command extended a white flag to Pepe. "If you wave the white flag Norris is offering to you and forget the duel, you are welcome to remain here in peace. I would like to make your acquaintance. Do you agree with these stipulations?"

"Oy feminist planets" said Pepe as he took the flag in hand and started to wave it.

"You and Sondra are welcome to join me for dinner in my quarters. Just a moment. Uhura Sondra is indicating that there is a message for you, Sondra."

"I regret to inform you that your mother is on hailing frequency one. She is coming in loud and clear," said Uhura Sondra.

"Where are you? Get married," said Herbert -- again.

"I am married. You remember. I had a wedding. You know, the one where you told me to get married even though I was getting married. I'm on a starship with Pepe and my clones. They just agreed to rescind his status as alien patriarchal invader. They just agreed not to kill him. Hence, it will not be necessary for me to undertake a new husband-hunting initiative."

"Mazel tov. Why can't you be normal, Sondra?"

"I always wanted to ask how you define 'normal.'"

"You're an English professor. I'll answer your question in terms of fiction. In normal fiction, women kiss frogs, the frogs turn into princes, and the women get married. Oy Pioneer! and Oy Feminist Planets are not normal texts. Anyone would back me up on this assessment. You are not normal. Get married."

"'Bye, Herbert."

Norris jumped into Pepe's arms and purred. Pepe smiled. I took advantage of the armistice between my first and second husbands to enumerate the starship's positive aspects. "We can have a great time on this ship. It has a wonderful Holodeck. We can use it to go anywhere and to meet anyone. Best of all, the ship's food processors can materialize calorie-free food. In all of the science fiction I've read, none of the science fiction worlds have calorie-free food." I pushed a food processor start button. A cheesecake appeared. This is my novel. I can go one better than real-world-low-carb cheesecake. Eureka. Calorie-free cheese cake, here I come." I ate an entire calorie-free cheesecake and offered one to Pepe. He had something to say between mouthfuls.

"Now I have something to say to you."

"Oy."

"I have a surprise for you. You did not count on me being a supernatural creature. I am Prince Charming."

"Really?"

"Really. I am of royal blood. Historians believe that the son of Marie Antoinette and Louis XVI emigrated to Canada. He did. It just so happens that he intermarried with the Le Pews. I am descended from both the Bourbons and the Le Pews. Don't worry. In the future, if you do something to aggravate me, I won't chop your head off. You, with all of your science fiction made real, married an authentic Prince Charming under non-fantastic auspices. So there."

"Honoré Amoreuse Le Pew the third didn't tell me about your Bourbon family connection."

"You met Honoré Amoreuse Le Pew the third?"

"Let's not discuss that now. I don't have time. I have a sex appointment in exactly two minutes and twenty seconds. You have already moved the Captain's Chair next to our bed. I have to finish writing Oy Feminist Planets. Let's see. What to write? Oh yes: The End.

And: Sondra and Prince Charming Pepe, while commuting between their Manhattan apartment and their Holodeck timeshare beach house castle, lived happily ever after.

Herbert was forever unable to access the beach house castle's unlisted telephone number.

That is a stretcher, mostly.

About the Author

Marleen S. Barr is known for her pioneering work in feminist science fiction and teaches English at the City University of New York. She has won the Science Fiction Research Association Pilgrim Award for lifetime achievement in science fiction criticism. Barr is the author of *Alien to Femininity: Speculative Fiction and Feminist Theory*, *Lost in Space: Probing Feminist Science Fiction and Beyond*, *Feminist Fabulation: Space/Postmodern Fiction*, and *Genre Fission: A New Discourse Practice for Cultural Studies*. Barr has edited many anthologies and co-edited the science fiction issue of *PMLA*. She is the author of the humorous campus novel *Oy Pioneer!*.

NeoPoiesis: *a new way of making*

1) in ancient Greece, poiesis referred to the
process of making: creation - production -
organization - formation - causation

2) a process that can be physical and
spiritual, biological and intellectual,
artistic and technological, material and
teleological, efficient and formal

3) a means of modifying the environment
and a method of organizing the self,
the making of art and music and poetry,
the fashioning of memory and history and
philosophy, the construction of perception
and expression and reality

4) an independent publisher with a steadfast
goal to print and promote outstanding
poets, writers and artists that reflect
the creative drive and spirit of the new
electronic landscape

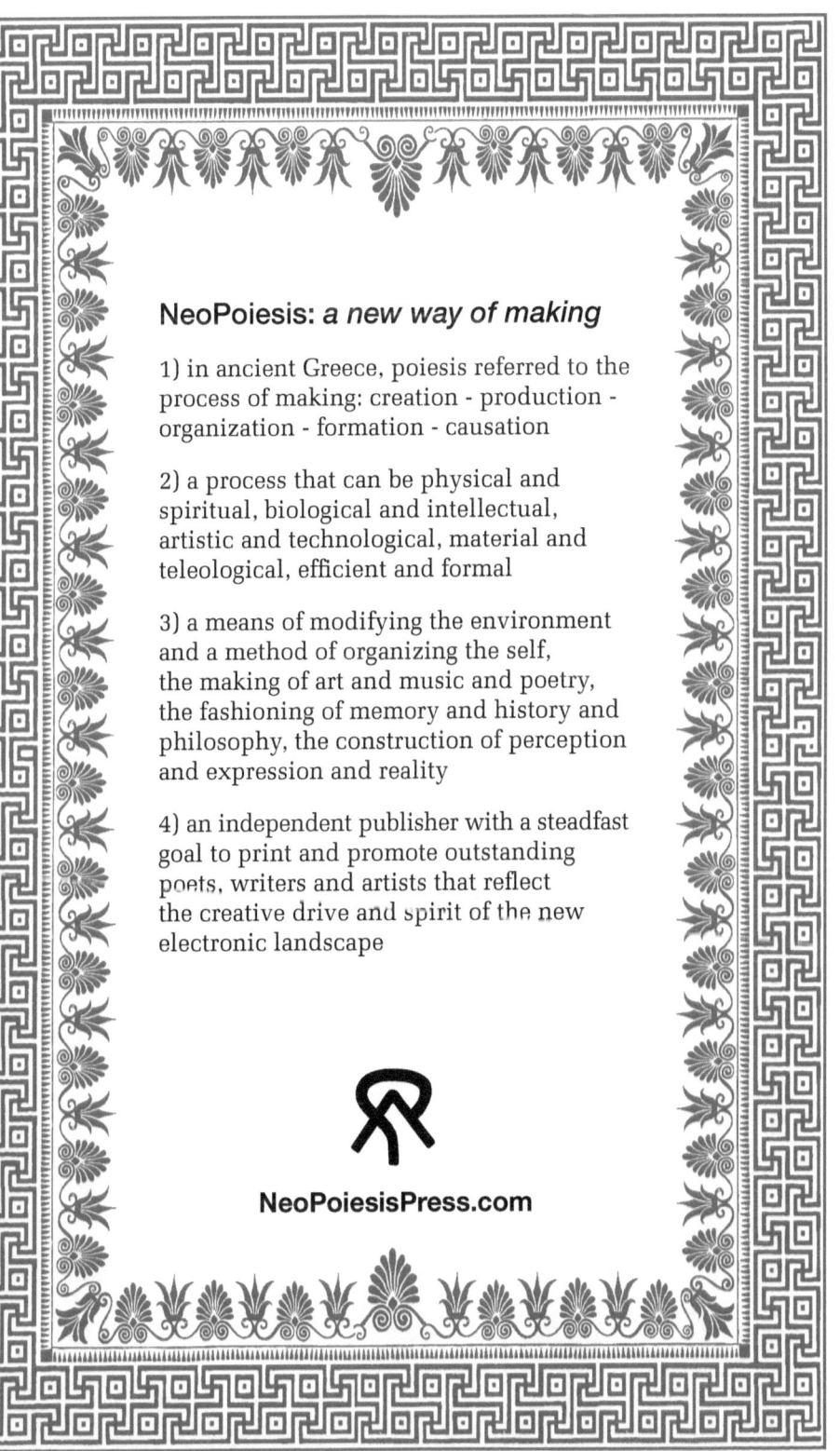

NeoPoiesisPress.com